THREE PERFECT MEN

EVELYN PALFREY

MOON CHILD PRESS
Austin, Texas

THREE PERFECT MEN

Copyright © 1996 by Evelyn Palfrey
Second Printing 1997
Third Printing 1999

For information:

Moon Child Books
P O Box 142495
Austin, Texas 78714-2495
512-452-0042; Fax-512-452-5130
moonchld@flash.net
http://www.flash.net/~moonchld (no 'i')

ISBN: 0-9654190-0-2
Library of Congress Catalogue Card Number 96-94883

Cover art and design by Dale Wilkins Art, Austin, Texas
Back cover text by Delma Lopez, Tina Allen & Sue Coburn

MANY THANKS

To Cynthia and Joyce, for being my fast friends, and sharing the good times. Full moon in September. Always.

To Delma Lopez and Christina Sanchez, for your encouragement, probing questions and blushing cheeks.

To Tina Allen and Jeannye Polk, *the* romance experts.

To Judge Ken Vitucci and Detective John Hutto, for teaching me everything I know about guns, except they go 'pow.'

To Detective John Sisson, for teaching me to fish.

To Eric Mitchell and Judge Ron Meyerson for showing me how to play basketball. (Hey guys, I *did* know the ball was round.)

To Nigel Gusdorf, for getting me on the net. Check it out at **http://flash.net/~moonchld.**

To Paul Williams, my computer consultant. Couldn't have done it without you.

To D. Kirk Johnson, Bess Cofer, Peggy Evans, Dawn Tisdale, Bill Stanley, Cindy Trautmann, Myra Green, Florence Vann, Donald McKee, Velva Price, Nigel Gusdorf, Sue Coburn, Vickie Carrouthers, Johnella Franklin, Stephanie Chretien, Arthuryne Dailey, Twanna Landers, Cline Armstrong, Cynthia Cooper, Teresa Nichols Tate, Judge W.E.B. Blackmon, Cynthia Kidd-Harris, Beth Fagin, Almaree Owens, and Dexter Guilford for your criticism and encouragement.

SPECIAL THANKS

To Lois Palfrey, my mother, for always being there. For everything.

To my sister, Vanessa, who always straightens my view up, when it gets a little skewed.

To Meredith, my daughter, for believing from day one that I could actually write a book.

To John, my son, for forcing me to finish it, by refusing to read a line until I did.

To Darwin, my husband, for tolerating the late nights and wee hours away from him, for understanding the story would only come then, and for indulging me in yet another dream.

PROLOGUE

"Where's my money?!"

"Man, I'm gonna git you yo' money," the boy said.

"I need my money now!"

"You don't *need* the money."

The big man gave him a back hand lick across the mouth, almost knocking him down. Stunned, the boy grabbed the sawhorse to keep from falling.

"I don't need no junior flip like you telling me what I need. Give me my stuff back. I'll find somebody else who can do the job. Gimme the stuff," he said, holding out his big hand.

"I, uh, didn't bring it," the boy stammered, still reeling from the blow.

"You what!" the big man exploded. "Where is it? You smoke my shit?" He advanced on the boy menacingly.

"No sir. You know I don't fool with that stuff."

"Then where is it?"

"I'll bring it to you tomorrow. I promise."

"You sold my stuff. And you trying to beat me out the money, ain't you? I thought you were smarter than that. You buy those fancy tennis shoes with my money?"

"No, sir," the boy said, glancing down at his feet. "Mr. Ike bought these for me. I swear."

Fear was rising in his gut, just like the time the cops almost caught him in Houston. He could taste it in the back of his mouth. The smell of it mingled with the mustiness of the house.

"I'll bring yo' money tomorrow."

"I thought you said you'd bring my *shit* tomorrow. I should have known better than to fool with you. You think you slick— just like yo' ol' lying mama."

"Don't talk about my mama. I don't play that," the boy said, with as much bravado as he could muster.

"I'll talk about yo' ol' ho-ass mama, if I want to. Me and her go way back, before you were even born. If she'd stuck with me, she wouldn't be having to sell her stuff now, to pay her rent. That bitch…"

The boy charged into him, butting him in his stomach with his head and wildly flailing at him with his fists. The man grabbed him by the back of his neck, held him out at arms length and stuck the big gun in his stomach. When he fired it, the boy's body jerked backwards and his eyes popped wide open before he went limp. The man dropped him in a heap on the floor.

"*I'm* the one that don't play, you stupid mother fucker," he said, breathing hard. He drew his leg back and kicked the boy's writhing body, to release his anger. Turning to the grinning man on the other side of the room, he ordered, "Take care of this fool, Jimmy. I'll see you down at my place tomorrow." Jimmy nodded, and never stopped grinning.

The man knocked the sawhorse out of his way, went outside and eased his bulk into the big, old Cadillac.

ONE

They were strangers. Obviously lost. Otherwise why would they be here—on this back road, cut through the East Texas pine forest? And in this back-woods store? The motorhome—the only vehicle parked outside the store, other than his Range Rover—said "lost." There was no public camping on this side of the lake, so there was no reason for the big rigs to travel this road. When one did, it was always lost.

Jones recognized most everybody from these parts, and they all knew *of* him. He kept his distance—just enough contact to get his supplies, as he was doing now. He wasn't even curious about the people around here, but he couldn't help but be curious about the two women. They weren't mother and daughter, and not sisters—the age gap wasn't right either way. Didn't look alike at all—different coloring, built different. He was surprised that he'd noticed their builds.

As he went about selecting his items, Jones caught snatches of the conversation between the women and the storekeeper. They *were* lost, and not making any headway with Gill. He didn't know if Gill was playing dumb, or really didn't know what they were looking for. The thought that Gill would purposefully mislead the women angered him. He had the urge to intervene, but easily shook it off. It was his habit to mind his own business.

As they turned to leave, the younger one stopped at the snack shelf. He watched her out of the corner of his eye, as she took enough chips and cookies to the counter to fill a grocery bag, paid Gill and left with the sack. He thought 'city women,' then turned his thoughts to his own business. He picked up enough supplies, of the more basic kind, to last him another month. He usually tried to arrange things so that he didn't have to leave the island more often than that.

"What'd you make of that?" Gill asked, as he rang up the items.

"Make of what?" Jones responded nonchalantly, as if nothing unusual had happened. The clipped speech pattern that showed his New England roots, was a stark contrast to the storekeeper's twangy Southern drawl.

"Don't even pretend you didn't see those gals. Don't get many in here look like them. And where you reckon they got that RV? I bet they stole it off somebody, and they on the lam. Probably down Houston way, maybe Dallas. The big highway runs both ways. Sheriff's probably looking for 'em now," Gill said contemptuously.

Jones didn't like the man. They usually didn't have much conversation. What little talking they did only emphasized how ignorant and uneducated Gill was. Jones had rarely been exposed to his kind, until his stint in the Army. His wealthy family, and Ivy-League education, had assumed he never would be. He only dealt with Gill at all because the next store was in town, fifteen miles away. The few times he'd driven in, he'd been the subject of stares and whispers. They were all curious about the man who lived on the island. They probably retold old yarns about ghosts or some such nonsense about the island. Pine Branch, Texas was a small town and not much happened.

"Maybe. More likely they're just some ladies down from the city for a nice weekend on the lake. Getting away from the husbands and kids for a few days. They look harmless enough. How much do I owe you?" Jones responded, trying to cut the chat short.

"What would a couple of gals be doing on this side of the lake anyway? It's all private property," Gill said, bagging up Jones' items, putting the heavier ones in cardboard boxes. "The only one of 'them' that owns any of it is that Evans boy and they weren't asking about him. They didn't even know him. I asked 'em. That map they had didn't show his place. I couldn't really make heads nor tails of it anyway. That'll be $75.20. Didn't see no rings neither."

Jones frowned as he pulled a hundred dollar bill out of his wallet and handed it to Gill, hoping he had enough change in his register. He was getting desperate to get out, and was willing to let him keep it if he didn't.

"Rings?" he asked.

Jones didn't want to encourage more prattle from a fool, but he had to wait as Gill laboriously counted out his change, in ones.

"Rings. Rings. You said they were married. You know how women are. If they *are* married, they sure as hell will wear a ring. Flaunting," he snorted, re-positioning the wad of tobacco in his cheek. "Want the world to know they got some man by the balls. Bet you a quarter them two ain't married. I can tell by the way they move their hips. Like they asking for it. Boy, if I could get in that trailer house with them, bet I could show them a thing or two."

"Thanks Gill, see you next time," Jones curtly cut him off. Enough of his stupidity. He couldn't get over the man. One minute spewing racism and sexism, the next, talking of bedding them. He was sure Gill didn't see the contradiction. Amazing. He thought, Gill would probably use the same language if Jones had been Black, and then would have been offended that his customer felt insulted. He grabbed two boxes, pushed the door open and stepped outside.

The bright sunlight helped clear his eyes of the darkened interior of the store, and his head of the stupid man's chatter. He opened the back door of the Rover and loaded the two boxes. Out of the corner of his eye, he saw the two women standing by the RV, talking into it and gesturing toward the map in the younger one's hand. Then he saw the third one in the passenger seat through the RV window. She sure as hell wasn't the mother! Resisting the urge to turn full face and stare, he walked back to the store for the sacks.

On the return trip with the remainder of his supplies, the women were still there. He got a full view as he walked toward the Rover. The younger, shorter one was leaning back against the side of the RV on one foot, a soda in one hand and an opened bag of chips in the other. When she pressed the soda to her forehead, he noticed for the first time, the film of perspiration on his own, and the trickle that had started in his armpit. He rolled the sleeves of the t-shirt over each shoulder, revealing the fading tan lines around his biceps. He ran his hand across the back of his neck, through the gray hair that was curling on his neckline from the sweat. Usually, he let his hair grow long after summer passed, then cut it off, ponytail and all, in the spring. When he first came to the island, it had been red with golden highlights. Now it was gray, with silver highlights. He'd expected it, having watched his father make that same transition in his early fifties. He *hadn't* expected the gray hairs that appeared in other places on his body. It occurred to him, as he wiped his hands on his khaki shorts, that sandals may have been a better choice than the hiking boots and thick socks he wore.

Fall days in Texas were hotter than summer back in Connecticut. Of course, fall nights here were another matter. It would be heavy-jacket cool two hours after sundown. The taller, darker one was now sitting in the driver's seat with her feet dangling out the open door. Her head rested on the steering wheel, a look of utter resignation on her face. He could see the third one through the windshield, in the passenger seat with her elbow listlessly propped on the dashboard, hand under her chin. There was no indication that they were leaving. He suspected they didn't know where to go. His natural inclination was to climb into the Rover, and get on about his business. The boat trip back to the island was still before him, and he could see the sun was on the down side. He started the engine and moved the gearshift into reverse.

Remembering Gill's comments, he felt his anger turn up a notch. Before he could stop himself, he pulled the Rover toward the RV and stopped by the gas pumps, opposite the open driver's door. He got out and reached for the squeegee, hoping his windshield was dirty enough to make his actions appear natural and necessary.

"Afternoon ladies. Are you lost? Maybe I can help," he said as he spread the wet side of the squeegee over the windshield, that was already clean. The first two appeared wary, but relieved. The third eyed him hostilely.

"What makes you think we're lost? And why do you think we need your help?" she asked from inside the RV.

Jones was taken aback. He regretted he had gone this far, but he would regret even more, having to answer Gill's stupid questions on his next trip to the store. He felt Gill watching through the dusty window, and knew he would find it curious for him to have approached the strangers. The thought of Gill sneering at his being rebuffed was more unpalatable to him, than facing the challenge in this woman's eyes. He turned the squeegee over and dragged the rubber blade across the windshield, gathering his crooked smile before he turned to them.

"Well, madam, I thought you were lost because your friends have been puzzling over what appears to be a map for some time now. Experience tells me that a map is unnecessary if you know where you are, and where you're going. Experience also tells me that intelligent people would not camp here by these gas pumps—with a beautiful lake so close by. It's much more suitable for the weekend camping experience. I thought you needed my help because I didn't think you ladies would want to be here at Gill's store when the sun goes down. He was talking about wrangling an invitation into your motorhome. But if you don't need any help, I'll just be on my way." He spoke without flinching from her hostile stare.

The wide-eyed looks on the two Black women's faces assured him they were more receptive to his offer. The short one quickly moved the two steps around the gas pumps to stand beside him, placing the map in a position where he could see it.

"Don't mind Eleanor. Any fool can see we're lost, and you don't have to help her. You can help me. It's Eleanor's map, but I'm the official navigator. I'm Angela Reeves. We're looking for the Taylors' place. It must be around here somewhere. I'm good at my job—when I have a decent map," she said, rolling her eyes toward the RV. "I'm sure we're on the right road, but we can't find the place to turn in."

Jones studied the crude, hand-drawn map for a second to get his bearings. No wonder they couldn't find it. He knew the exact spot when he saw 'red mailbox' written inside a square. He knew of the Taylors too, although he'd never met them. He had bought his land from them. Some city folk—from Houston, as best he could remember. They had never come to the property since he lived here. He guessed they had bought the large tract on the lakeshore with intentions to retire on it; but perhaps they thought it was good investment property. When he bought the island, his lawyers had arranged the purchase of the Taylor's southern-most acreage. It abutted the road on the east end, and the lake on the west, providing him a place to park his Rover and launch his boat. He still used their turn-in, never bothering to erect a fence dividing his property from theirs, or to make a separate gate or driveway. The only improvement he had made, in fact, was to erect a plain metal mailbox with no name on it, just '305', in the place of the fancy red one the Taylors had put up, back when their dream was fresh. It looked like something Mrs. Taylor might have picked up at one of the city arts and crafts shows. Although he thought the thing was hideous, he had used it, until a couple of years ago when it died at the hands of someone with a shotgun—some of the local high school boys out for mischief most likely. He remembered—it was his fiftieth birthday and he thought it was nice of them to give him a present. Looking at the 'red mailbox' on the map now, he thought the Taylors probably couldn't find their own property now. He felt vaguely responsible for the women's plight.

"I know exactly where you are trying to go. Follow me. It's not out of my way at all. Just turn in behind me off this road. Then when I head left, you follow the road to the right. About five miles from here." Without waiting for a reply, he hoisted his lean body into the Rover and started the motor.

From the driver's seat, Sondra was listening intently to their conversation, and started the RV motor as soon as she heard 'Follow me.' She was tired, and anxious about getting the rig set up before dark. She was always anxious about something. It was just her nature, although her always-calm demeanor belied it. The three of them had taken many trips together, usually for a long weekend, but sometimes longer. Each trip had its own start-up problem. She usually took all the little set-backs in stride, keeping the group's spirits high for the coming adventure. She could always stimulate a good-natured argument among them over which set-back had been the worst. Eleanor always voted for the time when the RV wouldn't budge above 45 mph—a broken spark plug it turned out—and it took them nine hours to make the four-hour trip to the beach. Angela singled out the flat tire, 80 miles from home. Neither of them ever had a clue about the agony each problem caused Sondra, including this one. But today, she was just tired. Tired of being responsible. Not only tired of being responsible for their pleasure, but even for her own. It was the being lost, after coming so far, that did it. She absolutely could not stand being lost. It conflicted hard with her need to be in control. She was angry too, but took pains to hide it from her friends. She had driven up and down this stupid road for too long, back and forth, and with each turn-around of the big rig in tight spaces on the narrow road, her vision of setting up early and putting her feet up, had receded.

A broad grin spread across Angela's face as she hurried around to the passenger door, giving the two-finger victory sign as she passed the big windshield. Eleanor moved back to the couch, as Angela swung into the passenger seat. They all had a way of making room for each other, not getting in each other's way. They worked well together. It had been that way from the very first.

Sondra and Angela—each for their own reasons—had shown up at the Women's Empowerment Group meeting that Eleanor held weekly at her bookstore. Then, Angela was in her junior year in college, and had a paper to write on the contemporary women's movement. On campus, she had seen a notice for the meeting, and thought attending might give her some material for the paper. Sondra happened in the store looking for a particular book by a Black woman judge. Although she didn't have it in stock, Eleanor had read it, and promised to order it for her. She invited Sondra to stay for the meeting, that was scheduled to start in ten minutes.

Although the fluid group usually numbered at least ten, Sondra and Angela were the only women to show up that night. It was storming, and they speculated the weather kept the others away. When it was clear that no one else was coming, the three of them dashed through the rain, to the little coffee shop at the end of the block. Over steaming cups of cappuccino, they shared their life stories until the coffee shop closed. They were different ages, different races, from different backgrounds. None of them could explain, or even questioned why, they became fast friends. More than friends. They were everything women can be to each other, except lovers. From that first night, they all assumed it would be that way always. Ten years had passed toward always, already.

Sondra eased the big rig onto the narrow two-lane road, following the Rover.

"I can't believe you two. A good-looking man comes along, offers you a little sweet-talk, and off you go, blithely following him to God-knows-where." Eleanor was working up her usual froth. "He could be an axe-murderer for all you know. Probably developed those arm muscles swinging an axe out here in these woods. And those strange hazel eyes. I'll bet. . ."

"You _did_ notice the good looks, the muscles, the eyes?" Angela deadpanned aloud, talking at Sondra, but they all knew the tease was meant for Eleanor. Angela was a quick-wit, dry and merciless in her teasing. Sondra felt the anger easing, and even smiled, as she saw the pinched look on Eleanor's face in the rear-view mirror.

"Don't worry, Eleanor," Sondra said, playing straight man to Angela's joke. "I've got my itty bitty gun—and I do know how to use it. I'll blow the bad ol' axe-murderer away if he tries to get you. And even if I miss, Angela'll stomp his brains out with that new technique she learned from Quinton."

No sooner than she said his name, she regretted it, as she saw the pained look on Angela's face. Sondra wanted to kick herself.

She hurried on.

"Girl, between the three of us, we'll get him before he gets any of us. Right, Angela?" Sondra prodded, trying to bring her back into the teasing mood. But it was too late.

"Right," Angela said quietly, staring at the road.

Eleanor felt the pain, as she heard it in Angela's voice. She saw Angela's reaction and retreat. That girl could pull so deep inside herself, it was scary. That was exactly why Eleanor had insisted they take this trip on such short notice—to pull her back from that place, before she dug in too deep.

Since she and Angela had their own businesses, they had more freedom about their schedules. But, Eleanor knew it would throw Sondra's life into chaos, having to rearrange her crowded docket. The defense attorneys would pretend they were angry at having their clients' cases put off, while in reality they would be delighted to have a little more time—to try to wrangle a better deal from the state's attorneys, and a little more of their fee from their clients. The prosecutors would grumble about backlogs, but secretly relish the unexpected free time to prepare for up-coming trials. As for her own business, a week's absence wouldn't make that much difference. She had capable and committed people working for her. Because they believed in the mission, they would do their jobs well, whether she was at her shop or not. Her only regret was missing the weekly meeting of the Women's Empowerment Group. Over the years she had only missed two meetings, both times for emergencies. But this was an emergency too.

Eleanor knew it the minute Angela burst into her office on Monday and crumpled into one of the overstuffed chairs oppo-site her desk, spewing forth a cloudburst of tears, along with her discovery about Quinton Rawlins. She had seen Angela disappointed by men before, but nothing like this. Angela was a level-headed girl. Eleanor guessed she was so good with computers because everything for her was either off or on, just like a computer. No gray shades, only black or white. She was very focused for a woman still in her twenties. That focus had enabled her to develop her software business to the point that she had secured a substantial contract with a bank.

Eleanor had been uneasy about Quinton Rawlins when he first appeared as the bank's point man. He was handsome as all get out, and smooth. *Too* smooth. She could easily see how he fit into the bank's operation. He could make himself fit in anywhere. But she didn't trust him from the first. She wondered if the bank had purposely sent a Black man to deal with Angela. She rarely saw people of color among the mostly-female staff when she conducted her business there. Eleanor didn't trust him. She didn't trust men in general. And she didn't trust big business, like the bank. But that day was not the time for 'I told you so.' When the cloudburst spent itself, Angela wiped her eyes, straightened her suit and walked out, head held high as though her world had not come to an end. Eleanor knew from the look on her face she was heading for that deep place. From her own experience, she knew it was a dark and dangerous place. It had taken years of therapy for her to recognize the signs and to force herself in a different direction. Within the hour, she had Sondra on the phone.

"We've got to do something. We can't let her do this to herself. Just when her company is about to take off. That contract is too important for her to flub it over some man. She just got blind-sided. Didn't see it coming. So, I've got an idea.

Let's take her away for a little while—for a little de-programming. You remember the woman I told you about who comes to the Empowerment meeting every now and then—the one I roomed with in college?"

"Maybe. Blanche something?"

"Yes, Blanche Taylor. She and her husband own some land on a lake. I've already talked with her, and she would be delighted for us to go up there for a little camping trip. She's always wanting to do something for the cause—as long as she doesn't have to get her hands dirty or miss any Garden Club meetings," she laughed. "She gave me directions and I drew a map. She said we can go any time. They never use it. How about Friday? Can you spare a week? This is too serious for just a week-end."

Eleanor spilled Angela's whole story out for Sondra.

Judge Sondra K. Ellis always took the calls that came in on the private line. She took, or returned, _all_ of her calls, but she would leave the bench mid-trial for calls on the private line. She'd had it installed and paid for it out of her own funds, to avoid any questions of impropriety. She was careful that way. Only the very special people in her life had the number—her girls, her parents, Angela, Eleanor. She had given it to one man she thought was special, but he wasn't special enough to use it. She grimaced when she thought of the several weeks she spent waiting for him to call—until she got over that bit of folly.

This time she wished she hadn't taken the call. But she was at her desk going through piles of pre-sentencing reports when the phone rang, and picked it up by reflex. Although she agreed that they had to do something about Angela, she was irritated that Eleanor didn't understand that cancelling her dockets for a week was damn near impossible. She had just within that hour, agreed to squeeze in an extra hearing on the docket for an attorney who had claimed his client had a special emergency. That alone would have necessitated her having to stay after hours on Monday. But with her girls away at college now, working after hours sometimes was preferable to going home alone. And besides, it gave her a really good excuse for skipping one of the many receptions and meetings she was expected to, and usually did, attend.

Quinton Rawlins had turned out to be a PhD cad. Sondra wasn't really surprised. She had not been comfortable with him from the first, but she never could quite put her finger on why. He was so charming, it was hard to dislike him. She tried to put the misgivings out of her mind, for Angela's sake. He seemed to be just what she needed. Articulate. Smart. A good dresser—but not too flashy. He seemed genuinely interested in Angela's work. As Chief Operating Officer of a New York bank, he obviously made good money, so didn't seem out to misuse her in that way. Sondra had been won over because she had never known Angela to be so happy. Sondra was enough of a realist to believe that anything that seemed too good to be true, probably was. But, she knew Angela was no fool. Her radar was so precise in picking up bullshit, that even the usually-skeptical Sondra trusted her instincts.

Angela was completely in love with Quinton. It was easy to see, just by the way she looked at him. Sometimes watching them, Sondra even thought about her daughters. She hoped—wanted to believe—someone just like Quinton would be there for her twins, Tiffany and Natalie, when the time came. Still, she had misgivings. And now it seemed that, once again, she was right. There was no joy in it for her. She would prefer for things to be as they seemed. But a wife and *two* children! How could Angela not have known all this time? How could Quinton have done such a thing! Poor Angela, going around, almost openly, talking about getting married when the contract was completed. He never said one thing to discourage it. Even encouraged her, talking about the pretty children they would have together. The jerk! When exactly did he plan on telling her about his other family? Maybe he didn't plan to tell her. He'd managed to pull this little scam off for nearly six months. Maybe he planned to have them both—like Mr. Sanders.

The state had prosecuted that case in her court, even though both the red-haired, bee-hived Mrs. Sanders had to be treated as hostile witnesses. Neither Mrs. Sanders had been aware of the other, prior to the indictment. Both ardently professed their love for Mr. Sanders, and invoked the Fifth. It took all Sondra had, not to burst out laughing in open court at their misunderstanding of the law. The only thing that kept her from doing just that, was a burning desire to take them both by the ears, right over to the bookstore. Eleanor would give them the what-for, until they both understood that they deserved better than sharing that pitiful-looking man. Eleanor would tell them they each could have a pitiful man to themselves—there were certainly enough pitiful men to go around. In the end, Sondra granted Mr. Sanders probation, and gave both wives the card to the Women's Empowerment Group meeting. There was no point to putting Mr. Sanders in prison and having the taxpayers support him, she reasoned, when *both* Mrs. Sanders were completely willing to do that, even after they were aware of each other. She thanked

Goodness neither of the Mrs. Sanders had been stupid enough to bring children into that mess.

"He's turning, Sondra."

Angela's voice brought Sondra back to the present. Sondra had seen the map, and as the Rover turned, she noticed the mailbox was not red—just plain old country silver. For just a moment, she wondered if Eleanor could be right about the axe-murderer. She was just so tired, and anxious to give up the wheel, that she pushed it to the back of her mind. She did, in fact, have the gun, and was in no mood for any mess from some axe-murderer, or anybody else. She had dealt with an axe-murderer before, too—and she wasn't even tired or angry then.

TWO

The Rover turned to the left just as he said he would, and Sondra kept on the road to the right. Angela was back on track, reading the map.

"Just keep on following the road 'til you see the lake. There's a big pole with an electrical connection. The water connection should be just beneath it. Ou-u-u, this is going to be perfect. I don't suppose we could hope for a level concrete pad," she said.

Eleanor spoke up. "I wouldn't hope for that if I were you. Blanche told me they hadn't been out here but twice since they bought the place. They haven't made any improvements. Will you look at that lake! Beautiful!"

Sondra eased the rig close to the pole and shut the motor off. The rituals began. The first was the key ritual. Sondra would ceremoniously hand Eleanor and Angela extra sets of keys—as though they might actually get separated during the stay. The second ritual was hooking up. Eleanor easily understood the need for electricity and water, but was befuddled by the process, and did her part by staying out of the way. Angela and Sondra removed cords and hoses from compartments and did whatever was necessary to accomplish the task. Eleanor walked to the back of the RV and unlocked the chain that held the folding chairs, removed three of them, and placed them wherever she thought appropriate. This was the one thing she was in charge of, and she took the responsibility very seriously. Sondra and Angela finished just as Eleanor selected the perfect spot, and the third ritual began. Sondra emerged from the RV with a tray holding a lead crystal carafe of wine and three matching glasses.

"Now this is living," she announced, as she poured the wine.

They clinked the glasses together, settled into their chairs and took a sip. After that, each trip was different, and delicious—to be savored like the wine.

The sun was low in the sky as the three women sat facing it, its reflection dazzling on the lake. They chatted about how beautiful the lake was, how the tall graceful pines were the perfect accompaniment, how quiet and peaceful the woods were. One of them started their favorite game—'This is the most beautiful place we've ever stayed.' Another would disagree, claiming that honor for a particular beach—say Biloxi or Port Aransas. Still another would cast her vote for the spot in the Hill Country, west of Austin, where they had parked in a shady pecan grove. The game grew longer with each trip, because the list of candidates grew with each trip. They had never been to the same place twice. There was no argument about their least favorite place—the beach outside of Galveston—where they were forced to park behind the dunes, out of eyesight of the water. Sondra would sum it up, "Nice level pads, good hook-ups, nice green lawn—we could have had *that* parked in my driveway." They always nodded in agreement. The game ended when they all agreed on the most beautiful place. The winner was always the place where they were at that moment. This time was no different.

The game over, Eleanor stood up and walked into the woods. Sitting most of the day had caused her to be restless, and she felt the need to stretch her legs. Before long, she returned and dropped an arm full of dry branches on the ground, then headed back to the woods for another load. No words were exchanged. They didn't need words to understand, or to assign roles and tasks. As was their way, each did whatever was required to get the job done. Angela and Sondra went searching for big rocks to build the fire ring. They helped each other carry or roll them into place. As Angela piled kindling to start the fire, Sondra retrieved the hatchet from the back compartment of the RV and walked into to the woods to help Eleanor with heavier logs. They had a nice fire going, just as the big red sun began its descent into the horizon across the lake. That done, Sondra re-filled their glasses and they all settled back down in their chairs. They sat in silence, just absorbing.

Angela heard it first. A twig snapping, pine needles being crushed underfoot. She turned her head in that direction, her eyes straining to see into the darkness. Sondra and Eleanor took immediate notice of her reaction, and turned too, just in time to see the figure of a man emerge from between two tall pines. None of them moved another inch.

"Evening, ladies," a deep masculine voice said. The man moved into the glow of the campfire. He wore a sleeveless down vest over the long-sleeve denim shirt. It had indeed turned cool when the sun surrendered to the lake. Sondra noticed the bulge of his arm and leg muscles, as he squatted and reached to warm his hands over the fire. She thought, an axe-murderer would have a body just like that. Remembering Eleanor's earlier reference to an axe-murderer made her uneasy. They *were* in the middle of God-knows-where. Had he lured them here? Was this even the Taylors' place? They'd been easy. She felt like a fool. Thoughts of the store owner increased her uneasiness. She had sensed at the time that he was being untruthful with them. Were they partners? Was the other one lurking behind one of the trees? They hadn't heard this one coming until it was too late. Oh, My God! Her rising fear was interrupted.

"What the hell are *you* doing here?!" The campfire was no match for the blaze in Eleanor's eyes.

"I was retrieving the last of the things I bought, and thought I'd come by and see if you ladies needed my help—again," Jones answered her question straight-forwardly. He threw the 'again' in just to remind her that she had indeed already needed his help.

"Can't we just have some peace and quiet without your interference?" she demanded.

Although fear was tugging at her hard, Sondra forced the calm on herself. She stood up and stared Eleanor straight in her eyes, her face expressionless. She hoped Eleanor would see that she had a plan.

"Now Eleanor, mind your manners," Sondra said evenly, with a touch of contrived sweetness. "We have a guest, and you are not being very gracious. We appreciate your thinking about us, Mr., uh?

"Gardner. Jones Gardner. Please call me Jones."

"It sure was nice of you to give us directions. This place is gorgeous. We never would have found it with Eleanor's map if you hadn't come along. Can we thank you with a glass of wine?"

"That would be nice."

"I'll get you a glass. And a jacket for me. It's getting a little chilly out here. Angela? Eleanor? Jacket?"

Sondra picked up the near-empty crystal carafe and walked to the RV in measured steps, hoping not to appear as hurried as she felt. She stepped into the RV and closed the door softly. Once inside, she nearly ran to the back closet. Her hands shook, as she rummaged in her bag, until she felt the smooth wood and the cold steel of the gun.

The gun had been a gift from Judge David Goldstein. They had a special friendship that had grown over the years she had been on the bench. She didn't like him at first—always talking about guns, hunting, killing. Always insisting that she get a gun. He had offered, not only to help her select one, but also to teach her how to use it. She had imagined him to be a week-end survivalist, perhaps even a wacked-out militia type. White men and their guns. Always made her nervous.

Shortly after she had been elected, and was still having to prove herself, Sondra walked out of her office to call a docket. Judge Goldstein was standing in his doorway twenty feet from hers. He raised his arm, his hand pointed at her in the shape of a gun, index finger extended, following her. As she approached him heading toward her courtroom, intent on ignoring him, he jerked his finger as though he had fired a gun, and simultaneously said "Pow." His voice was as eerie as his smile. When she was even with him, she stopped, looked him dead in his eyes without flinching.

"Rumor has it, you only shoot blanks," she said, and calmly walked on to her courtroom. To this day, she had never told him he had nearly scared the shit out of her.

After that, she had been coolly polite to him. But his attitude toward her was different—respectful and even friendly. That gained a measure of acceptance for her in the other judges' eyes. They respected him, or were afraid of him—she still hadn't decided which, after all this time. She wondered if he had pulled that little pretend gun crap with any of them, and had picked out several she was sure had flinched. Gradually, she became more comfortable with him as she learned more about him. He had come from a poor family, worked his way through college and law school, then did a stint in the Judge Advocate Corps. He had a wife he still adored after many years, and two kids he would have given his very life for.

Even though she and David ate lunch together nearly every day, and had shared many late dinners when court ran late, he always behaved as the perfect gentleman and husband. Sometimes she thought she saw something in his eyes—a longing, almost a pleading, for her to invite him. But she always dismissed this as the rambling mind of a woman too much aware of middle age bearing down on her, and resisting her apparent destiny of being alone. Inquiring about his latest gun acquisition would always bring her—if not both of them—back to reality. She didn't like guns, but they completely absorbed David. He would go on and on about his newest one, and they would both be safe.

The day that he saved her life, she knew she would always

love him. The courts had closed for the night, when the man came to her office unannounced. She just looked up and he was there, in the doorway. When she looked into his eyes, she sensed something was not right. She remembered she had let her bailiff go home for the night, while she stayed to catch up on paperwork.

"Can I help you?" she calmly inquired.

"I have a problem. Can I come in, Judge Ellis?" he asked— even as he entered her office.

"Sure. Have a seat. What can I do for you?"

But she wasn't sure at all. How did he know her name? She had refused to allow the maintenance man to attach the bronze nameplate to her door, taking to heart the lessons on court security taught in the first judge school she had attended. Her eyes never left the man's, and he began to look vaguely familiar, as he eased his boxer's body into the chair opposite her desk.

"I've actually been thinking about what you can do for me, Judge Ellis. And I've had a lot of time to think about it. To think about *you*. I still don't see how you could believe I done that to that little girl. I like fucking women. Women like you."

Fear gripped her from head to toe, but she remained stock still in her chair and her eyes never wavered from his. She forced the calm on herself, as she always did when facing a threat. As the man recounted all the ways in which she, and bitches like her, were responsible for the troubles in his life, Judge Goldstein walked past her still-open door.

"Hey, Goldstein. Got a minute? We could use some help in here," she called out, struggling to sound calm, but she heard the strain in her own voice.

"Long day, gotta go. G'night," was all he said, as he walked on by.

Sondra wanted to scream to him, but didn't—couldn't. That was the only time she took her eyes off the man. He didn't seem to notice Goldstein's passing—too absorbed in his story, his misery. When her eyes returned to him, the man was clenching and unclenching his fists as he spoke, his pock-marked face full of rage. She knew this was serious, and she was not going down without one hell of a fight. Under her desk, she eased the high-heeled shoes off her feet. Mentally surveying her desk for a weapon, she settled on the lead-crystal letter opener that she kept in her lap drawer. When she received her parents' gift to celebrate the opening of her law office years ago, it had not occurred to her all the uses to which it might be put. As the man continued to talk, she eased the drawer open, her movement so slight he didn't notice.

The man was now describing his years in prison and the ugly things that had happened to him, in a sexually explicit way. She wasn't surprised at the abuse. Child-molesters were generally low on the totem pole there. He began talking about what he planned to do to her as the pay-back. The man stood and started around her desk. Her hand closed tightly around the letter-opener as she also stood. She would not be at that kind of disadvantage. As he advanced on her, she pushed her chair between them, backing up. It was then that she saw the knife in the man's hand and the ugly sneer on his face. Just as he lunged for her, the whole world exploded. The sneer froze into a look of shock, and the man fell across her chair.

Sondra looked up and saw Judge Goldstein walking toward her from the doorway, the gun in his hand still trained at the man. When he reached the place where she stood, she fell into his arms. As she realized what had happened, and that she was safe, the calm abandoned her. Her body began to tremble. The trembling gave way to violent, uncontrollable shaking. David put his arms around her and held her tightly, until it gradually subsided. It seemed like hours, but it must have only been minutes. The sound of gunfire had brought two deputies, their guns drawn, squatting just outside the doorway. David heard them, and continued to hold her with one arm as he held the other straight out to clearly show the gun in a position of surrender.

As one of the deputies edged forward with his gun trained on them, he commanded, "Put the gun on the desk! NOW!"

David complied, then put his free arm back around Sondra and said soothingly, "It's OK now. It's over."

It wasn't until the deputy reached the desk to secure the gun, that he saw the man's body sprawled over the leather chair, then recognized the judges.

"Judge Goldstein? Judge Ellis? What the hell? Who the hell is this? What happened here?"

The sound of his voice brought Sondra back. Her face was pressed into David's chest. He was much taller, and she couldn't see who was asking the questions. She stepped away from David's zone of comfort and sank into one of the guest chairs— not the one the man had sat in. Before long the room was filled with chaos. All manner of law enforcement types invaded, barking orders, radios crackling. David, continuing to protect her, took her into his office next door to give her statement to one of the investigators. He had put himself between Sondra and the news reporters they passed in the hall, shielding her face from their cameras.

A week passed before Sondra could bring herself to enter her office again. It looked just as it had before the incident, except for the new chair behind the desk. She supposed the old one was taken for evidence. When she opened her bottom drawer to put her purse in, she saw the beautiful and ornately carved wooden box. In it, the gun that she later learned was a Ladies Smith & Wesson .38 Special, lay nestled in blue velvet. She thought it was pretty, shining like new chrome. The handle was smooth, and of the same wood as the box—polished Texas mesquite. David knew she liked light colored wood. He never admitted that the gift was from him, even on the many trips they took to the firing range for him to teach her to use it. But she knew in her head—and in her heart. She carried the gun everywhere after that, and it did make her feel safe.

Sondra felt almost safe now, as she pulled the gun from the bag and tucked it into the waistband of her denim shorts. She had never used the gun anywhere except at the firing range. This was the real deal. She could hear her Daddy saying "Don't pull a gun on a man unless you're willing to kill him. Don't ever use it to scare him. A scared man will tremble a bullet into you." She could also hear David's more aggressive version of that same thought, "Fire twice at the stomach, then once at the head. Ask your questions later."

Would she really kill this man? He hadn't done anything except help them—or maybe lure them to their own deaths. Maybe she was over-reacting. He seemed so nice. Would he really try to attack all three of them? Maybe he had a partner— or partners. Better safe than sorry. Her mind raced back and forth, as the seconds passed. She yanked her jacket off the hanger in the closet and put it on, relieved that it was long enough to cover the bulge in her waistband, but loose enough for her to have easy access. She pulled the other two jackets down and went to the cabinet to get the last glass in the set.

At the campfire, Jones was trying to make sense of his behavior. Why had he even come back across the lake? As he had put his supplies away, he couldn't get the women out of his mind. Or Gill. Gill knew where they were headed, he was sure of that. What if Gill tried to make good on his desire to join them? Somehow, Jones knew Gill was wrong about the women. They weren't on the run. If the map didn't prove that, the lace curtains at every window did. No question the RV belonged to a woman. A man would never put up with lace curtains. He had no curtains at all at his own windows. There was no need. As the only inhabitant of the island, he had nothing to hide, and no one to hide it from.

Earlier in the evening, on the island, he had tried to focus on something else, first some little chore that needed doing, then the investment reports that arrived on the fax. But the women kept popping into his mind. He guessed Angela must have been in her late twenties. She had been friendly and open. Would Gill approach her because she was the youngest—and the most approachable? Or the driver? He guessed she was about 10 years older than Angela. She seemed very observant, but not very approachable. The one he now knew as Eleanor, appeared to be about his own age. Maybe Gill would pick her because she was the only White one. She'd eat Gill alive. She'd probably piss him off, and there was no telling how Gill would react. Jones couldn't decide whether he was going back to protect them or Gill. As he'd listened to the drone of the motor on the boat, he persuaded himself he was just going to check and make sure they were *all* OK.

Now he wished he hadn't come. But he had to, at least, have the glass of wine before he left. He couldn't understand why this Eleanor was being so hateful.

"I'm sorry you think I'm interfering. I just thought you might need something. But it appears that you've settled in quite nicely. I admit I'm a little surprised. I had the impression you were real city women, with no idea how to handle yourselves out here. Obviously, I was wrong. Nice fire."

"We do this a lot," Angela spoke up. "Been doing it a long time too. Believe me, we know what we're doing. And we're an awesome team. This is a beautiful place. Do you live next door?"

"You might say that," he chuckled softly, and pointed. "See those trees in the middle of the lake? That's where I live. It's an island."

"So what are you doing *here*?" Eleanor asked bitingly.

"I've already answered that question. But don't worry. I won't be here long, now that I know you're OK."

Sondra backed out the RV door, with the jackets over one arm, using both hands to balance a tray, with the re-filled carafe, a bowl of chips and a smaller one with picante sauce. She took a deep breath to steady her hands. She wanted to appear calm and normal, in case Mr. Gardner was what he appeared to be. She was ready—in case he was not. She turned around and booted the door closed with her foot.

"Eleanor, you mean in all this time you didn't get Mr. Gardner a chair? Mr. Gardner, why don't you get yourself a chair. There's another one on the back of the RV," Sondra said, calmly, as she set the tray in her chair, and handed the jackets to the women. Angela immediately reached for the chips. As he walked off, Sondra moved to where she could watch him, but turned her body to face her friends. She pulled her jacket back showing them the gun, then pulled it closed around her. Angela's eyes widened and she nearly dropped the chip from her mouth. Eleanor rolled her eyes upwards and crimped her mouth.

"For Christ's sake Sondra, you don't have to shoot him. He's not dangerous. Just on the make. If you just quit being so damned friendly, offering him wine and everything, he'll be on his way."

"You were the one who said he was an axe-murderer," Sondra hissed. She could see him returning with the chair.

Jones unfolded the aluminum chair and sat down, as Sondra poured wine into the fourth glass and handed it to him, then re-filled the others. He took a sip.

"This is nice," he said.

He really meant it, and not just about the wine. He realized it had been a very long time since he'd had company. Since his son left for college several years ago, he had been alone—sometimes these days, lonesome. Before that, while Philip was in boarding school, he had been alone, but the boy was home on holidays and summers, and even some week-ends—filling the house with boyish whoops, and later rock music. Looking forward to those visits kept him from feeling lonesome. He actually enjoyed the solitude. But he was enjoying this, too.

"You say you do this often?"

"Oh yes," Angela answered. "Four or five times a year. Whenever we can coordinate all of our schedules. We've been lots of places, but this is the first time we've been here. It definitely won't be our last tho'."

Jones had placed his chair opposite Eleanor, he didn't think on purpose, but it did give him a clear view of her in the campfire light. The look on her face was of determined exasperation. Her dark auburn hair, laced with silver strands, was pulled up in a long ponytail. The simple hairstyle and the V-neck shirt she wore under the open jacket accentuated her long neck. She must have a thing for silver, he thought, noticing the necklaces, the Canterbury cross earrings, and wide ornate bands clasped around her wrists. She was tall for a woman, although not as tall as he.

Earlier, he had watched her gathering wood among the pine trees. He had stood very still, watching the women, from a vantage point where he knew they couldn't see him. He had been relieved to see Gill was not there, but couldn't persuade himself to get back in the boat. So he continued to stand and watch. Once when she bent over from the waist to pick up a piece of wood, he noticed how long her legs were. She would be a perfect fit in that position. The tug in his loins caught him by surprise. He hadn't felt that sensation in so long. Or thought those kind of thoughts. Really not since Rebecca's murder. As he rubbed the heel of his hand on the slight swelling in his groin area, he knew he should leave right then. Maybe it had been too long. The thought came back to him now, looking at her with her arms folded across her breasts.

"Your husbands don't object to your leaving that much?"

Eleanor's response was blistering.

"I see you are a man of many assumptions Mr. Gardner—like most men. First you assume we are damsels in distress, waiting for you to ride up on your Rover and rescue us. Now you assume our knights in shining armor are cooling their heels back at the hearth. I don't suppose it could have occurred to you that a woman could live a happy and fulfilled life without a man and all that macho bullshit."

"I suppose that could happen," Jones returned, in a quiet voice and sardonic smile. He hadn't come to fight with her, but he wasn't one to back down either.

His smile infuriated her even more. Eleanor turned and glared at her friends.

"Ya'll invited him. Ya'll entertain him. I'm going in. Just beware of sweet-talking axe-murderers!"

She stood, yanking the chair into a folded position and stormed off. The sound of the RV door slamming in the quiet night, jarred them all a little.

Sondra and Angela looked at each other out of the corner of their eyes. They knew Eleanor was the most jealous of their time together, and the most resentful of any intruders. But this was beyond the pale, even for her. Sondra was embarrassed at her friend's behavior—and at her own. She had leaned against the big pine tree rather than sit, so as to have the advantage—if she needed it. She was aware of the now-warmed metal, pressed against her bare flesh.

"Axe-murderer? What the hell is she talking about? What's wrong with her anyway?" he asked them.

Sondra felt compelled to defend her friend.

"Don't take it personally. Eleanor's a little out of sorts tonight. She didn't take well to our ribbing her about the map—and the red mailbox." She hadn't forgotten.

Relief flooded over her when Jones explained the circumstances of its demise. She felt a little silly now about the gun, but not too.

Angela, laughing at their earlier conversation, chimed in.

"I can't wait to tell Eleanor about that—but not until she gets over her little snit. I swear, she's just jealous that we're not spending all our time listening to her lecture."

"Do you really live on that island?" Sondra asked, abruptly changing the subject. She was fiercely loyal to her friend, even though she agreed with Angela's assessment.

Jones nodded, then told them the story of how he had come to live there. They were spell-bound as he recounted it. He and his wife had driven to New York City for a long weekend. It was a warm spring night and they decided to walk back to their hotel from the late show. The man must have been following them. As they crossed the alley, he grabbed Becky from behind and dragged her into the darkness. Her yelp of surprise had drawn Jones in behind them.

"Your wallet and your jewelry!" he barked. "Now! Quick, don't make me kill her!"

Despite the warm weather, the man shivered intermittently. Between the tic-like shivering and the vacant grin on the man's face, Jones knew he was a drug addict. He handed over his wallet and watch. The man released Becky to receive them.

"Gonna get me some rocks now, ba-beee," the man laughed.

Jones was relieved it was over, and his mind was already racing ahead to how to cure it—reporting the credit cards stolen, calling his father to wire cash. Then the man's expression changed, his little ferret eyes narrowed.

"The ring. Give me the ring, bitch." Becky refused. He stuck the gun between her breasts, shoving her back against the wall. She still refused. The sound of the shot echoed in the alley. Jones and the man were both shocked, then he ran from the alley. Jones was torn between chasing after the bastard and going to Becky. He cradled her in his arms as she drew her last breath. He still had the ring. That and Phillip were all he had left of her.

That was the first time he'd heard the term 'rocks.' He told them how he'd known drugs, mostly marijuana. With the peaceniks he occasionally hung out with on campus in Cambridge, and with his fellow soldiers in Nam, it was almost always a communal affair. He noticed a change in the drug scene by the time he went to work on Wall Street. The young brokers and investment bankers preferred cocaine, but like the rest of their lives, it was all about money. No sharing. No sense of community. You were only 'in' as long as you had the big money required to play that game. He'd observed how the powder took some of them down, losing everything—the big bucks, the BMW's, the women, the upscale condos. And how the others contemptuously turned their backs on the falling one. None of them would have made it a week in Nam, where mere survival required the men to cover each other's backs. He'd declined to play that losing game. Instead, he concentrated on making the contacts and gaining the knowledge his father had sent him there to acquire.

Later, back in Connecticut, he spent his time applying what he had learned to the business his father had built. He expanded it, and the bottom line, by buying several of the suppliers. He always made a fair deal, and kept the former owners and employees on. According to his plan, he took the company public, then sold it, just months before the big market crash. It was incredible timing really, but he had seen it coming and planned for it.

While he had been so absorbed with putting his plan into

effect, the world outside his Connecticut compound had changed in a deadly way. The drug scene had moved way beyond even the selfishness he had seen on Wall Street. Crack cocaine and blood were beginning to flow freely in the streets in the big cities of America. Becky was just one of the thousands of hapless victims, and with all his experience and wealth, he could not protect her.

After her death, he had brought his son, Philip, to the island. He spent the first couple of years teaching him manly things—fishing, hunting, self-defense. But he realized he couldn't keep Philip there forever, under his protection. To be whole, Philip would have to break from him and make his own way, be his own man, just as Jones had done before him. So he found the best boarding school in Texas, and enrolled him. The director had assured him that the individualized instruction that only money could buy, would fill in whatever gaps that existed in Philip's academic education, and that he would surely follow in his father's footsteps right up to the ivy-covered gates of Harvard.

Jones couldn't figure, for the life of him, why he was pouring out his life story to these women he had just met. Maybe it was the wine. He hadn't had alcohol in a long time. During his story, he had moved the tray out of Sondra's chair for her to sit down, and had assumed the task of pouring the wine. It was just in his nature to quietly take charge. Now, feeling overcome by a sense of urgency to leave, he abruptly stopped talking and stood.

"I apologize for drinking all of your wine, not to mention bending your ears. I'm sure this is not what you had planned for your trip. I'll help you put the fire out, and see to you locking up safe inside."

Neither of the women moved. Jones had kept the fire going through his visit, by occasionally adding to it from the pile of branches Eleanor had brought. Although it now was dying, the embers were bright red, and cast a nice glow. The near-full moon was visible between the pine trees.

"Thanks, but I think we'll sit here by the fire a little longer. It's too nice to go in just yet," Sondra said.

"Well, if you're sure. I'll build the fire up a little for you before I go."

After he did, he said, "Say 'goodnight' to Eleanor for me. And assure her that I won't 'interfere' again—and most of all that I'm not an axe-murderer. Thank you for a most pleasant evening. Perhaps I can return the favor before you leave."

Jones waved back at them before walking into the woods.

THREE

Isaac Evans watched the brick red sportscar drive up. A Nissan 300 ZX. He didn't know anybody around here who drove a fancy car like that. Whoever it was must be lost. Still, they were a brave somebody to have followed the driveway so far off the road, past the clearing and 'The Mansion', near the spot where he sat on the grassy edge of the lake, fishing. His boldly-lettered "Trespassers Will Be Shot On Sight" sign was clearly visible at the gate that he was sure he'd closed. He never left the gate open, even when he was here.

Ike rose to his feet, as the driver brought the car to a stop, and unfolded his long body from under the wheel. Ike found himself staring into his own face—ten years ago. The same chocolate complexion, the same shining black eyes, the thick black moustache, the same white teeth showing in his smile. He hadn't seen his little brother, the one he'd raised like a son, in three years.

"Say, man, can't you read?" Ike inquired with a big grin.

"Well, what you gonna do? Shoot me with that fishing

pole?" Donnell returned the same broad grin, as he walked toward his older brother and grabbed him in a bear hug.

"What you doing here? Man, I'm glad to see you," Ike said, after lots of hugging and back-slapping.

"Oh, I just had a little time coming, and what better place in the world to take a vacation, than home?" Donnell asked, his black eyes shining.

"How'd you know where to find me?" Ike asked.

"I went by the house and didn't see your truck. Where else would you be, but here?"

"You bring your rod?"

"You know as well as I do that I left it in 'The Mansion' the last time I was here. You didn't catch that big ol' cat while I was gone, did you?"

"Boy, me and that old cat been waiting for you for years. His whiskers are probably gray by now. You know we both want you to be here when I catch him, so you'll really know, once and for all, who the best fisherman in the whole state is."

"Nah, nah, nah. Mr. Charlie's been waiting on me all this time. Today just may be the day. Let me go get my rod. Be right back."

Ike chuckled to himself as he watched his younger brother walk toward 'The Mansion.' That was the name Donnell had given the Quonset hut Ike had bought at an Army-Navy surplus sale and set up years ago when they outgrew the tent. A tent was all they had, when Ike first bought the land. The name was their little joke. Donnell may have wanted a mansion. Ike never had. He'd had something simpler in mind. A two-bedroom A-frame was more to his taste. But he had always encouraged Donnell to dream his dreams. Donnell had accomplished most of his dreams—and some of Ike's as well.

When Donnell returned, Ike was again seated on the grassy edge of the lake, watching his cork. He took a couple of practice casts, before settling down next to his brother on the bank.

"You've really fixed 'The Mansion' up since I was here. I like it. I see you left the basketball hoop up. You been shooting?"

"Nah. I leave it up for the kids. Every once in a while, I bring the Explorer Scout troop from the Church out here for the weekend—usually when I need some cleaning and clearing. I pass out the shovels and rakes and stuff—and the keys to the mower. They fight over a turn on that riding mower. They have a good time, and I get some work out of them. It's a 'Jesse deal.' Good for both of us. When they finish the work, I let them play ball as long as they want. You see the lights? They put the lights up themselves. I told them I would buy the stuff if they figured out how to do it—without getting anybody killed. And, by God, they did it," he said, laughing and slapping his thigh. "Of course, I think they all got a shock or two before it was done. It was good for 'em. Made them have to study, have to think, work as a team."

"So what do you do—other than use those poor boys?" Donnell asked with a mischievous grin.

"I ref for them. I show them some moves, how to improve their game. Some of them are real star quality. One in particular, Derrick Woodall, puts me in the mind of you, at that age. Best body among the bunch. Smart as a whip; knows everything. Thinks he's slick. Still, he'll listen—most of the time. But, lately…" A frown crossed his face, then he shook it off. "Oh, well. How long can you stay? Maybe I can get them out here and let 'em play with a real NBA star. They'd love it. You owe it.

A 'Jesse deal.' How about next Saturday?"

"Sure. Sounds like fun. I'd planned to stay that long—maybe even longer. I could get used to this," Donnell said, looking at the tranquil beauty of the lake, ringed by tall pine trees.

All the while, Donnell had been watching his cork, bobbing lazily on the placid lake, so his eyes narrowed when it dipped under a couple of times in rapid succession. His body tensed as he got ready. It dipped again—longer this time. He held his breath and didn't move. He bided his time. Soon, the cork went under completely. Ike noticed too, and resisted the urge to tell him, again, how to do it. Instead, he just watched as his little brother showed him he'd learned his lessons well. With a flip of his wrist, Donnell jerked the rod solidly, but not too hard—just enough to imbed the hook—then relaxed it. He let the fish run a while, then reeled in some of the line. When he felt the resistance, he released the tension on the line and allowed the fish to run some more. He could tell it was a nice sized fish, but he also knew it wasn't the one he was looking for. He repeated the sequence several more times, 'til he felt the fish wearing out. He smiled as he heard Ike saying "Easy, easy" under his breath—still being coach and father. Each time, Donnell reeled the fish in closer, until finally it was just below the surface of the water in front of them. He held the pressure now, stood up and reached into the water, grabbing the fish behind his gills, and held him up for Ike to see. The fish was a good size, although not enough for dinner for the two of them. Still, he was beaming.

"Just like catching a woman. Like you said, 'Give 'em some line, let 'em run, then reel 'em in.' If you can manage to catch one near this size, we'd have enough for dinner. I know you haven't put a phone in yet. You can use the phone in my car to call your lady to come on over and heat up some grease. Well, I guess we both need to catch a couple more so there'll be enough for her too. Tell her to bring a friend. You still messing with Jackie? When ya'll gonna hook-up? Man, that woman's too fine. Nah, she's three fine."

As Donnell removed the hook, put the fish on the stringer, and baited the hook again, a wry smile crossed Ike's face.

"Nah man, she got tired of waiting on me. Married some dude from Houston and moved. She wanted kids and all that. Been there, done that," he said as he looked knowingly at Donnell.

Now in his early forties, Ike knew he was still young enough to raise a family, he just wasn't sure he wanted to. He had done well enough with the ranch and the other investments, that money wouldn't be a problem. He had the stamina to do it. Thanks to his early training, and the work he had done for years, his body still maintained its muscular form. In fact, in comparing his body with Donnell's younger, slightly taller one, Ike was pleased.

Ike saw that Donnell had kept fit through the four years he had been out of the pros. Many of the pro athletes let themselves go, when they were pushed out by younger, faster players, eager to make a name for themselves, or when the lifestyle took its toll on their play. Donnell had been one of the smart ones. He'd left at the height of his career, while the fans were still calling his name. The surgeons had told him that, with proper rehabilitation, he could play as good as ever. Ike hadn't quite understood why he then took a government job. With the FBI or DEA, something like that—Ike could never remember. In a couple of years, Donnell had quit that too, to open his own security firm. It had actually been a sharp move. He'd used his NBA connections to get security contracts for several arenas. Initially, his employees protected the parking lots and the dressing rooms. Soon he had expanded to provide the team escorts and, seeing the need develop, offered personal bodyguard service. His most recent expansion was into computer security. Donnell was doing well for himself. A father's pride shone in Ike's eyes when he looked at Donnell now, in the dimming light.

It hadn't always been that way. Ike remembered Donnell as a brash young kid. Then, Ike himself had been too young to be a father, when the mantle of fatherhood was thrust on him. Didn't have a clue how to do it. But he had no choice. When their Dad died, Ike was in his senior year in college. The future he'd planned was finally unfolding for him. It had taken him too long to get there. And a circuitous journey it had been. He had been 21 years old when he finally enrolled. He had never given up his dream, even through the dark days in Viet Nam.

Ike had been a good athlete in high school–one hell of a basketball player–and had dreams of his own. Wilt Chamberlain had been his hero. Ike had planned to use his athletic prowess to get the degree he coveted. But he'd planned to get an education—as well as a degree. He would be a biologist, specifically a geneticist. He planned to return home and partner with his Dad. He chose the school where he would have access to the best-equipped lab in the country. He knew Black athletes–hell, all the athletes–were usually steered into the easy courses. He knew what he'd planned wouldn't be easy, but he was accustomed to hard work and it did not scare him. He was smart and he knew it. All that was blown away when he got the letter from the Draft Board.

Although he suspected they'd pulled some funny business, there was nothing he could do about it. Instead of college, he was going to the Army. At that time, only Whites could serve on the Draft Board. He knew Joe Crowley, who headed it, was put out when Ike got more notice in the local paper than his own son. Big Joe absolutely went into a rage when the Houston papers started following Ike. Ike believed to this day that Big Joe had had more to do with his being drafted, than bad luck had. Little Joe didn't get called. Ike believed Big Joe had something to do with that, too.

Little Joe was a fairly good basketball player, but he had such a soft life, he didn't have the real hustle in him. Ike actually liked Little Joe. They were a good pair on the court when Little Joe followed his lead—and he always did. They hadn't grown up together, because the schools, as well as everything else, were segregated then. When the school board had been forced to de-segregate the schools—like most places in Texas—it was done by closing the Black high school, Paul Lawrence Dunbar. Ike and Little Joe both had been in 11th grade. Ike would have excelled wherever he was—in the classroom and on the court. Robert E. Lee High School was no exception. Little Joe had done what he could to make things easier for him in the locker room and on the court, and Ike appreciated that. Those were tense times for everybody. On Ike's part, he'd shown Little Joe some moves to improve his play. Ike had worked out the plays for the two of them that no one in the district, or region, could defeat. Ike received the credit for catapulting Robert E. Lee into the State Finals down in Austin, and he deserved it. Big Joe could never see that his son wasn't a natural athlete. Little Joe hadn't had any passion for the game until Ike came to Lee. Before that, he was only walking in the path that his father's ranching money had paved for him. He wouldn't have made the B-team at Dunbar. But he was a stand-up fellow anyway and Ike thought of him as a friend, even now.

Ike had been courted by many of the major universities, even the University of Kansas where his idol had played. But his sights were set higher. He nearly turned himself inside out when the letter came from his chosen school. When the coaches came down to meet with his parents, he could hardly contain himself. But he had to. He respected his parents that much. They knew how much he wanted to go to that school and they would see that he did, even though it wouldn't have been their choice for him to go so far away—up North.

His Dad, Jesse Evans, had been North when he was a young man. After high school, he'd studied animal husbandry at Prairie View Normal and Industrial College. He'd been able to stay there long enough to know what he was doing, when his funds ran out. He went North to work, planning to send for Esther when the time was right. Esther stayed and got a degree in elementary education. She returned to her father's home, secured a teaching position in the Colored School—and waited for Jesse. Their love was deep and patient.

Jesse found the North to be not that much different from the South—for a Black man. So he had returned to the only roots he knew, and with the money he'd made up there, bought some land of his own. Esther's father had married them in his church in the Springtime. They lived with Reverend Walker until Jesse finished building their house on his land. When they moved in, Esther was already pregnant with Ike. Their pretty brown baby was born the next Spring. They lost two babies, then much later had another son, Donnell.

Esther—they all called her 'Muhdea'—had taught at the elementary school until the school board closed it. Like many Black teachers at the time, she was summarily fired. But unlike most of them, she did not have to move to another town to find work. She and Jesse owned their own land, and he made a good living, having developed a reputation over the years as having the best breeding stock in those parts.

The White coaches who came from the school up North had expected they would be dealing with some ignorant share-croppers, and it showed in their condescending smiles. It didn't take Jesse long to relieve them of that notion. He was accustomed to doing business with White men on an equal footing. And he always had superior knowledge of the goods subject to the deal, be it a yearling—or his son. In the end, he got the deal he knew was best for Ike. The coaches went away happy about the deal, too. That was the way Jesse did business. He called it a 'Jesse deal.'

None of it had mattered, however. Two weeks before Ike was to leave for school, the letter came from the Draft Board. When Jesse called the coaches for their intervention, they claimed to be as disappointed as he. And they probably thought they were. But they had a whole team of good basketball players—Jesse only had one Ike. Jesse refused to go to the local White men, despite Esther's pleading. He knew they would only take some primeval joy in his pain. He would have borne that too, and gladly, if he thought it would save Ike from the killing fields of Viet Nam that he saw on TV news each night. But he knew they wouldn't help. In the end, Jesse had told his first-born to 'be a man', do his duty, learn as much as he could—and come back ready to go to school.

After the farewell ceremony for Ike at the bus station in town, Muhdea let Donnell go home with the Wilsons. Their sons were about the same age and played together often. She anticipated she would be inconsolable, and Jesse would be her strength, as he had always been. Instead, she had to be his. Jesse sat mute in his big chair, staring into space for hours. Then he cried—first tears of abject sorrow, then tears of absolute rage. It was the only time in their life together Esther had seen Jesse in this state—out of control, beyond her reach.

Unlike so many other mothers' sons, Ike made it through Viet Nam without much more than a flesh wound. Some had left limbs in that fertile place; others had left their minds; some didn't come back at all. Esther and Jesse thanked God theirs had come back whole. Ike had followed his father's advice. He had indeed become a man. When he refused to talk about the war, Jesse understood and left him alone, except to continue to teach him what he knew about animals, and the land.

Ike submitted his application to the same school, the day after he returned. Having veteran's benefits to help pay for his schooling would make getting his degree a lot easier. No need to play basketball. He was too old then to play games—of any kind. He was a man with a mission. He'd faced death. School would be a snap—just longer.

Ike entered college with a zeal unmatched by any of his classmates. Against the advice of his advisors, he signed up for the maximum hours allowed each semester. It was only at the upper class level that students were allowed into the lab and to interact with the researchers. When he reached that point, he enjoyed school. It was no longer just a chore he had to get through to reach his goal. It wasn't long before his constant presence in the lab had been accepted. He'd come there with more practical knowledge than any of them had at that point in their lives—things Jesse had taught him. They shared everything they knew around him; but he didn't. Ike had learned the hard way that they would claim credit for what he shared with them.

Late one night, just after his final semester began, the phone was ringing as he entered his tiny apartment. As soon as he heard Muhdea's voice on the telephone, he knew something was wrong. She wrote him long letters regularly, always enclosing several bills—"here's a little something for you." But a long-distance call was an extravagance for her that was reserved for births and deaths. He packed immediately and went home. They buried Jesse on his own land—the only place he would have been happy.

In the week that Ike was home after the funeral, he worried about making up the school work he was missing. He was anxious for the semester to be over, so he could return home for good. But he worried more about the change he saw in the town, and in his little brother. It was easy to see that Donnell, at fourteen, could have been every bit as good an athlete as he had been. But Donnell was hanging out. Muhdea didn't know who his friends were. He'd abandoned the Wilson boy that Muhdea thought so much of. Ike had tried to talk to him several times, but Donnell was good at avoiding him—getting out of the house early and coming back late. He especially didn't like the way Donnell talked to Muhdea, the few times he *was* around. Ike was certain Jesse had not known how Donnell addressed his mother.

Jesse would have killed a grown man with his bare hands for disrespecting her. Muhdea had always been over-protective of Donnell, in a way she had not been with Ike. Donnell had been her baby, and had come late in her life, after losing two. Ike didn't want to bother Muhdea with what he was thinking. She was grieving hard.

At the end of the week, he returned to New England and plowed back into his work. He tried to call Muhdea at least once a week to check on her. He could tell from those conversations that the ranch was going to hell—and Donnell, too. He found he couldn't concentrate on his studies, for worrying about what was happening back home. In the end, he withdrew from school, a semester short of his dream, and went home. It was his duty to all of them, especially Jesse. Jesse had taught him about duty.

Ike arrived home on a Monday. After visiting with Muhdea a while, he unpacked, then spent the afternoon and evening surveying what had to be done to get the breeding farm back in tip-top shape. Tuesday morning he spent with Muhdea going over the finances of the operation. She had kept their books, and because she was so organized, all that was in order. Together, they decided the most ground could be covered by leaving that function with her, while Ike concentrated on the farm. Thursday came, and he still hadn't been able to catch Donnell. When Ike had asked Muhdea about him, she became vague and quiet. She said maybe he was just having growing pains. Although Ike thought something different, he kept his counsel. He knew what he had to do.

After a hard day Friday, Ike came in, showered and dressed. He told Muhdea he was going to town, try to catch up with some of his old friends. He drove straight toward 'the cuts'. That was a block-long area which contained the only night spots on the Black side of town. It had been there as long as he could remember, and hadn't changed much. This night was no different than endless Fridays before. Most of the men had their pay in their pockets and were feeling like 'real men' for the first time that week. Testosterone was flowing. It would be much later, after too much alcohol, when the fights started. Sometimes blood flowed. The women were there for a good time, the dancing, some trying 'to catch.' The law only came when summoned, and they were only summoned when the trouble was so big that even Big Mike couldn't quell it—or when there was a body. Big Mike ran the enterprises. He was mean as a snake, and carried a pistol at all times. He also had a shotgun behind the bar. Rumor had it Big Mike had killed two men and had never spent a day in prison. Rumor also had it that Big Mike had killed more than ten men. The truth probably lay somewhere in between. The red and blue tattoos said he had definitely spent some time in prison.

Ike parked down the block a ways and watched all the activity. He recognized most of the people coming and going. He recognized Donnell, leaning against the corner of the building, amid a knot of young men, most several years older. Donnell was big for his age and did not look out of place in a cursory glance. Every now and then, someone would approach the group. Shortly one of the young men would stroll off nonchalantly toward the back of the building, return and give the newcomer the 'Black handshake' and send him on his way. Sometimes a car, usually containing a couple of young Whites, would pull up near the group. One of the group would approach the car, chat a moment, then stroll toward the back of the building. He would return, give the handshake and the car would leave. Ike knew immediately what the deal was.

When Ike regained control of his anger, he got out of the car and strolled up to the group.

"Hey, what's up? Ya'll know where I could get a little smoke?" he asked, not giving a hint of recognition to Donnell.

"Might. How much you want?" one spoke up.

With his thumb, Ike pushed the bill in his fist up enough to show the denomination.

The fellow walked off and shortly returned. In the handshake, he exchanged the bill for the plastic bag.

"Thanks, man," Ike said, and strolled back to the car.

Donnell was the only one in the group that noticed the car did not drive away. Ike waited. After thirty minutes had passed, Donnell could stand it no longer. He walked down the block to the car and got in.

"Why you tripping, man?" Donnell spit out, his mouth in a pout.

Ike said nothing, staring straight ahead.

"Who you think you are, man? The big war hero. Been off fightin' the White man's war. Now here you come taking over everything, trying to boss everybody around, messing in everybody's business. You should have stayed up there in the White man's school. Me and Muhdea were doing fine without you."

Ike was seething, but it only showed in his flashing black eyes and the tension pulsating in his jaw.

"Yeah, I can see that," he said, his voice tight and hard. "Did Dad know what you're up to?"

"That old man didn't know nothing, but them ol' cows," Donnell said, still pouting.

Ike thought the car would explode with his anger. He took three deep breaths, started the engine and drove off toward home.

"What you doing, man?! I ain't going home. It's too early. You can't make me go home," Donnell protested all the way.

Ike didn't say a word the entire distance. When they reached the driveway, Ike drove to the back of the house. As he shut off the engine, he turned to Donnell.

"Get out. Go in the house and go to bed. We'll talk about this in the morning."

"You can't tell me what to do," Donnell shot back, not moving.

Ike just shook his head. He got out of the car, walked around to the passenger door, snatched it open, and grabbed Donnell in the chest with both hands. Ike dragged him out of the car and dropped him onto the ground. Donnell was so shocked, he didn't resist at first. When he did, it was to no avail. Although they were nearly the same height, Ike was stronger, his anger was greater, his body had been trained—he had killed. Ike grabbed him again and alternately dragged and pushed him out through the back yard and deep into the pasture, where he threw him down on the ground and sat beside him. Ike was breathing hard, more from trying to control his anger, than from the exertion. By now, all the fight was out of Donnell.

"You look at these 'ol' cows' real good, boy. These ol' cows are what has kept you alive. They provided you with a nice house, all the food you wanted, new clothes and everything. Let me tell you something, you better make damn sure, as long as I live, I *never* hear you saying anything disrespectful of these 'ol' cows'—or my daddy—again." His nostrils flared and lightening flashed in his eyes. "And another thing, if I see, or even hear of, you treating Muhdea any other way than the queen she is, you won't even be able to live long enough to regret it enough. Understand?! Now you get yo ass up, go in the house and go to bed."

After a minute, Donnell did just that.

The next morning Donnell awoke to the sound of his name. When he opened his eyes, he saw Ike standing over him. He sat bolt upright, the grogginess vanished instantly.

"Get up and get dressed. We've got a lot of work to do today," Ike said.

"We?" Donnell demanded.

Ike gave him a menacing glare. "Yes, WE. Muhdea is fixing breakfast and you better have your butt in a chair and a smile on your face when she sets the last plate on the table." He walked out and closed the door.

Donnell grumbled under his breath—way under his breath. He thought about digging back under the covers and forgetting about Ike. He thought, "I ain't scared of that dude. Muhdea won't let him do nothing to me." Then he remembered the fire in Ike's eyes the night before. Ike had been to a war. Maybe it drove him crazy, like ol' Grinnin' Jimmy. Maybe even Muhdea couldn't stop him. He thought maybe it was best to just play along with this crazy dude for a while. He smiled to himself. They didn't call him 'Slick D' for nothing. When the last plate was set, he did indeed have his butt in the chair.

"Morning, Muhdea," he said, with a smile.

Although Ike's expression did not change, Esther nearly dropped the coffee pot when she saw Donnell sit at the table. She couldn't remember the last time Donnell had been up for breakfast on a Saturday morning—and especially at this hour. He usually slept 'til the afternoon, dressed, gave her a peck on the cheek—promising to return early—on his way out the door. It had started right after Jesse died. Of course, he never came back early. At first, she had waited up for Donnell. But that only ended in loud arguments and slamming doors. She even resorted to sabotage. Once, in a fit of anger and desperation in the middle of the night, she tore the sheets off his bed and left them in a pile on the floor. The next morning, she found him asleep on the bare mattress. In the end, she walked that last mother mile—turned him over to the hands of The Lord.

After that, she'd slept a little better, but still she worried. She didn't dare say it, but she wondered why he couldn't be more like Ike. Ike had never given her a minute's trouble. He was so much like Jesse. It almost brought tears to her eyes to look at him now. She was heartbroken that Ike had quit school. She knew how much it meant to him—and he was so close. She tried to persuade him she could manage for the few remaining months, but he had made up his mind. When he folded his arms across his chest that certain way, and set his mouth just like Jesse, she knew it was no use. She would get back to that, when things settled down. She was so glad Ike was home. In just a week, he'd come so far in repairing the damage to the ranch, wrought by several months' neglect. She hadn't neglected Donnell. If anything, maybe she had spoiled him too much. Maybe Ike could fix Donnell, too.

And Ike did fix him. Or maybe Donnell fixed himself when

a firm hand was applied. Ike made him help with the ranch work. He taught him basketball, how to fish—and how to be a man.

"It's him! It's him!" Donnell's shouting brought Ike from his reverie. "Told you I'd be the one to get Mr. Charlie."

Donnell had gotten too excited by the prospect of besting his big brother. Losing control of his emotions had caused him to lose the coveted fish. Regaining his composure, Donnell played the whole thing off. "I was just kidding. Today's not the right day. We'll have Mr. Charlie to dinner the last day I'm here. That'll be the right day."

They continued to fish until they had a nice mess. When the sun got low, Ike suggested they eat. They went into 'The Mansion,' and while Ike cooked their catch, Donnell talked about his company and how excited he was about his newest venture. Ike listened with mixed emotions. He had long had a vision of a sign that read EVANS BROTHERS CATTLE COMPANY, ever since Donnell had made the decision to leave the NBA. Nothing in this conversation gave him any hope that would happen soon. They returned outdoors with their plates full of fried fish and potatoes to the long picnic table Ike had built to accommodate his Scout troop. Ike had switched on the light on the side of the hut that shone directly on the table. They ate heartily.

"My boys wired this too," Ike said proudly.

Donnell hated to admit that he felt a twinge of jealousy. Ike had been a good brother, father and friend to him. Why shouldn't he be the same to some other boy that needed him as much now, as he had then. It was the first time Donnell had thought of Ike as a man of a certain characteristic, and himself as the happen-

stance beneficiary. Until now, he always viewed their relationship as being driven by his own need, to which Ike was only
responding.

"Wanna brew?" Ike asked.

When Ike returned with the bottles, they sipped and talked
about old times. Ike brought Donnell up on his old friends—who
was working at the plant, who had been to prison, marriages,
divorces, births, and deaths.

The huge moon was directly overhead when they heard the
piercing scream reverberating through the pines.

"What the hell!" Ike knew no one lived that close, and that
the adjacent property was vacant. Before he made up his mind,
Donnell had already started off, in a full sprint, through the
woods.

FOUR

Eleanor flopped down on the couch, her arms folded tightly across her chest, her brow in a knot. She knew there were white ridges around her lips because she felt the tension of them pressed together. She recognized it. The old pattern. She thought that was all behind her, that she had control over it.

Doing the exercise Dr. Martinez had shown her, she forced her lips to relax. She had found the perfect therapist in Lydia Martinez. Her therapy sessions were infrequent now—only when she felt the need. In her last session several months before, Dr. Martinez had asked whether she had reached the stage that she could have a relationship with a man. Eleanor had given her a non-commital 'maybe,' but at her age the prospects were few. Dr. Martinez, taking her response as a positive, had warned that she'd have to guard against the old pattern at first. The two dinner dates she'd had hadn't evoked it. Maybe it was the fact that balding heads and bulbous bellies weren't attractive to her. This fellow certainly didn't suffer from either of those. She'd noticed *that* when she saw him emerge from the store. She had been surprised at her reaction to him, as though she would punish him for her attraction to him. Then, she realized it wasn't that he was a man that brought it on. It was that he'd used the H-word.

She didn't need his help. She didn't need anybody's help. To hell with all of them. She felt the ridges. She crossed one leg over the other and jerked it in a tense rhythm. There it was again. The old pattern. She felt foolish about the way she had acted. She had seen the curious look on Angela's face, fleeting as it had been. And she knew Sondra had been embarrassed, even though she was good at hiding it. For a moment, she wondered if they were talking about her around the campfire, and the way she had behaved. No. They would talk *to* her about it—she was sure of that. She was equally certain they would never talk *about* her to a stranger. Feeling the softness of their caring, she toyed with the idea of going back outside. She wanted to be with her friends. She walked to the front of the RV and moved the windshield curtain back just a little. He was still there. She wondered what he was saying that held their attention so. When he stood abruptly, facing the RV, she quickly closed the curtain.

Sondra and Angela waved back to Jones as he walked into the woods.

"You think he made that story up? About his wife and all?" Angela asked.

"Why would anybody make up something like that? No. I don't think so." Sondra answered. She had seen the loss on his face, and recognized it.

For a time, they were both quiet, sipping their wine.

"You worried about Eleanor?" Angela asked.

"No. Are you?"

"Well, kind of. She hasn't done that in a while. I thought she was...you know...over it."

"Yeah, me too. I don't know what set her off. Don't worry, she'll be OK."

Angela rose from her seat. "I'm going to get her. Maybe she's cooled off enough to come out—now that her axe-murderer is gone," Angela said, laughing at her own little joke.

"Good idea. No point in her missing this beautiful moon. You know how she loves it. Always plans our trips by it," Sondra replied, without taking her eyes off the reflections on the lake. It was so beautiful, so peaceful. Her days were usually spent refereeing between warring factions. Peace was precious to her.

Shortly, the two women returned, Angela carrying a bottle of wine, Eleanor carrying her chair. She wasn't ready to talk about it, but she was practical enough not to let it keep her from enjoying her favorite sight—the full moon—and her favorite company.

"You OK?" Sondra asked, examining her face as she would one of her daughters'.

"Yes. I'm fine." She knew that would be enough for Sondra, for now.

"Talk about fine," Angela said. "That Jones is the one that's fine. I like that kind of rugged, Clint Eastwood look. I saw the way he was looking at you, Eleanor. You ought to go for it, girlfriend."

"Leave it alone, Angela," Sondra said, her voice quiet and stern.

Eleanor was the first to see the boat drifting their way. "Oh, no. Not him again," she groaned.

The others saw it too. They watched the little flat-bottomed fishing boat drifting closer and closer, propelled by the gentle waves.

"I don't see anybody in it. And I don't hear a motor. Doesn't look like it even has a motor," Angela said, straining to see.

"Maybe it's some fisherman, fell asleep. He'd have to be drunk tho' not to feel the motion. Maybe it just broke loose. But this little breeze wouldn't be enough to do that," Sondra said.

Then they were quiet, watching. When the boat first began to softly bump into the bank in front of them, none of them said anything.

"Let's go check it out. The least we can do is tie it up until morning, then find the owner," Eleanor said, rising from her chair and lazily stretching her body.

"It's genetic," Angela said.

She and Sondra exchanged glances and giggles. Eleanor laughed, too. She knew their little joke, about how only a White woman, always wearing high heels, would unlock a door and leave her safe home, go outside to investigate whether the sound she thought she heard was made by a knife-wielding madman. How it always was. How she would always stumble on the high heels and fall—and how her slashed and blood-soaked body was found the next morning. No Black woman in her right mind would act like that. Eleanor preferred to think that she was just the more curious of the three. But she had to admit, she *was* always the one to initiate an investigation. On the other hand, she was too much of a feminist to *ever* wear high heels.

Shaking her head and smiling, Eleanor rolled her eyes

heavenward. Dismissing them with a flick of her wrist, Eleanor sauntered to the edge of the lake. She reached down to gain control of the boat by pulling hard on the rope dangling from its bow. She didn't notice that the rope was not attached to the boat, but instead to a cheap plastic tarpaulin. She fell backwards from the strength of her pull against the unexpected weightlessness of the material. She clasped her hand over her mouth to stifle a scream, at what she saw underneath it. On reflex, Angela and Sondra sprang from their chairs and ran to where she had fallen into a sitting position. They saw the young Black man sprawled on his back inside the boat, his vacant eyes seeming to stare at the bright moon, his mouth open. The blood that had pumped out of the jagged cut across his throat, was a shiny pool under his head on the seat of the boat.

Much later, they had good-natured arguments over who screamed first—a blood-curdling scream. No matter, the first was joined by a cacophony of screams, before they all collapsed in a shaking heap, their arms around each other. They were still in that position when the large man came crashing into the clearing from the woods, another on his heels.

The women and the men were equally shocked to see each other. The women immediately connected the men with the hideous sight in the boat. Sondra was on her feet in a flash, the gun drawn.

"Stop! Or I'll shoot!"

The men were so completely shocked, they did—skidding to a stop. Both put their hands up, as if to push themselves backwards.

Ike was the first to speak. "We won't hurt you, lady. Point the gun down."

Donnell started toward her, youth and training giving him confidence that he could easily overtake her. The sound of gunfire shattered the quiet night, echoing through the forest, startling them both. He recovered quicker and lunged at Sondra, grabbing the gun, throwing it away from them, and taking her to the ground in one movement. Angela scrambled after Eleanor into the fray, clawing, scratching and pounding on the man who had attacked their friend.

Momentarily shaken by the sharp sound of the gunfire, Ike stood watching. He walked over to the gun and picked it up, containing the real danger. Watching the comic scene unfolding before his eyes, Ike let out a deep, whooping belly laugh. Donnell still had Sondra in the bear hug he'd used to take her to the ground, rolling her this way and that, using her struggling body as a shield against the other women's blows. Ike laughed so deep and hard that tears came to his eyes. The sound was so incongruous to all of their ears, that, one by one, they quit the fight, to stare at him. Not one of them, covered in red dust and pine needles and breathing hard, thought anything funny had happened.

Seeing all eyes on him, and the non-plussed looks, Ike was finally able to contain himself. He wiped his eyes with the heels of his hands.

"What on earth are ya'll doing here?"

"We might ask you the same question," Eleanor responded huffily, rising and dusting her clothes off. She raked her hand through the ponytail to dislodge the pine needles.

"We live on the next cove. We heard ya'll screaming. What happened? You see a snake? Lots of them around here. That's no call for you to shoot at us—then beat my brother up," he said, chuckling again.

"That isn't funny, Ike. You didn't even help me, man," Donnell said, pouting, as he stood and dusted off his clothes. He reached a hand to help Angela up.

"Well, sir, if you think *that* was funny, you'll find the body in that boat down there downright hilarious," Sondra said calmly, still seated, jerking her thumb toward the boat.

"Body? What boat? What?" Donnell asked.

"Come see. It's horrible," Angela said, pulling him by his hand.

Eleanor followed Angela and the men toward the edge of the lake, where the boat was still bumping against the shore. Sondra wrapped her arms around her knees and put her head down. She didn't want to see the body again. She was disgusted with herself. All that target practice, and for nothing. When she was confronted with real danger, she choked. She wasn't sure whether she had purposefully fired the gun, or trembled the shot off. The one thing she *was* sure of, neither David nor Daddy would ever know she had disobeyed their teachings. Watching the little group by the boat, she was relieved she had.

Ike recognized the boy immediately. A tortured "No-o-o." escaped his lips, trailing off into the night, as he jumped into the boat. He shook the boy, vainly hoping to bring him back. But he knew, even as he hugged the boy's body to him, that he was dead, and there was nothing he could do.

Donnell didn't recognize the boy, but he could tell Ike did, by his reaction and the pained expression on his face.

"Who is he, Ike?"

"Derrick," Ike said, his voice breaking, as he gently laid the boy down.

Seeing his brother's tortured face, Donnell was ashamed of himself for the jealousy he had felt earlier, when he'd first heard the boy's name. It seemed so inappropriate now, with the boy dead. He also felt bad for Ike's having belittled the women. Finding a body is a long way from finding a snake.

"You got some rope we can tie the boat up with?" Ike asked toward the women. "Donnell, you go to your car and call the sheriff."

"There's a phone in the RV. You can call the sheriff from there. It's probably closer. C'mon I'll show you," Sondra said to Ike, then emphatically, "And *give* me my gun. Angela'll get the rope."

With all the commotion, neither man had noticed the big vehicle nestled among the tall pines.

"You know that kid?" Sondra asked Ike, as they walked toward it.

"Yeah, he was in my Scout troop. Good kid, basically. I don't know why in the world somebody would do this to him." He shook his head. "My name is Isaac Evans. Ike."

"Pleased to meet you Mr. Evans. I guess. Under the circumstances. I'm Sondra Ellis. You two must be brothers. Watch your step."

Conscious of his height, Ike bent slightly to go through the doorway, as he followed Sondra up the steps. He had never been in an RV before. Once inside, it looked larger than it had from the outside, but his large frame took up a lot of space. A quick glance around showed him all the amenities of home—sofa and two chairs, a small kitchen, tiny bathroom, and a bedroom. It was clearly a woman's home—soft pinks, blues, mauve. And lace. The soft strands of a jazz guitar drifted through.

While Ike placed the call on the phone she'd handed him, Sondra went to the kitchen area and started a pot of coffee. When she approached the couch to get the cups down from the overhead cabinet, she saw the dejection on Ike's face and his body. He was bent over, forearms on his knees, dangling the phone between them in his hand. She had the urge to put her arms around him, to comfort him. Instead, she stood watching him, as he slowly shook his head back and forth. She didn't even know this man. But she *did* know the feeling, and knew it well.

Memories flooded over her—of seeing her husband's still, and blood-splattered body lying on the edge of the narrow roadway. Her reaction had been the same then as Ike's at the boat—only to a greater magnitude. She had screamed Michael's name and reached for him, but Maxwell, the big detective who had brought her there, pulled her back. She resisted and fought like a mad-woman, completely out of control. She screamed and railed, deep guttural sounds, until she was hoarse. She pounded on Maxwell's arms and chest and tried to break free. When she went limp, he gently led her to Michael's body, dismissing the uniformed officers standing by, with instructions to keep the press and the curious at bay. Sondra knelt beside Michael and pulled his head into her lap, completely mindless of the blood staining the white silk pantsuit she wore. Tears fell silently, as her body rocked rhythmically back and forth, and her fingers stroked his temples. After a time, she heard Maxwell's soft voice.

"Sondra, the ME's here. Come on, I'll take you home. There's nothing more you can do here. You'll have to tell the girls."

Sondra nodded she understood, but didn't move immediately—not until she bent over and kissed Michael on the lips. Then she allowed Maxwell to take her back to his car.

Sondra knew there was never enough she could do to thank Lt. Kirk Maxwell for having been her rock during those times—and others as well. He always said no thanks were necessary. He liked her, respected the way she did her job. She didn't look down on his men, like some of the judges. Not that she was the 'cops' judge,' like some of the others tried to be. She would no more countenance shoddy or underhanded police work, than she would an unprepared attorney in her court. In those cases, she had never once upbraided either one in open court, but her rulings clearly reflected what was on her mind. Leaving the bench, she would pause, and ask with a smile, "Officer Jones, (or Attorney Smith, as the case may be), can I see you a moment in my chambers." Her voice held more demand, than invitation.

Whatever went on in there, although the subject of much speculation and teasing among the offender's peers, was never repeated outside those doors. After those little chats, she would escort the errant one to her door with a handshake saying, "I know you're busy. I appreciate you making time to see me," as though they had done her a favor. In the very few cases there had been of repeated offense, she had taken swift and appropriate action, be it a letter to the State Bar Association, or a commanding officer.

A couple of weeks after the funeral, Maxwell told Sondra of how he had heard the broadcast about the accident—one apparent fatality, lone occupant—on his police radio. He instantly recognized the car from the description and plate number. He had tailed that car many times, sometimes on official assignment, and sometimes out of personal concern. He immediately turned his big cruiser around and headed for her house. He radioed in his destination and purpose, so that her family wouldn't hear this terrible news from a stranger on the phone, or at the door. He then called his wife and told her how to reach the house. She would arrive shortly after he did to take charge of Sondra's girls. The car was not in the driveway—as he knew it wouldn't be. When Sondra opened the door, greeting him with a smile, he was so relieved—then saddened by the task before him. As he told her the news, her face first registered disbelief, then shock, then calm.

They rode to the scene in silence, except for the crackle and static from his police radio. When he moved to turn it off, she reached over and stayed his hand. He couldn't tell by the calm look on her face whether the intermittent broadcasts disturbed her. "Driver-unit one—DWI. Slight injuries. Being transported downtown for booking. Driver—unit two—fatality confirmed— ME in route." She had winced then—the only emotion she showed until she saw Michael's body. She had never, before or since, felt a pain so bitter.

Sondra hated to disturb Ike, but she had to. "Excuse me. Don't move. I just need to reach over your head and get some cups."

He leaned back and allowed her to step between his long outstretched legs, to open the overhead cabinet.

"You care for some coffee? It should be ready in a minute."

"Yes. It might steady my nerves."

He accepted the first three cups, as she handed them down. When she brought her arms down with the other two cups, and saw the look on his face, she was embarrassed at the way she was standing, and by the way Ike was looking at her midriff. He was embarrassed at being caught. He hadn't tried to look, but in the position he was sitting, he couldn't help but see under the blouse as she reached up. Her skin was a pretty color, smooth and taut, but soft-looking. Under other circumstances, he would have been tempted to put his hands around her waist, pull her to him, and kiss her just above her navel.

"I was just noticing that you still have the gun," he mumbled, turning his face away from her so she couldn't see the lie in his eyes. Maybe she'd buy it. He had in fact noticed the gun, so it wasn't really a whole lie. Sondra quickly stepped over his leg and set the coffee cups on the counter. She self-consciously straightened her blouse, pulling it down over the gun. She knew he was lying.

"Does the gun bother you, Mr. Evans?"

"Only when it's pointed at me," he chuckled.

"What do you want in your coffee?"

"Black, thank you. And call me Ike. Everybody does."

He handed her the cups he was still holding and she handed him a full one. Just then, the door opened, and Donnell stuck his head in.

"You get the Sheriff? It's been enough time for him to get his tired butt out here, don't you think? We tied the boat up and covered the body with the tarp. These ladies even have a lantern, so we got that lit and hung up. Is that coffee I smell? I could sure use some."

"I'll have you a cup ready when you get back. Take these to Angela and Eleanor. How do you take yours?" Sondra asked.

"Black. Nice place. Cozy. Are you sure you even called the

Sheriff?" Donnell asked, giving Ike a knowing grin, as he backed out the door with the two steaming cups.

Ike could tell from the expression on Sondra's face, she hadn't missed Donnell's comment. He would strangle that boy later. He stood up and with his free hand, picked up the cup she had poured for Donnell.

"Grab your cup. We'd better join the others. No telling what outrageous thing Donnell will tell them if we don't."

When Ike and Sondra rejoined the group, she could tell from the 'wise and otherwise' looks on Angela and Eleanor's faces Donnell must have said *something* outrageous. The headlights of two vehicles through the trees, approaching rapidly, turned their attention to more serious matters. The Sheriff's patrol car pulled right up beside them, while the funeral home station wagon stopped a ways back, by the RV. Sheriff Billy Perkins and his deputy, emerged from the patrol car and walked toward them.

"Evening, Ike. What's going on out here? What's all this about a body? Ol' Man Johnson ain't gonna be real happy if there's not one, after I roused him outta bed this time a night."

He took Ike's large brown hand in his own, just as large, pale one. The men had known each other since high school.

"Donnell? That you?" Sheriff Perkins asked, extending his hand to Donnell. "Well, I never thought we'd see a big star like you in these parts again, after yo' mama died and all."

"Yep, it's me alright. Just down for a few days to visit Ike, and enjoy some peace and quiet."

"Evenin' ma'ams," he said, tipping the brim of the big gray Stetson toward the women. Then to Donnell, "I see you brought you some company."

It was more of a question than a statement.

"No. In fact, we just met. They actually found the body. They nearly killed us." Donnell realized how that sounded and hurried to correct it. "I mean, they shot at us, but they weren't really trying to kill us. Well, they may have been trying to kill us, but just 'cause they were scared." He gave up.

"Shot at you? Who shot at you?" Sheriff Perkins asked, eyeing the women suspiciously.

"I shot at him. Them," Sondra spoke up. "But I wasn't trying to kill them. I was trying to stop them. When they came crashing out of the woods, we didn't know who they were."

"Well, where's the gun, little lady?"

Sondra, knew without even looking, that Eleanor was bristling at his reference. She shot her a dirty look, and said to the Sheriff. "It's right here. Why?" She pulled back her jacket to show him.

Ike didn't like the turn of the conversation. Or the way Billy was looking at Sondra. Ike knew what Billy was thinking. The resemblance to Laura hadn't been lost on him either.

"The body's out here, Billy. C'mon."

The sheriff followed Ike out to the boat, looking for tracks that might have been left by the killer. The rest of the group followed them. He pulled the tarp all the way off.

"That's that Woodall kid, ain't it?"

"Yes. Derrick," Ike answered.

"Somebody really meant to do him in," the sheriff commented, almost to himself. "Cut his throat *and* shot him."

They all peered into the boat then. The bullet hole in Derrick's stomach, now fully uncovered, was clearly visible in the light cast by the lantern.

"Jake, get that camera out of the back seat. Use the whole roll and get everything. We may have to send some to Austin. While you're up there, tell Johnson to bring his wagon on down here."

He took a small spiral notebook and a pen out of his pocket and moved closer to the lantern.

"Have any of you touched the body?"

"I did. But he's pretty much in the same position we found him," Ike said.

"And you ladies found the body? That right? Tell me about that."

Eleanor spoke up, describing the boat's approach, and her gruesome find, as the sheriff scribbled in the notebook.

"So, what were ya'll doing out here?"

"We're on vacation," was Eleanor's simple explanation.

He looked at them with one raised eyebrow.

"I'll need to get all of your names, addresses and phone numbers—home and work."

He passed the notebook around, and they complied. He took the notebook back and scanned the page, curious as to where they were from, before stuffing it back in his pocket. He then turned and looked directly at Sondra.

"Mind if I see that gun?"

Sheriff Perkins took a white handkerchief from his breast pocket, laid it over his palm and extended it toward Sondra. She took the gun out of her jeans and laid it in his up-turned palm. He examined it from several angles, turning it over and admiring it. He flipped the cylinder out and then back, taking note that a bullet was missing.

"Nice gun. Where'd you get it?" he asked.

"I beg your pardon," Sondra responded indignantly. She

was not accustomed to being questioned, and it showed in her face.

"I was just wondering what a nice little lady like you would need with a gun? And on vacation?" he added pointedly.

Now it was Sondra's turn to bristle. She put both hands on her hips and leaned back on one leg.

"A nice little lady like me! A nice little lady like me needs a gun for the same reason as a big man like you," she said, nodding to the gun on his hip.

Sheriff Perkins didn't like the impertinent tone in her voice, or her attitude.

"Well, I'll be taking the gun with me," he said, matter-of-factly.

"What! You can't take my gun! Why would…" She stopped mid-sentence, when she felt the pressure on her shoulder.

When Ike saw the expression on Perkins' face, he had walked up behind Sondra, put his hand on her shoulder and squeezed very firmly to hush her. There was nothing to be gained by pissing the sheriff off. She got his message, but didn't like it one damn bit.

"That's alright, Billy. I'm sure you have to check it out. We'll come 'round tomorrow and get it. It'll be OK," Ike said. He was talking to Billy, but his words were meant as much for Sondra.

"Don't ya'll touch that boat. I'll send a tow truck for it. And another thing, don't any of you leave town until I say so," he ordered.

Sheriff Perkins got in the patrol car, turned it around and drove away, the hearse following with the body.

FIVE

None of them said anything for a long time. Finally, Eleanor broke the silence.

"After all this, I could use something really stiff. Sondra, where do you keep that cognac?"

"Last cabinet on the right, over the couch. Why don't you make a pot of decaf while you're in there," she said to Eleanor, then to nobody in particular, "Can you believe that ignorant back-water jerk—taking my gun. I'm going up there tomorrow morning and if he doesn't give it back—with an apology—I'm gonna... "

"Now just calm down Sondra. You'll get the gun back. You fellas want some coffee?" Angela asked, heading in to help Eleanor.

"Not coffee. My nerves are already shot," Ike said.

"Yeah, I'll have a cup. Thanks," Donnell said, when she looked in his direction.

Sondra flopped into a chair. "'Calm down', she says. Humph! I'm so mad, I could just . . . spit! I just can't believe that big, dumb, yellow-headed peckerwood took my gun. Probably'll try to keep it. Who the hell does he think he is! He just doesn't know..."

"Don't worry about it, Mrs. Ellis. Billy's OK. We go way back. It's probably just some procedure he has to follow."

Ike's voice was so soothing, she did calm down, but just a little bit, to about a half-pout. The sound of 'Mrs. Ellis' irritated her. She hadn't been called that in a long time. It no longer fit. These days it was most often 'Judge Ellis.' She jerked around and faced him squarely.

"You should call me Sondra."

Then she realized they were alone.

"What happened to your brother? Did he go inside?"

At that moment, they heard sounds of a scuffle, then Donnell appeared from among the trees, pushing a White man in front of him. He had one arm around the man's neck, using the other to push the man by the arm that he had twisted behind him.

"Jones! What. . .?" Sondra gasped.

"You know this man?!" Donnell asked incredulously.

"Let him go! He's a friend. I mean, I know him. Just turn him loose!"

Donnell slowly released his grasp. Jones coughed a couple of times to clear his throat, then straightened his clothes.

"Thanks, Sondra. I thought the man was going to kill me."

"I thought you went home."

"I did. Then I heard the gunfire. I had to come back to make sure you were all OK again." He looked around. "Where's Eleanor? I don't want her to hear me say I came to help."

Sondra laughed a little. "I know what you mean. Don't worry. She's inside getting some coffee."

She introduced the men to each other.

"Sorry 'bout that, man," Donnell said to Jones. "I just didn't know. After all that's happened here tonight, when I heard you moving over there in the trees, I didn't know what to think."

Jones thought he had been exceedingly quiet, while watching from the woods. He thought the fellow must have some Indian blood in him, being able to sneak up on him that way. In fact, Donnell did.

Jones told them how he had arrived just as the sheriff did, but waited in the woods. Watching. Not wanting to be questioned.

Angela and Eleanor emerged from the RV with the cognac, glasses, cups and the coffee pot.

"Look, girls. Our savior has come to the rescue once again."

"Eleanor, why don't you get off it," Sondra said irritably, returning to her pouting.

Angela, the light-hearted, served as hostess, passing around glasses and cups, and pouring. As the strong liquids warmed them, the talk under the glow of the lantern centered around speculation about the body.

"Reckon drugs had anything to do with it?" Donnell asked the group, none of whom were in a position to know.

Ike had his suspicions, but kept his peace. He was aware that Derrick had been acting different lately, hadn't been playing with his heart. Ike had run into the basketball coach just Wednesday, who told him that he was worried Derrick would fall victim to the 'no-pass-no play' rule if he didn't get his grades back up. Ike had promised to talk to him. He was about the only one Derrick might listen to. Ike knew who Derrick's daddy was, but either the man didn't know, or didn't care. His mama did the best she could with him, but she had others to worry about, too.

A boy his age just needed a firm male hand to control him—and to show him the way. He remembered he'd actually planned to go get Derrick that afternoon and take him fishing, but forgot when Donnell showed up. It may have been better for Donnell to talk to Derrick. It was his own fault he hadn't thought of that earlier. Maybe then this wouldn't have happened. Maybe Derrick would have made it through that increasingly treacherous passage to manhood.

He heard Eleanor responding to Jones' question.

"I own a small publishing company and bookstore."

"What do you publish?"

"Books. For women."

"Love stories?"

Eleanor's laugh was almost a sneer. "You might say that, but not the kind you probably think. My books are about women loving themselves."

The brothers looked at her with the same curious eyes—then at Sondra—then at Angela—then at each other, their eyebrows raised.

"She didn't mean that," Angela said, noticing their reaction.

"Yes I did. I meant just what I said. A man who lives on an island should understand about self love."

Jones took her jab, handed it back to her.

"Well, Ms. . . Eleanor—I don't know your last name—it always seemed to me that a woman who had a man to love her, wouldn't need to spend her time being concerned about loving herself."

"I'm not the least surprised you'd think something like that. Fits you perfectly," she said, not retreating from his amused gaze.

Although he was interested in their repartee, Ike couldn't keep his eyes from wandering to Sondra. She sat sideways, leaned back on the arm of the chair, one leg swinging over the other arm. He wished she would stop fuming about the gun. He planned to get it back for her tomorrow. Right now, he wanted to know more about her.

"And what do you do, Ms. . . . . Sondra?"

"I work for the government," she said, not looking at him.

"Oh, yeah? What do you do for the government?"

"I'm basically a paper pusher," her tone indicating she didn't want to continue the conversation.

He wouldn't let her go. "So, what does a paper pusher do?"

"I push the stack of files on one side of my desk each morning to the other side of my desk by evening," she said absently, irritation showing on her face.

"Doesn't sound like you like your job much."

Ike wondered how she could afford that nice motorhome on a secretary's salary. She must be married, he thought wryly.

"It's OK. These days it consumes my whole life," she said, realizing at the same time just how true that was.

Sondra thought about the seemingly endless cycle of campaigning and fundraising, the meetings, receptions, the speeches she was asked to give to every imaginable group. Of course all that was easier to do now, with the girls gone. Then she realized it was all she had left. The big house she and Michael had built was clean all the time now—and quiet. She only slept there, really.

"So does your boss know how you feel?"

"I don't have a boss," she said, a little too emphatically.

She *did* have to contend with demanding lawyers and

disgruntled cops all day. Then there were the reporters always looking for a story—or some dirt. And the special interest groups—victims' rights were the vogue these days—demanding harsher punishments. There was an increasing number of truly deviant, scary defendants—the ones with the vacant eyes, void of any regard for human life or pain. She worried whether there would be enough space in the prisons for them. Then, the steady stream of young men, mostly Black, probably like Derrick, with bad attitudes, dancing their way to prison, either nonchalantly or in resignation—as though it was a badge of honor. Not understanding they were the defeated foot soldiers in the celebrated War on Drugs. And the accompanying stream of mothers, and a few fathers, who *did* understand—most of them broken-hearted, some angry and defiant. Their eyes accused her of having the power to, but refusing to, save their sons. Sondra didn't have a son, but she *was* a mother, and as she watched the parade go by, she wondered what the future could hold for her daughters. Most days, she felt she was under constant attack by baby piranha. Maybe she just had more bosses than most people. To hide the emotion she was feeling, Sondra put on her polite face.

"What do you do, Ike?"

"I have a little farm up the road a piece."

Sondra thought about the only farmer she knew—the one with the huge, rough-looking hands—who had come to the city to retrieve his wife. The lady hadn't wanted to be a farmer's wife anymore. In his efforts to persuade her, he had killed her with a hunting knife.

"Oh. I see," was all she said.

There was a lull in the conversation, as their attention was drawn to the tow truck that slowly passed them on its way to the lake's edge. Angela started off in that direction to watch. Eleanor, Donnell and Jones trailed behind her. Sondra followed them with her eyes, but didn't move. Ike noticed her wince at the grating sound of the wench, pulling the boat onto the bed of the truck.

"How long do ya'll plan to be here?" he asked, trying to keep her from withdrawing back into her funk.

"We had planned to stay a week. But now, I don't know. We haven't had a chance to talk about it. I know I'm not leaving 'til I get my gun from your friend." She was pouting again.

"I don't suppose you had in mind finding a body on your outing. But what *had* you planned to do while you were here? Fish? The fishing's great here," Ike said, trying to lighten the mood.

"Heavens, no," Sondra said. "Angela and Eleanor brought work with them. I don't believe in that. As far as I'm concerned, a working vacation is an oxymoron." Her eyes followed the tow truck as it passed.

"So what had you planned to do while they're working?"

"Just BE. Right now, I think I'll just go BE in the bed."

As the others approached, Ike rose. "I think it's time for us to let these ladies get some sleep. Tomorrow's likely to be a long day for them." He certainly intended for it to be.

The men walked their separate ways into the woods.

SIX

As Sondra sat by the lake's edge, sipping coffee, she was mesmerized by the big white bird stepping gingerly at the edge of the lake. She could see why Eleanor loved watching birds. She thought this one was putting on its graceful performance just for her. They seemed to be the only ones up, on the whole lake. She loved the sunrise time, and the clean pine scent wafting through the crisp, cool air only added to her pleasure. Even though it wasn't necessary, she had been careful not to wake the others—jealously guarding her quiet time.

The clacking sound of the diesel engine startled her. She turned around and watched, as the big extended cab truck wound its way through the trees. She self-consciously pulled the fluffy chenille robe tighter around her when she saw Ike jump down from the driver's seat, grinning.

"Mornin'. I didn't expect to find you up so early—after last night. Thought I'd treat you all to fish and rice for breakfast. I've got the rice already, but we'll have to catch the fish. You game?"

"Angela and Eleanor'll sleep 'til noon. I'm just enjoying the quiet."

"Fishing is quiet. Same view," he said, an expectant look on his face. "Come on. It'll be fun. I won't even ask you a bunch of questions." His expression was serious, but his black eyes were shining with anticipation of spending the day with her.

"Oh, alright. Why not? Give me a minute to throw some clothes on. Be right back."

It took longer to drive the distance out to the road and back than it would have taken them to walk through the woods. The truck didn't seem so big with him in it, his body taking up so much of it. The long guns on the rack behind her told her he was a hunter, as well as a fisherman. She liked riding up so high, but hated the noisy engine. She got her first good look at him in the early morning sunlight. The ruddy undertones in his skin had not been apparent the night before. They spoke of a time when Indians and Blacks had shared more than a common oppressor. His coal-black hair—strong, and cropped short on his head, long and neatly trimmed on his upper lip, nearly hiding it—also showed that earlier melding of bloodlines. When his white teeth showed in a slight smile under the long moustache, she knew he'd caught her staring at him. She quickly looked away.

When they arrived, he got all the gear together and showed her to his favorite spot, at the edge of the lake.

As he sat and baited his hook, he noticed she continued to stand, holding the rod he had handed her.

"You want a chair?" he asked.

"No. It's OK," she answered.

"Well, what's the matter? You scared of worms?"

"Scared? Of course not."

He knew she was lying.

"Here," patting the ground next to him. When she sat, he took her hand and pushed it into the little cardboard bucket.

"Just grab one."

He laughed when she squeezed her eyes shut and scrunched her nose and mouth.

"You're funny, lady. Last night you were 'Ms. Tough.' Now you're scared of a little ol' worm. Here, let me show you how to do it."

As he expertly guided her hands to get the worm on the hook, and showed her how to cast, the morning sunlight sparkled colors off the large diamond on her wedding band.

"You married?"

"No. Why?"

"Just wondered," he said, relieved, looking pointedly at the ring.

"I *was* married. My husband died some time ago. Car wreck."

"I'm glad you didn't shoot him."

He laughed at his own joke. She didn't, instead pursing her mouth and rolling her eyes in mock exasperation.

"So why you still wear the ring?"

"I don't know. Protection I guess."

"Protection? From what?"

"From people who ask too many questions. What about you? Married?"

"Nope."

"Ever?"

"Nope."

"Why?"

"Never found the woman I was looking for."

"Kids?"

"Only Donnell."

"Donnell's your son? I thought he was your brother."

"He's both." He told her about his father's death, and him being the surrogate.

"Watch your cork!"

Knowing she hadn't done this before, he quickly moved to sit behind her, choo-choo style, putting his arms around her and enclosing her brown hands in his own. He taught her how to fish.

"Give him some line, let him run, then reel him in."

The excitement of catching the fish made her forget the offense she felt that the farmer had the nerve to invade her personal space—and the tingling she felt, where his body pressed against hers in so many places.

They caught several more, then quit as the day warmed up. He showed her how to scale the fish. She handled them very gingerly, as she followed his instructions. He cleaned the fish on newspaper spread on the big picnic table, while she watched. When he made the slit in the fish' belly, he laughed at the 'ugh' look on her face as the blood, eggs, and guts spewed out.

"And you think you can shoot a man. Humph!" he said, smiling derisively.

Sondra walked away from the table, stooped down and picked up two pine cones. She studied them, before dropping one back on the ground. After a few more steps, she picked up another one, studied it, then dropped the one she had picked up earlier. She continued doing that until he called out to her.

"Whatcha' doing?"

"Getting my souvenir. I bring one from every trip. My rule is, it has to be something natural from the area. I have red rocks from Arizona, shells from every beach I've visited, plants from California. I'm searching for the perfect pine cone for this trip."

"There's plenty to choose from. I lived here all my life and I never thought about what a perfect pine cone would look like," he chuckled. "I'll help you look later. It's bound to be around here somewhere. The fish is ready. Come on, let's go inside, so I can get this breakfast started."

"No. Let me. I don't get to cook much any more," she said, setting the largest pine cone she'd found on the table, where she wouldn't forget it.

Inside, Ike sat at his table with his feet propped up comfortably in a chair, watching her move expertly around the end of the Quonset hut that was his kitchen. He breathed in the wonderful aroma of the spices and herbs she'd used to dress the fish. He felt calm and peaceful. He wondered if this was what it was like to have a wife.

"There's tin foil in that cabinet. We can wrap this all up and take it back to your camper."

"I told you, Eleanor and Angela'll sleep 'til noon. This will be too cold to be good by then. I guess they can heat theirs up in the microwave. I want to eat mine now."

They enjoyed the broiled fish and rice on the big picnic table. Over their second cup of coffee, she asked, "Could I use your truck to go to town? It won't take long."

"Girl, you can't handle that big truck. Why don't I take you?"

"I beg your pardon?! I've driven that RV all over this state—several states in fact. And it's bigger than that truck. Much bigger."

"Well, I guess you got a point. But, I know the way, and you don't. Just let me take you. I'd just rather go with you to talk to Billy anyway."

She wondered what he meant, but let it go. She just wanted to get her gun, and the sooner the better.

The Sheriff's office was the only one open in the courthouse on a Saturday morning. Billy Perkins sat with his feet propped up on his desk. He'd spent a restless night on the cot in the back. He expected them, and was waiting. Through the dusty blinds, he watched the familiar black truck ease into the space outside. He was struck again, by how much the woman looked like Laura, how Ike looked at her—just like he'd looked at Laura. This time would be different. He had what she wanted. He was the star. He had the power now. As he took the pretty gun out of the drawer and laid it on his desk where she could easily see it, he was conscious of the slight paunch he had developed somewhere on his way to his forties. He was sure he carried it well, with his height. He ran his fingers through his hair. It was so blond—and full—that the few strands of gray didn't show. He knew he still had his rugged good looks, by the way the women chased him. It had been that way since high school. But then, he'd only had eyes for Laura.

Billy hadn't understood why it had been such a scandal—his inviting her to their senior prom. Even his staunchly religious parents, he bitterly remembered, tried to explain it to him. But they couldn't reconcile their explanation with their earlier teachings. They had the same worried look on their faces that he saw on Laura's parents' faces when he walked her home from school, or showed up at the Black Baptist church for evening services. Watching Sondra and Ike walk into his office now, only reminded him of seeing the two of them together—how pretty Laura looked, how the white dress was such a nice contrast against her brown skin, how he wanted to die, as he watched her walking into the prom on the arm of the big basketball star.

After that, her parents wouldn't let Laura come to the phone when he called. At the end of the summer, they sent her to some college over in Tennessee he'd never heard of. The last he'd heard, she was still married and teaching somewhere out East.

"Morning Ms. Ellis. Ike."

"Sheriff Perkins," she nodded. "I'm here to get my gun."

Sondra saw it laying on the desk and resisted the urge to reach for it. She wanted him to hand it to her, just as she had handed it to him.

"Sorry, ma'am. Can't give it to you."

"You mean, won't," she said evenly, to hide her anger.

"Standard procedure, Ms. Ellis. I've got a body with a bullet hole in it, and a gun. And a suspect," he said, watching for Ike's reaction.

"Suspect?! What are you talking about?! Are you trying to suggest…"

Ike stepped to her side and cut her off.

"Don't do this Billy. It's over. It's _been_ over a long time. Neither of us won. You know she doesn't have anything to do with the murder—or the other thing. Give her the gun, Billy," he said tightly.

"What other thing?" she asked, looking from one to the other.

Neither of them answered—blue and black eyes glaring at each other. She saw fire and lightening in both.

"Maybe Monday. Austin's closed 'til then. I sent the slug from the body to the lab up there this morning. Check with me Monday. May even be Tuesday before I know anything. These things just take time. This may have to go to the grand jury."

Billy was trying to sound official, but the condescending smile infuriated Ike.

"Grand jury?!" Sondra said incredulously.

"That's bullshit! And you know it. Give her the gun Billy," Ike demanded, his eyes still blazing.

"Ms. Ellis, check with me Tuesday. Oh, and Ms. Ellis? Remember. Don't leave town 'til I say you can," Sheriff Perkins said, smiling down at her, and ignoring Ike.

Sondra turned and stormed out. Ike gave a hard look at Billy, before he turned and followed Sondra to the truck.

The quiet, but insistent, knock at the door wakened Eleanor from her sleep on the couch. It took her a minute to recognize Donnell. She grabbed her robe and opened the door.

"Good morning. You seen Ike?" he asked.

"You woke me up. What time is it?" she asked sleepily.

She heard Angela stirring in the overhead bed, and pulled the curtains to shield her from his view.

"Come on in. Want some coffee? Somebody already made it. Sit down," she said, pointing to the chair across from the couch with the rumpled quilt and pillow.

"Yeah. That'd be good. I slept late too—'til nearly eleven.

Ike was gone. He wasn't over by the lake, so I thought he might be here."

She poured two cups and handed him one.

"Excuse me a minute."

When she turned to go in the little lavatory, she noticed Sondra's bed was made up—and empty. She turned back to Donnell.

"You see Sondra outside?"

"Nope." The expression on his face told her they both thought the same thing.

"What had ya'll planned to do today?" he asked, sipping the coffee she'd handed him.

"Very little. Just enjoy the lake. Thought I'd take a little swim if it warms up enough. I'll probably work on a speech I'm giving next week at the Women Against Violence luncheon. I know Angela brought some computer program to work on. It's been giving her fits. What about you?"

"I'd planned to spend the day messing around with Ike over at the ranch, but looks like he had other plans. Guess I'll just go on back over there and see if anything needs doing. Hey, why don't ya'll go with me. I'll show you around the place. Ike's got quite an operation over there. It's a big place now. We could see it all, though, if we ride some of the horses."

"Ou-u-u, you've got horses. Sounds like fun," they heard from overhead. Angela poked her head through the curtains, the bronze curls tousled about on her head.

"Morning, Sleepyhead." Donnell smiled up at her.

"Sounds like you're the sleepy head. Come on, Eleanor, let's do it. It'll be fun. I'm sure as hell not getting in that cold lake with you! And Sondra won't either. Where *is* Sondra?" she asked, craning to see to the back bed.

Then she saw Eleanor and Donnell exchange knowing smiles.

"What? Where is she?" Her eyes narrowed. "And where is that brother of yours?"

Donnell shrugged his shoulders innocently.

"I can't believe she went off with him somewhere. That's not like Sondra." Angela wrinkled her brow, then smiled. "Well, she's grown. Time for her to have a little fun. Give us a minute. Go outside. We'll be dressed in a flash."

When Angela saw the sportscar, she laughed. She thought it was slick, but knew it would be cramped for the three of them.

"Since I'm the shortest, I'll sit in the back."

"You might want to put on some long jeans, like Eleanor," Donnell suggested, wondering if she had ever ridden a horse.

Angela looked down at the spandex shorts she was wearing.

"Nah. I'll be alright," she said, climbing into the excuse for a back seat.

The driver's seat was pushed all the way back to accommodate Donnell's long legs, so Angela had to sit sideways, stretching out in the seat. She watched the tall pine trees whiz by, as Donnell expertly maneuvered the car along the winding road. From her position she couldn't see Eleanor's face, but she could imagine the pinched look. The one she usually wore when she rode in Angela's car. She wasn't surprised when she heard Eleanor's question.

"You get many tickets?"

She *could* see the mischievous look on Donnell's face, when he answered sweetly, "No ma'am. I never speed. The car is just so low-slung, it *seems* like we're going faster than we are."

Angela felt Eleanor's relief when the car slowed down and they turned into the driveway, by the big sign that read EVANS CATTLE COMPANY. She watched the cloud of dust following them down the long driveway, past the house and overtake them when he stopped in front of the stable.

After Donnell helped her out of the back seat, he led them around until he found the teen-ager stacking the bales of hay.

"Hey, Trey. I need you to help saddle up the two gentlest horses around here. I'll saddle up Buck myself. Ike doesn't let you handle him, does he?"

"I don't even want to fool with that crazy horse. Nobody but Ike can control him," the boy said, eyeing them curiously.

"You hear about Derrick?" Donnell asked him, as they put the saddles on the horses.

"Yeah. I heard."

"Ike told me he was a Boy Scout."

"He was in our troop, but he wasn't no boy scout."

"Looked like a drug deal gone bad to me," Donnell said, searching.

"Probably. Since that crack come here, all these people gone crazy—the ones using and the ones selling it."

"You hang around with Derrick?"

"Nah, man. I got no use for that stuff. He hung around up there at Big Mike's, on the cuts. You know where it is? 'Bout the only place to go 'round here. But Ike told me he'd kill me if he ever heard about me being up there. I believe him, too."

"You should," Donnell said, with a wry smile. "I know."

Listening to their conversation, Angela remembered that Donnell had asked about drugs last night too. Surely he wasn't into crack—he looked too healthy. Still, these days you couldn't always tell. He was about the right age. Despite what the media portrayed, she knew the young boys weren't using it—just selling it. Maybe he was into powder. That would be more fitting with the expensive car and designer jeans he wore. She remembered the sheriff calling him a 'star,' and wondered what he meant. She couldn't place his name, so he probably wasn't an actor or singer. She searched his face, but couldn't place it either. Must be some private joke between them, she thought.

When the horses were ready, Eleanor mounted hers easily. She was long-legged, and had grown up on a farm. She hadn't ridden in a long time, but it was like riding a bicycle.

Angela eyed her horse cautiously. She could raise her foot high enough to reach the stirrup, but couldn't hoist her body up.

"Looks like you need some help, Shorty," Donnell said, laughing at her attempts.

"But it's so big. I had something in mind more like a pony. What if he doesn't like me?" she asked, eying the horse warily.

"I like you. He'll like you too. Just put your foot in the stirrup and grab the horn."

Before she could say anything, he put his large hands around her waist from behind, and easily raised her up. She worked herself into place, still looking uneasy. He instructed her how to use the reins to guide the horse. He could tell Eleanor didn't need any instruction, as she and her horse went off at a gallop. He mounted Ike's big stallion.

Donnell walked the horses first, to give Angela time to practice and to get accustomed to handling the big animal. When Angela got the swing of the thing, she enjoyed it. The three of them spent a long time riding through the pastures, Donnell pointing out the different breeds of cattle, the strengths and weaknesses of each. To Angela, they all just looked like cows. She was fascinated, though, by the huge black bull, in its own special pen. He explained how it had taken Ike a long time to breed him. 'Big Jesse' was so valuable, Ike had installed a surveillance and alarm system at the pen, and hired men to watch him night and day.

Angela was disappointed when Donnell suggested they head back. She planned to ride again before they went home. She would definitely wear her jeans the next time.

When they returned to the stables, Ike still was not there. Donnell suggested they get something to eat. This time Eleanor folded her long legs into the back seat, saying "If I'm gonna get killed in this little car, I don't want to see it coming."

Donnell drove to town, past the '305' mailbox, and stopped at the Dairy Queen on the main highway. They feasted on greasy burgers. Eleanor had manipulated the seating so that Donnell and Angela sat together, across from her in the booth. When she returned from getting a refill on her milk, they were talking and laughing. This little trip was turning out even better than she had planned, in spite of the ugliness the night before. Even that had brought this tall gorgeous man to Angela—just the antidote she needed to Quinton Rawlins. Angela was having fun, and Eleanor was happy to be cheated out of the lectures she had planned to give her.

When they finished their meal, Donnell took them on a tour of the little town—main street, the courthouse square, the oldest neighborhood with the huge trees and beautiful Victorian houses. When they crossed the railroad tracks and came to the area he called 'the cuts', Angela laughed. Every town had one. She noticed that Donnell seemed especially alert, driving slowly and looking hard. When he drove around the same block twice, she was convinced she had pegged him right. Angela wondered if his brother knew.

Once, she had dated a cokehead—for way too long before she figured it out. He always had an explanation for his lack of money, even with a good job. The little investment he'd made didn't quite pay off. Getting kicked out his apartment, was a dispute with his landlord over repairs. Eleanor had been the one to comment on his mood swings. Angela had been miffed with her about that, even after the time he had pushed her around, scaring her. She'd thought then, that Eleanor just didn't understand the pressures that a young upwardly-mobile Black man faced every day; that she was just so wrapped up in that feminist oppression shit, she couldn't see.

When the flat gold chain her father had given her—the one she always wore—came up missing, Angela kicked him out and apologized to Eleanor. Angela thought she would never be that blind again. Then she thought about Quinton.

When Donnell suggested that they all come back later for a little dancing, Angela just shook her head. Not only in response to his invitation, but also to what she was thinking. That she was going to end up just like Sondra and Eleanor—alone, no man, no kids.

SEVEN

It was almost dark when the three of them arrived back at the campsite, and there was still no sign of Ike and Sondra. Donnell knitted his brow.

"Looks like we just missed them," Angela announced, pointing to the dishes drying by the sink. "She changed shoes too."

Despite his disappointment at not seeing his brother, the day had been so pleasant, Donnell didn't want to leave. He liked the little pixie girl in the spandex shorts.

"Let's go down to Big Mike's and I'll show you how we country folk party."

"Thanks, anyway. I didn't bring a dress or anything," Angela said.

"Just put on some long pants. It's pretty casual."

"You two go on," Eleanor said. "I'm worn out. Besides, I need to work on my speech. Anyway, Angela, you know how you love to dance."

Angela shot her a cold look. She knew what Eleanor was up

to. Eleanor just didn't know what Donnell was up to.

Angela grumpily showered and changed her clothes.

"I promise I won't keep her out too late," Donnell said to Eleanor as they went out the door.

Donnell first drove to Ike's house, so he could shower and change too. The drive didn't seem as long to Angela this time, since she knew where she was going.

"Make yourself at home. This won't take long. Want something to drink?"

"No, thanks," she answered curtly.

Angela was irritated at his earlier remark—acting like Eleanor was her mama or something. She felt like a prisoner. Eleanor's prisoner. She would rather have suffered Eleanor's lecturing, than spend the evening with a dopehead. She'd probably have to drive back, so she paid attention to the road as they drove toward town.

"What's the matter? I thought you liked to dance."

Angela had her arms folded across her chest. "Why do you think something's the matter with *me*?"

"Well, I don't know. You were so talkative all day, now you're not saying a word."

"OK, then. Where do you live Mr. Evans?"

He was confused by her use of the formal term.

"I've been living in D.C. for several years."

"And what kind of work do you do?" she asked, staring at the road as though she wasn't really interested.

"I'm in security."

"Oh, a security guard? That's nice."

"Yeah, sort of," he said, trying to be as short with her as she was with him.

He almost wished he hadn't insisted she come with him, but he was determined to go down to 'the cuts.' There was something there he needed, and the busiest night of the week was the best time to find it. They rode the rest of the way in silence.

It took their eyes a while to adjust, when they entered the dark, smoky place. The music on the jukebox was almost too loud, but not loud enough to drown out the laughter and shouts. All eyes were on them.

"Donnell! Hey, man! When'd you get back?"

Donnell guided her over to the table where the men were sitting. He slapped palms and bumped fists with each of them.

"Just got in yesterday. What's going on?"

"Same ol' shit, man. You know. Good to see you. This your wife?" he asked, eyeing Angela appreciatively. "Man, you doing alright for yourself up in the big city. How long you gonna be here?"

"I'm not sure. A few days. I'll come back and talk to you. Let me get my ol' lady a table before they're all taken."

Angela felt self-conscious as the men eyed her, noting that Donnell didn't answer their question about her. She didn't like him calling her his 'ol' lady.' But she thought maybe he was trying to protect her, establishing her as his possession, so the men wouldn't approach her. She walked stiffly, as he guided her to a table.

"What do you want? They only have beer, wine, and set-ups here. I forgot to check and see if Ike had some whiskey. I rarely drink it."

"Me neither. Wine will be fine."

Having been in places like this before, she knew it would be the cheap kind that gave you a headache. She would take care to sip it very slowly. She watched Donnell as he stopped at several tables on his way to the bar. He seemed to know everybody, and they all seemed glad to see him. He was the tallest man in the room besides the big bartender, and by far the best looking. Of course, there was no real contest. Most of the men were balding, or had big stomachs, or gold teeth. Even the young ones had a gold. Too country, she thought. She was glad when he returned with the glass of wine for her, a beer for him.

"Come on. Let's dance," he said.

She took off her jacket and followed him onto the dance floor. She was surprised they had the latest records on the jukebox, mixed among the oldies. He was a smooth dancer, but she was better. As soon as they returned to their table, he said "I'll be right back." She watched him walk outside. He wasn't gone long, but when he returned she looked into his eyes for a sign that she'd been correct. Then he snapped his finger as the next song came on and took her back to the dance floor, smiling at her. It seemed to her that after every dance, he'd go outside again. She was convinced she knew what was happening. After a while, a slow oldie came on the jukebox, and he pulled her onto the floor, enveloping her small body in his arms. He was easy to follow, rocking her back and forth, hardly moving his feet. That his body showed no sign of how sensuous the music was, with her body pressed so close to him, only went to confirm her suspicion. She remembered how Freddie lost interest in sex, as he was dragged deeper into the drug.

Donnell wondered if Angela had any idea how much effort it took for him to control himself, as she swayed with him. When he felt that natural sensation, he would back away from her a little. But she would press her body into his, as if trying to feel it. He just couldn't figure her out. She'd hardly said a word to him in the car, or at the table. Now she seemed to be coming on to him. What was with her?

When they got back to the table she said, "I'm ready to go."

He searched her eyes for a sign, but she didn't seem interested in him now. He was confused. But he still didn't have what he'd come for.

"Well I'm not. I'll get you another drink."

After he did, he went back outside.

Feeling conspicuous sitting alone at the table, Angela nearly dropped her teeth when she saw Ike and Sondra walking toward her. She was relieved to see them. Now she had an escape. She would get a ride back with them, and Donnell could just have whatever it was he was so interested in outside.

"Fancy meeting you here," Ike said, as they sat down. "Where's Donnell?"

"Outside. Didn't you see him?"

Ike frowned and pursed his lips as he left to get drinks for him and Sondra. Angela declined his offer, as she had hardly touched the last one Donnell brought.

"You don't look like you're having a good time," Sondra said.

"I'm ready to go, but Donnell seems to be having a good time. Maybe I can get a ride back with you, if you're not staying too long."

"I don't think we'll be here long. Ike wasn't particular about coming here, but I didn't want to sit around the campfire either—after last night. He says it's the only place in the county to party. I had to practically drag him down here. I had such a good time today. I just wanted to hear some good music, a little dancing."

Angela looked at her with raised eyebrows.

"Maybe it's something about being in a place where nobody knows me. I don't have to watch everything I do or say. Don't have to hear about somebody's little run-in with the law, or how some judge...What's the matter with you?"

"Nothing. I'm just ready to go, that's all." Angela said, looking off, exasperated.

After a minute, Sondra said, "I went to get my gun today, but that dumb jerk sheriff wouldn't give it to me. Can you believe he said I'm a suspect! And he even talked about taking it before a grand jury!"

"You told him you were a judge, didn't you?"

"No. That's not his business. It seems to me, he really has a beef with Ike. But Ike said I was just imagining things. Maybe so. I'll tell you one thing, if I don't get my gun Monday, I'm calling the Colonel over at DPS. I'll fix that dumb jerk. He'll wish he never fucked with me!" Sondra squeezed her hands together, rubbing one thumb in the palm of the other, like she always did when she was buffeted by any strong emotion. It had started as a trick her mother had suggested to stop her thumb-sucking when she was six. Now, nearly forty years later, it was a habit more ingrained than the other had been.

The Dells' "Stay in My Corner" came on the jukebox just as Ike returned with the drinks. He took Sondra's hand and led her away. Angela watched as they began dancing, like very proper strangers. The dance floor filled up, blocking her view. The next time she was able to catch a glimpse of them between the other couples, they appeared more relaxed, laughing and talking. Before the long song was over, they were nearly indistinguishable from the other couples, embraced and swaying. When the song ended, Sondra and Ike returned, quiet and subdued.

"Ya'll 'bout ready to go? Sondra said I could get a ride with you," Angela said perkily.

"We just got here. I'm sure Donnell will be back in a minute," Ike said frowning, thinking about how long the song was. "In fact, maybe I'd better go check on him."

Just then, Donnell walked up, a big grin on his face. "Say, look at you! Out on the town, huh? Wish ya'll had come earlier. We were just leaving."

Angela turned and looked at him in shock. From the big stupid grin on his face, she *knew* she was right.

"I'm enjoying the music so much. I think I'll just stay here with them. You go on."

Now it was Ike and Sondra's turn to look shocked.

"Nah, come on. Gotta' go. I promised Eleanor I'd get you back early. See ya'll," he said, firmly gripping Angela's arm and nearly pulling her up from the chair. Not wanting to make a scene, she didn't resist.

"Well at least let me drive," Angela said, when they got to his car.

"Are you kidding?" he laughed. "It's a stick shift. Get in," he said urgently, opening the door.

"I can drive a stick shift." She changed her tack. "Besides, I've always wanted to drive a snazzy car like this." It had worked on drunk dates before.

"Maybe tomorrow. Just get in!" he ordered, in a hurried voice.

She reluctantly complied, and he sped off.

Donnell drove even faster than he had that morning. At each

turn in the road, the tires screeched, and she had to brace herself, one hand on the console and the other on the handgrip in the door, to keep her balance. She couldn't fathom the expression on his face, as she desperately tried to think of something to say, to get him to slow down. She nearly panicked when he passed the now-familiar silver mailbox—'305'. He sped on, past the EVANS CATTLE COMPANY sign on the other side of the highway, almost overtaking his headlights on the moonlit road. When he came to the highway intersection, he slowed down just enough to make the right turn, and took off again. Fear was gripping her now, but she held on. After a couple of miles, he turned off onto another small road at the 'Scenic Outlook' sign and turned off his headlights. She felt the bump when the pavement ended, and they coasted the rest of the way. He stopped abruptly in a dirt clearing in the tall pine trees, just at the edge of the lake. The place looked well worn, tire tracks everywhere. He removed his seatbelt and sat back, peering into the rearview mirror outside his door, through half-closed eyes, as though he was expecting someone.

"What the hell is this all about? What is this, the local Lover's Leap? You're acting like a crazy man. Take me home, right this minute!" she demanded, her arms folded across her breasts protectively.

"Hush," he ordered quietly, never taking his eyes off the mirror.

When she saw the headlights of the slowly approaching car in the mirror, she looked at him out of the side of her eye. From the sly smile on his face, she figured this must be his connection. She was angry with herself for not insisting on staying with Ike and Sondra. She couldn't believe he would bring her along for the drug buy. He didn't need her for that.

As the big aging Cadillac pulled in front of them and parked, she saw another set of headlights in the mirror. Just then, he leaned over her and put his mouth on hers, as his hand released her seat back. She pushed against him with her hands. The weight of his upper body and the seat belt held her to the seat.

"Put your arms around me," he said.

She didn't move.

"NOW!" he ordered, and plunged his tongue into her mouth.

Angela didn't know whether she complied out of shocked reflex, or in response to the harshness in his voice. Out of her wide-opened eyes, she could see his eyes were open too, looking calmly into hers. She couldn't read them, but she realized that whatever this was about, it wasn't about sex. Her relief didn't make it any easier to breathe with his weight on her. She wanted to bite his tongue hard to make him get off her, but she was afraid of what he might do. She'd never been in a situation this weird.

Angela heard a voice saying, with a chuckle, "That Donnell. I swear, he ain't changed a bit." Then muffled laughter. She could hear conversation—men's voices—but couldn't make out what was being said. When she heard the two vehicles drive off, he raised her seat back and sat back in his own seat, watching her. She stared straight ahead, her fists clenched, her body trembling with too many emotions. Relief and anger were the only two she could name.

"I'm really sorry," he said quietly, not taking his eyes off her.

"Take me home."

"Please, let me explain. Angela, I know I shouldn't have used you that way, but in the business I'm in . . . ."

"Just take me home!" she yelled, her voice filling the small car.

The set of her jaw, and balled fists told him there was no use. The cautious side of him told him he really couldn't afford to tell her anyway. He'd just met her. Still, he wanted her to understand. He reached over to take her hand, but she jerked her hand away. After a minute, he started the motor and turned the car around. When the silence got too much for him, he put a tape in. Soft ballads. She wasn't soothed.

Angela opened the door, even before he brought the car to a complete stop. Her hand was shaking as she put the key she had already taken out of her purse, into the little keyhole. Inside, she climbed the ladder and flopped down, on her back, on the upper bed. When she felt Eleanor staring up at her from her pile of papers, with that little 'worried mama' look, she snatched the curtains shut. She didn't want to talk about it. In fact, she just wanted to go home.

Eleanor tried to be satisfied with the thought that whatever the problem was, her plan had not been for naught. She was *certain* Angela wasn't worrying about Quinton Rawlins.

EIGHT

The aroma of the strong coffee roused Angela. She realized she had fallen asleep in her clothes. She also realized she owed Eleanor an apology, and dreaded having to face her. She steeled herself for it, trying to think of what to say. They didn't keep secrets, but she certainly wasn't ready to tell either of her friends what had happened. Not yet, anyway. She opened the curtains, and threw her legs over the edge of the bed, trying to appear bright and perky, only to find herself alone in the RV. She rolled over on her stomach and looked through the small upper window at the foot of the bed. Eleanor, Sondra and Ike were sitting outside, talking and laughing. She was relieved Donnell hadn't had the nerve to come here. When she saw Eleanor heading toward the RV, she drew the curtains, and lay very still.

Angela heard Eleanor making more noise than was usual for her.

"Angela. Are you awake?"

Angela didn't respond.

"Angela, I know you're not sleep. It's too late, even for *you,* to be asleep. You can't stay up there all day. Ike brought a canoe and we're going for a ride around the lake. You want to go? We'll wait for you."

When Angela realized Eleanor wasn't going away without an answer, she said sleepily, "You all go ahead."

"Suit yourself," Eleanor said and left.

Angela watched through the little window as Ike held the canoe for Eleanor and Sondra to get in, then hopped in himself and used the oar to push the little boat away from the shore. She climbed down, washed up and changed into shorts and a t-shirt. She made a slice of cheese toast and poured a cup of coffee. She was glad to be alone. She got the papers from her briefcase, and stretched out on the floor, her back against the couch. She had gone over this a hundred times and still couldn't find the source of the error. She couldn't bring her system on line until she figured it out. Now she was really anxious for this contract to be completed.

Six months ago, Angela had been so excited to get the contract with the bank. It had been awarded in open competition. This one was for real money—not like the little jobs she had gotten as a 'qualified minority contractor.' If only she could have been paid by the hour for the time she spent filling out forms to prove she was a minority, she'd be damned near rich. She was always tempted to send a snapshot of herself hugging her computer instead. She rankled at having to provide her tax returns and other business records. She was aware that those were not required for the other vendor list, the one she bitterly referred to as 'the unqualified list.' It galled her, that while she was spending hours filling out forms and making copies, those on the 'unqualified list' were receiving contracts.

Angela was good at what she did, worked hard and put her all into every project. She did all the networking, read all the trade periodicals and the business pages every day. She attended all the meetings and luncheons of the trade organizations. It was at one of those, that she overheard a conversation about a contract for converting the operating system at Homestead State Bank. First American, a larger New York bank, was negotiating to buy Homestead and the deal would be sweeter if Homestead's system was compatible with theirs.

She'd submitted her proposal to Homestead's committee in charge of selecting the contractor. She took red-headed Bill Devane with her to the initial meeting at the bank. Bill and she had had classes together and she recognized his genius. But he'd gotten bored with school, and dropped out. She subbed him from time to time in a crunch because they worked well together— when he wanted to work. He was a strange fellow. He was so intrigued at the idea of putting one over on a bank, he didn't even make her pay extra for having to cut his hair. She knew the style was anathema to him, but it made him look like he'd just come from lunch at the country club. The new suit she'd bought him was worth every penny. It worked just like she had planned. She had schooled him enough to get him through the initial phases of the presentation. They assumed she was his employee, so when he turned it over to her for the more technical aspects, they were comfortable with her. Even after the contract was signed, when they called Financial Technical Software Development, Inc., "Mr. Devane was in a meeting, but she would be happy to connect them with his assistant, Ms. Reeves." When honey-colored Quinton Rawlins showed up from the headquarters in

New York, as her contact in the bank, she wondered if they were on to her.

Although he didn't seem to know much about computers, Quinton was First American's trouble-shooter, and knew the bank's operations like the back of his hand. They made a good team. He kept telling her that. She believed him. At first, she kept him at arm's length. But he was so nice. When he told her how hard he'd had to work to get his position, she could identify. She was continually surprised by how much they had in common. They were both ambitious and self-motivated. They had similar family backgrounds, held the same religious views, both loved to dance, both wanted children—a boy and a girl. She should have stopped it when they first began having the late dinners. But she didn't. From there, they went to having take-out at her condo or his apartment. When the relationship became intimate, they had agreed that it was better for both of them if their co-workers were not aware. They had laughed about how suspicious Whites became when Blacks worked together. They worked together all day, maintaining a professional distance, not revealing a hint of how well they worked together at night. He was a skilled and considerate lover. She took him to the hottest dance clubs in the city. Introduced him to her friends. Angela saw the reservation in Eleanor and Sondra's eyes at first. But it meant a lot to her for them to like him, and before long, it seemed he had charmed them too. They even agreed that it was wise for them to keep their relationship under wraps until the contract was complete. The night he took the three of them out to celebrate her birthday, he presented her with a ring with a big birthstone, promising to replace it with an even bigger diamond when they could end this charade. Eleanor and Sondra were down-right misty eyed.

Of course, Quinton had to go to New York regularly—usually once a week—to report to the Board of Directors on the progress of the new system. He persuaded her that it wouldn't be wise for her to go with him until they were ready for the final conversion. It might raise suspicion. He always called—usually late at night—to tell her how the report had been received.

It was late one Sunday night, when she first hit the snag. She was far enough along to do a test run, in preparation for the final installation. She knew that it would be in the bank's best interest to have a complete conversion, rather than running two parallel systems, until the old one died a natural death over time. Otherwise, it would be confusing to the bank's clerks, as well as its customers. The program ran fine on the test data, but when she ran it on the production data, it bombed off. She went over the flowchart and compared it to her program until she was bleary eyed. Finally, she decided to call Quinton. Maybe it was something she didn't understand about the bank's operation.

The long distance operator gave her the number for Quinton D. Rawlins. When she first heard the woman's sleepy voice, she thought she must have the wrong number. Maybe there was more than one. Not likely—his was not a common name. She was shocked at the thought Quinton might be playing around on her. But why would he let a woman answer his phone? Her inner voice made her ask, "Mrs. Rawlins?" When she heard "Yes?" her body went cold all over. When the woman asked, "Who is this? Hello?" Angela heard a man's voice in the background asking the woman who was on the phone. Angela hung up. She sat for a long time staring at her telephone in disbelief.

Finally, she went to her computer and used the modem to

connect to the bank's main computer. The security code she'd been assigned wouldn't allow her access to the personnel records. Then she entered the code she had watched Quinton use so many times. When his file appeared on the screen, her heart fell to the bottom of her stomach—12 Fallen Ash Place, Long Island. Wife—Jennifer. Two dependents—one male, one female. When the sun came up, she was still staring at the screen.

Angela first decided that she would tell him she called very late and he didn't answer, see what his reaction would be. No, she wasn't good at playing games. She would just tell him what she knew from his file, see what his response was, then act accordingly. Maybe, just maybe, it was dated information. He had worked for the bank for several years. Things change. Maybe he didn't want his Board of Directors to know. But why hadn't he told her? Being divorced was nothing to hide from her. Then she thought it would be better to play along with his little game. It might jeopardize her contract to confront him. She didn't know what he would do. She would make excuses to not see him after work. All she had to do was make it until Friday. Then he'd go back to New York for the end of the week report. In the end, she did all of it.

Angela wore her most expensive suit, the coral one that made her look and feel her most confident, and the matching pumps. She took extra care with her make-up, especially to camouflage the little pimple forming on her chin. It had been a long time since she had been happy to know her period was coming, but now she looked forward to it. It would give her a good excuse to keep Quinton at arm's length. On her way out the door, she was pleased at her reflection in the long mirror. She looked like a woman who could handle anything.

When Quinton strode into her office late that morning with the white paper bag in his hand, a broad smile on his face, Angela had the appearance of being absorbed in her work.

"Hey, baby. I couldn't wait to get back and tell you about the Board meeting. They are very pleased that the new system is coming on-line way ahead of schedule. There may even be a bonus—for both of us," he said, with a big smile still on his face. "I brought something for us to celebrate. I wish it could be flowers, but you know. . ." his voice trailed off.

He opened the sack and placed the Danish and coffee cups on the table behind her desk. Then he kissed her on the forehead.

"You're always so thoughtful," she said coolly, pulling away from him and glancing at his hand for the telltale sign of a missing ring. His long delicate finger was the same honey color from knuckle to knuckle.

"What's the matter? Is something wrong?"

"No." Then after a moment, "Quinton, I called you last night."

"You called me?"

"At your house. You didn't answer," she said quietly.

"Well, you knew I wouldn't be there," he said nonchalantly, emptying the little cream containers into the cups. "You know I always take the early flight on Monday."

"Not your apartment here."

"You called me in New York? Where'd you get the number?" he asked, looking at her with one eyebrow raised into a question.

"You didn't answer."

"Oh, I was going to tell you that I took Randall for drinks to discuss the meeting. He's the CEO. I told you about him. To celebrate. The Board was so . . ."

"A woman answered," she said, cutting him off.

"Well, you must have dialed the wrong number. Baby, I thought you'd be excited. We're almost there."

She was supposed to let it go, but she couldn't. She noticed his eyes were rapidly scanning hers. And he was talking too fast. Damned near babbling.

"I mean, you should have seen the looks on their faces. They didn't really believe I could do it. Nothing but doubt, at first. But now, I'm their hero. They'll be able to cut a lot of employees. Greedy bastards. It's really going to make a big difference to the bottom line. And mine too," he said, smiling. "Oh, and yours too. As soon as the system's up, I'll get my friend at *Bankers Quarterly* to do a story. Your name'll be in it. They'll be beating your door down. Your..."

"I'll bet your wife will be proud of you." Angela stopped him cold.

"Wife? What wife?" Quinton asked, his eyes widening.

"You know. The one who lives on Fallen Ash."

A frown crossed his face, then relief.

"Oh, *that* wife. I see. You must have called my *old* house. My new number is unlisted. I should have figured it out when you first said you called. I used to be married. Well, I guess I'm still married—technically. It's a long story. I wanted . . ."

"Get out of my office. Right now. Don't ever come in here again. I'll have all the reports sent to your office. Any further communication between us will be through email," she said evenly.

"But Angela, you don't understand . . ."

"No, *you* don't understand. If you don't leave here this minute, I will make a scene that your Randall will hear about before his three-martini lunch. Get out. And close the door behind you."

She didn't take her eyes off him. He raised his palms as if to say "OK", then tilted his head with a hang-dog look. When her glare didn't waver, he turned and walked out the door, closing it softly.

Angela didn't know why she went to Eleanor first. Sondra's office was closer. When she walked into Eleanor's private office at the back of the shop, away from the hubbub of the bookstore up front, and beneath the drone of the machinery above them, she was relieved that she had. She couldn't hold back any longer. Eleanor immediately comforted her, mothered her. She understood, took her side, assured her she had done the right thing. Together, they wished a pox on his house and all the generations to come.

Angela couldn't have let it all hang out that way in the austere courthouse office. Besides, Sondra would have tried to get her to look at the thing from all sides—it was that lawyer training, she guessed. Sondra would say she should have heard him out, get the whole story before jumping to conclusions. Anyway, Sondra had had a long, happy marriage to a man she had met in college. She would not be able to imagine a man acting this way. She'd never really been on the dating scene—before her marriage or since Michael died.

Angela had. She prided herself in being able to spot the married men on the prowl—something about the way their wives dressed them. And the hair—usually not as meticulously groomed as the more self-centered, single guys. For Angela, it was black and white. The bastard. He had betrayed her. He had not been honest. When she left Eleanor's, she felt a little better. She agreed that a week away, in the shelter of her friends' caring, would be just the balm she needed to get through the final phase of the contract. After that, Quinton D. Rawlins could kiss her ass.

The rest of the week was hell. Quinton didn't try to contact her at work. But when Angela got home at night, the light on her answering machine was blinking. She didn't bother to play the messages. He called every hour until midnight. She let the machine answer. Each time she heard his voice, she was tempted to snatch the phone up and curse him for all he was worth.

"Angela, please. Pick up the phone. I know you're there." Then a long pause. Then click.

Tuesday was no better. She couldn't concentrate at work. The fact that the program was still bombing, didn't help at all. It gave her a headache. And if that wasn't enough, her period came. Just what she needed. She was miserable. She kept the door closed to her office. She left early, went home and got in the bed. She didn't even play the messages when she saw the little red light blinking on the machine. Asshole!

Wednesday was just as bad. The only bright spot was when Sondra called. She didn't have to try to disguise it. Angela could tell she knew. Of course Eleanor would have told her—they were just like that with each other. Sondra tried to sound upbeat as she rambled on about how she was getting the RV ready, and how excited she was about going to the new place. It did make

Angela feel a little better. She didn't look at her email all day. She went home and went straight to bed.

It was the same on Thursday. The light was blinking again when she got home. She pressed the button on her way to the coffee table with the pizza and chocolate bars she'd picked up at the grocery store. She heard his voice, "Angela, please. Call me." As she went in her bedroom, she heard, "Angela, you don't understand. Baby, please let me explain" She turned to the machine and said, "Fuck you."

As she undressed and put on her silk pajamas, she could hear the voice, but couldn't make out the words. She didn't want to hear it. Lying bastard! By the time she settled on the couch for her feast, the messages had finally ended and the machine was rewinding. She turned on the TV with the remote control.

When the doorbell rang, she just rolled her eyes. She knew it was Quinton, so she ignored it. She didn't move. Then he knocked. And knocked. Finally she went to the door and opened it.

"How dare you come to my house! And quit calling me!"

"Can I come in for a minute?"

"No!" she said emphatically, her arms folded across her chest.

"I won't leave, Angela, until you hear me out. Then if you still want me to leave, I will. And I won't call you anymore, or bother you at work."

"If you don't get out of my face, I'll call the police. I'll have your ass arrested for trespass."

"Now Angela, you know that won't be any good for either of us. The folk at the bank might get wind of that. I could lose my job. And you could lose the contract. You don't want to do that. Just hear me out, then I'll leave."

She stared at him, thinking about what the loss of the contract would mean. Then, she walked away from the door and sat back down. He closed the door and followed her to the couch. She stared at him with her arms crossed over her chest.

"So? Say it."

"Angela, I know I should have told you. You just don't know how many times I wanted to. It's been hanging over me like a sword. But the time was never right. When we first met, it didn't occur to me to tell you. I mean, why? I didn't like Texas that much. It's too hot. And the people act funny. This was only a temporary assignment. I was planning to do this deal, then go back to New York. I thought the divorce would be over by then. Then, when you and I . . . well you know. There just wasn't ever a good time. I was afraid you would leave me if I told you. It would look like I had been hiding something. I decided to wait until I had those papers in my hand. Then everything would be OK. You and I could get married the next day if you wanted. I've already put in for a permanent transfer here. I hate that you found out this way. Please forgive me."

"Well, if that's all there is, why didn't you just tell me?" Angela asked, skeptically.

"Oh baby, I don't know. I was just thinking stupid. It's my own fault. I just should have told you."

"But you've been here six months. How long does it take to get a divorce?" she asked, still not convinced.

"That's just the thing. It should be over by now. After I fell in love with you, I told my lawyer to get it over with, no matter what it took. I agreed to give her everything—the house, the resort property, the stock, everything. All the stuff I worked my ass off to get, while she just laid up on hers. All the stuff she said she wanted." He shook his head. "Everything, but my Porsche. I figured you and I could start fresh. It will even be better for us that way. Don't do this to us, Angela. I've given up everything for you. I love you."

Seeing her soften, he took her hand in his and held it to his cheek.

"So, now what's the problem?" she asked.

"She's trying to take my kids from me. She won't let me see them. We've been to court over it once already. She'll do anything to hurt me." The expression on his face hardened. "I'll fight her to hell and back for my kids. I just can't give them up. They're so sweet and innocent. You'll see when you meet them. Don't leave me Angela. I need you."

She saw the pain in his light brown eyes. Quinton looked so sad, she couldn't help but reach over and pull his head to her breast. After a moment, he began caressing her. She enjoyed the feeling a while, before she stopped him.

"Not tonight. I'm . . . I can't."

"Can't I just stay with you tonight?"

"No. It's best if you don't. I need time to think about all this. Call me before you leave tomorrow."

When he called her from the airport the next morning, he sounded so happy, she didn't tell him about the problem with the program—or that she was leaving town.

Angela opened another folder, spread the printouts over the floor and began wading through the code again, although she was certain the problem was not with her program. She thought about starting from scratch. Just pretend she hadn't written this program, and write an entirely new one. That would take too long. And what would she do different? In frustration, she put two slices of cheese toast in the oven, refilled her coffee cup and sat back on the floor amid the printouts. She wished she had brought her laptop, since as it turned out they did have electricity. It hadn't sounded like they would, from Eleanor's description of the place. She put her hand on her forehead, and started at the top of the flow chart she had made from her conversations with Quinton.

Angela jumped when she heard the soft knock on the door. When she opened the mini-blinds, she saw Donnell's face through the lace curtain. She closed the blind and sat back down among the printouts. She didn't need any more problems. He could just go to hell.

But he wouldn't. He kept knocking softly and calling her name. She couldn't concentrate.

"Go away, Donnell. They're not here," she finally yelled.

He kept knocking. "Angela. Can I talk to you?"

Finally she unlocked the door and pushed it open.

"What the hell do you want?!"

"Can I come in? I need to talk to you, just a minute."

"No." She looked down on him from the doorway, not budging.

"Don't you even want to know what happened last night?" he asked.

"I already know what happened last night. I was there. Or don't you remember?" she said, folding her arms.

"Of course I remember. That's why I came. I just wanted to explain."

"You don't have to explain anything to me. I know the deal.

Thanks for coming by. Excuse me," she said reaching for the door handle.

He held the door. "What deal?"

"I'm not stupid. I know what's happening."

"What? What deal? What are you talking about?"

"Never mind. Why don't you just go on. I've got work to do while it's quiet around here."

"What kind of work? Maybe I can help."

"I doubt it. It's computer stuff. Thanks anyway."

"Well, can't I have a cup of coffee? I'll just watch. How 'bout that?" he asked, hopefully. "I don't have anything else to do. Ike's gone again."

Although he looked clear-eyed and harmless in the bright daylight, she didn't want to be bothered.

"I know. He took Eleanor and Sondra for a boat ride."

"Can I come in? Just 'til Ike gets back. I won't bother you, I promise."

"No. I don't want any company. Just go on," she insisted.

"What's that burning?" he asked, sniffing.

Angela turned around, and saw the smoke pouring from the little oven.

"Oh, Lord! Now look what you've done!" she said rushing to the oven and jerking the door open. In her hurry to get the toast out, she stuck her fingers into the burning cheese. She immediately jerked her hand back and put the burned fingers in her mouth to suck the melted cheese off, and soothe the pain.

Donnell rushed up the steps behind her, snatched the towel off the rack and used it to remove the smoking pan from the oven, then set it on the stove.

"I don't believe *I* did this." He smiled sympathetically, as he took the ice container from the freezer, took hold of her hand and rubbed her fingers back and forth across the cubes.

"Do you have bandages?" he asked.

"Probably. Sondra has everything in this place. Look over the sink in the bathroom," she answered, taking the container from him with her good hand.

She winced as he wrapped gauze and tape around her fingers, tying them to each other.

"A couple of days, and they'll be good as new. You should even be able to write by then."

"Oh, God! I've got to write. I've got to finish this program! Dammit! I don't have a couple of days to waste."

Donnell saw the tears well up in her eyes, as she stared at her hand. He mistook them for tears of sadness, instead of fury. He pulled her to him and hugged her, rubbing her back in a soothing way.

"Don't worry about it. I'll write for you. I have pretty legible handwriting. My mama taught me."

Angela jerked away from him, eyes flashing, a frown on her face.

"I don't need you to write for me. You've done enough already. I need you to leave. If I see Ike, I'll tell him you're looking for him. Just go!"

Donnell leaned against the counter and smiled.

"Look at you, looking like a wet hen. You about a mean little heifer. I tell you what. I'll leave. If you need anything, just holler. I'll be waiting outside—for Ike of course."

Angela slammed the door behind him so hard, the windows rattled. She flopped on the floor and dug into her work. She reached for the pencil to mark a spot where the problem might be, and realized she couldn't bend her bandaged fingers to pick it up. She looked at the window, then pursed her lips and shook her head. To hell with him. She reached the pencil with her left hand and made the mark. She slowly wrote a note on the edge of the print-out to explain the mark. When she realized she couldn't read what she had written, she threw the pencil across the RV. She fumed, until she saw she had no choice.

"Donnell?" she called sweetly. " Would you come here a minute?"

Instantly the door opened, and he poked his head inside, a big grin on his face.

"You rang, ma'am?"

"OK. OK. You were right. I need your help. You don't have to rub it in. It's bad enough as it is."

"Aw, it won't be that bad. You'll see," he said, as he sat on the floor next to her, with his long legs stretched toward the door. She told him what to write and where.

"You do have nice handwriting. Was your mama a teacher?"

He smiled and nodded. She plodded on, having him write notes at different places.

Every now and then Donnell would ask her a question. She explained the problem to him in the simplest terms she could think of.

"Why are you doing it this way?" he asked.

"What do you mean?"

"Well, you said you've run this several times, and the test data worked fine. It's only the production data that makes it crash. It's obvious there's nothing wrong with your program. The problem must be in the bank's data. Why don't you write in a loop that will tell you where it's diverging."

She turned and looked at him, puzzled.

"You sound like you know something about computers."

"A little. I minored in computer science." His crooked smile told her he knew she had underestimated him.

"I know a little something about banks too," he continued. "I worked in one all through college. I went to college on a basketball scholarship. You know, the big alumni—'Sugar Daddies' we called them—could always find a little job for the athletes during the off-season. Mine was the president of a bank. I got to carry a lot of golf clubs, fetch a lot of coffee, but I also learned a lot about how banks operate. Let me show you something on your flowchart. See this. Now that's an unusual step right here for a bank. I'd put the first loop there. Where did you get this?"

"I drew it."

"Yeah, but where did you get the information? Do you work for the bank?"

"No. I'm under contract to do this program. The Chief Operating Officer is working with me. He's from New York. He explained the process to me for the flowchart."

"But I thought you said the bank is in Houston," he said, a puzzled expression on his face.

"It is. His bank is buying it, so he's here to oversee the transition."

"So how does he know so much about the Houston operation? Who do you work with from there?"

"Well...nobody. He deals with all of them. He's very knowledgeable. I guess that's why they sent him. He knows everything," she said, feeling herself defending Quinton.

"Humph," he said, still going over the flowchart. After a

while, he asked, "Can you connect to the bank's computer?"

"Way out here?" She rolled her eyes around the RV, as if the answer was obvious.

"What if you had a modem?"

"Well, sure."

"I've got one. Tell you what, I'm hungry. Aren't you hungry? Let's go grab a bite. We'll take this flowchart and your printouts. Bring a sweatshirt—it may turn cool before we get back," he said rising.

"I don't want to go to the cuts," she said warily.

"I don't either. I got what I needed from there last night. Come on," he said, reaching for her hand. "Another greasy burger? Or the blue plate special at Trudy's Cafe?"

This time he drove the country road like a sane man.

NINE

Jones was having his third cup of coffee, sitting on the deck above his upstairs bedroom—his favorite place on the entire island. He'd added it several years ago. It would have been a third story, except it didn't have a roof. He had a 360 degree view of the lake from here. It was so quiet among the treetops. He loved the whooshing sound the pines trees made when they let the breeze through. The clouds were gathering, and he could tell it would rain before the day was over. Whenever it came, he would move to the cover of the deck downstairs and watch it. He had no plans for the day, other than to watch.

The canoe across the lake drew his attention. It seemed to float aimlessly for a while, then it would seem to take on purpose, before drifting back into aimlessness. It was as if the oarsman was searching for something along the shoreline. It was the only craft on this side of the lake, so it held his interest. When the canoe headed straight toward the island, he reached for the binoculars on the table. He kept them there to watch the birds mostly. The lake was on a migratory path. Certain seasons, there was quite a variety of birds around the lake. Several years ago, he'd bought the book *Birds of Texas*, and kept a log in it of those he'd spotted.

As the canoe drew closer, he recognized them, and wondered what they were up to. He saw Sondra pointing toward the island and followed her arm with the binoculars, until he saw the large white bird perched on his dock.

Before he knew it, he was racing down the steps, through his bedroom, down the stairs and out the front door, past the two weimaraners who had been sleeping on the porch. As he ran toward the lake, dodging the trees, the large gray dogs caught up and loped excitedly alongside him, as though he'd come to play. He reached the dock just in time to see Eleanor stand up in the little boat, pointing to the big bird, as it rose in flight. The canoe began to rock. As she fought to maintain her balance, he saw Sondra lean over and reach for her, and Ike reach for Sondra. In the end, they all lost the battle. Jones hit the water about the same time as they did, swimming hard, the dogs right behind him. He didn't come up for air until he'd nearly reached the canoe. He heard them all laughing and saw they were safe, holding onto the capsized canoe. Then he laughed too, as he tread water.

He heard Eleanor say to Sondra, "Come on," and watched her swim off toward the dock, Sondra following.

"I don't see the oar. Let's turn it over and push it," Jones suggested to Ike.

By the time they reached the dock and tied the canoe up, the women were standing, watching them, the wet clothes sticking to their bodies and dripping. Sondra's arms were folded across her breasts, her shoulders scrunched up to her ears. Eleanor reached a hand down to Jones.

"Looks like I get to save you this time," she said, still laughing.

"Not funny, Eleanor. I bet you dumped us in this lake on purpose, just to have somebody to swim with. It's cold as hell out here," Sondra said, shivering.

Ike moved close to her and put his arm around her. She gave him a strange look, then shrugged and eased closer to him, still shivering. The warmth was more important than the invasion.

Jones started to put his arm around Eleanor, but didn't, not knowing how she'd react. The hostility seemed to be gone, but he wouldn't press it.

"Come on up to the house. It's warm. And dry."

The dogs, Jones just called them 'Boy' and 'Girl', had scrambled up the bank next to the dock and were circling around him, shaking water from their gray coats. Their yellow eyes watched him expectantly, eager for more play. He pointed and ordered, "Go. To the house." And off they raced.

When the four of them reached the house, Jones showed Sondra to the downstairs bathroom, promising to return with dry clothing. Passing through the den, he handed Ike a towel and asked him to stoke up the fire in the fireplace. He invited Eleanor to follow him and led her upstairs to his bedroom. Showing her into his bathroom, he handed her a washcloth and towel. He took one for himself and ran it over his head and body. From the bedroom, he heard her adjusting the water, as he hurriedly rummaged through the neat stacks in his drawers, pulling out pants and shirts for all of them. He leaned over the loft railing in his bedroom, and dropped two pairs of pants and two shirts to the den below.

"Ike. Catch. Make yourself at home."

Jones took the other dry clothes into his bathroom. As he laid them on the counter and turned to leave, he caught a glimpse of Eleanor through the lightly-frosted glass shower door. She was holding her head back, letting the water run through her hair, oblivious to his presence. Even knowing that he should leave, he leaned back against the counter and watched her. As the fragrance of the shampoo reached his nostrils, he drew a deep breath. He could see her slowly massaging it into her hair, piling it on top of her head as it filled with lather. He couldn't take his eyes away. Hers were closed, as she rinsed her hair and it fell down her back. Then she took the bar of soap and rubbed it, even slower, over her body. The movement was so sensuous, it seemed she was hearing some strange music in her head. He was titillated by it. He could almost hear it himself.

Jones imagined being in the warm steamy shower stall with her, rubbing the lather all over her—her breasts and stomach and hips—while she spread the lather on his back and chest, and lower. When they were both covered, he would press her back against the warm tile wall with the weight of his body. He could almost feel the force of the hot water on his back and the slippery feel of the thin film of soap lather that separated their bodies. In the trance, he didn't realize he was gripping the edge of the counter so hard, his knuckles were white. He was only aware of his rising nature. She would be so taken by the sensation of his mouth on her breast, she would stand on her tiptoes to thrust it deeper. Passion overcoming her, she would run her fingers through his wet hair, twisting strands of it around them. Then he'd lift her by her bottom and ease her onto him. He would move in and out of her rhythmically—until she set the tempo where she wanted it. Then he'd . . .The harsh metallic sound of the faucets being turned jarred him. The water went quiet, except for the last drippings as the pipes emptied. He eased out of the door, into his bedroom, before she saw him.

Ike caught the shirts and pants as they cascaded from the upper floor. He eased them through the bathroom door onto the counter, without looking. The fire was blazing now, and he no longer felt the chill—even with the wet pants still sticking to his body. He'd draped his wet shirt over the tool set in its stand by the fireplace, hoping it would dry soon. He felt naked standing there.

He admired the large room, the vaulted ceiling rising to the loft bedroom. The big stone fireplace on the interior wall had no mantle, only a two-tiered gun rack above it, holding the long guns. Through the opposite wall on the front of the house—almost all glass—he saw the day growing grayer.

It was clearly a man's room, nothing frilly, no bric-a-brac, no curtains. Even the furniture was masculine—large tan leather pieces. The only adornment was a collection of Native American artifacts and paintings that nearly hid the beauty of the rough-hewn wood of the far wall. When he walked closer to admire them, he saw the knife on the long narrow table against the wall. He knew its origin immediately. It was a common working knife used by the villagers. The crude curved blade ended in a foot-long wooden handle. The wood was worn smooth and oval from use. He stared at it—remembering—until he heard Sondra calling his name.

"Your turn."

"That was quick," he said as he broke away, and passed her

on the way to shower.

The bathroom was thick with warm steam. He thought the clothes she had spread on the towel racks would never dry that way. The hot pink bikini panties stood in stark contrast to the somber colors of her other clothing. He would have expected a paler pink, if not black.

The big sweatshirt fit him fine, but the jeans were too tight. He left the waistband unbuttoned. These would do until his dried. Sondra was standing by the fireplace when he came out.

"Nice house, isn't it?"

"Yeah. I have something similar in mind for my place on the lake. It's about time for me to start on it. Been planning it for a long time. Donnell will probably have a fit when I move The Mansion up to the farm. At first I'd planned to use it for storage. But maybe I'll just leave it where it is and convert it to a garage. I'm going to build the house closer to the lake anyway. Maybe close enough that I can fish from the porch," he chuckled.

"I can't believe you're that lazy. I thought farmers were industrious. Speaking of fish, I'm hungry. Wonder if Jones has anything in the kitchen."

"There's probably something we can put together. You really broiled that fish yesterday. It's a wonder you're not fat, cooking like that."

"I love to cook, but I hardly cook at all anymore, since my girls left for college. Let's see what we can find."

When Eleanor walked into the bedroom, her wet clothes bundled under her arm, Jones was at the fireplace, nonchalantly poking at the embers.

"Find everything you needed?" he asked.

"Yes. I enjoyed that." she nodded.

He thought, 'I did too', but he didn't say it.

"Sit down. I'll be right back," he said as he headed for the bathroom.

Eleanor didn't sit. She loved books, and there was a wall of them. She walked over to them and ran her finger along the spines as she read the titles. Many she recognized, some she didn't. That none of hers were there didn't surprise her. There was a set of leather-bound classics. And many modern ones, some very recent. She laughed to herself, thinking Jones was very well read, for an axe-murderer. Then she saw the pictures.

There was a collection of them on the opposite wall, over a desk. Some were framed, and posed. Others were snapshots, stuck to the wall with a push pin. Most were of a boy at various ages. The same crooked smile. Some were of Jones. The ones of the woman intrigued her most. She could have been Eleanor's younger sister.

"They're gone now," Jones said somberly, from behind her. "My boy is in Boston—in college. He hardly comes here anymore. He calls—sometimes. I miss him."

"He looks just like you. What's he studying?"

"I don't really know now. He's changed his major several times."

"Is this his mother?" she asked, pointing to one of the pictures.

"Yes."

"Where is she?"

"Gone."

"Must have been something pretty exciting, to make her leave a beautiful place like this." Eleanor said, turning to look at him.

He looked away.

"She never lived here. She's dead."

"I'm sorry. How long?"

"A long time."

"You still miss her?"

"Not as much—now," he said wistfully.

"Do I remind you of her?"

"She'd probably look a lot like you now. She isn't, I mean, wasn't as...blunt as you are."

"You don't like bluntness in a woman?"

"Let's go downstairs. They're probably wondering what's taking us so long," he said, abruptly, as he put his hand on her waist to urge her toward the door. Eleanor didn't budge.

"You didn't answer my question."

"I don't know. I'm not used to it. I think I like it. You're the only woman who's ever been in this house, in my bedroom," he said, his crooked smile showing.

Eleanor couldn't think of a thing to say, so she turned and started down the stairs, with the bundle of wet clothes under her arm.

"I hope you don't mind. We got hungry. We raided your kitchen," Sondra said, when Jones and Eleanor came in.

Jones was surprised at the array of food spread on the table. It didn't seem they had been upstairs long enough for a meal to be prepared.

"We've been waiting on you. I took a couple of chairs out on the deck. Grab a plate. This girl can *cook*," Ike said.

They loaded their plates and went outside. Jones went back

inside and returned with a bottle of wine and glasses. The sky was full of heavy gray clouds, and there was rumbling of thunder in the distance.

"Looks like its going to rain," Ike said.

"Yes. I've been expecting it all day. It's slow coming. From the South. That's not a good sign this time of year. I hope it's not a bad storm. Remember the one last fall? Damn near did my dock in. I spent most of the Spring repairing the damage. You get any damage over at your place?"

"Oh, yeah. It was awful. Lost some of my cattle. Had to replace the roof on my house."

"You don't have a roof on your house, Ike," Sondra broke in.

"Sure I do," Ike said querulously. "Oh. You think I live at the lake? No, I have a house up at the farm, where I stay most of the time. I just go over to the lake to fish and mess around. One day, I plan to sell the farm and move to the lake. Retire, sort of. I may do it sooner than I'd planned, now that it doesn't look like Donnell is gonna come back. I always hoped he would join me in the business. He's got his own business, and seems to be doing real well. Oh, well . . ." he trailed off.

The thunder was closer now, the sound menacing. Occasionally, the darkening sky lit up.

"I'll pull KP. Anybody for coffee?" Eleanor announced, as she gathered the empty plates and headed inside.

"I'll help," Jones said, starting up from his chair.

"No. I don't need help. I'll do it myself," she said sharply as she closed the door.

He eased back into the chair and shrugged his shoulders, looking to Sondra for an answer. She shrugged, too. But she knew the answer.

Sondra tried to make small talk for a while, but she had seen the storm gathering on Eleanor's face, as the dark gray clouds rolled across the sky. She couldn't do anything about the weather. Maybe she could stop Eleanor before she went too far.

"Excuse me. I'll go see if she'll let _me_ help," Sondra said, trying to signal Jones that it wasn't personal against him.

When she entered the kitchen, she saw Eleanor standing in front of the sink, staring out the window at the sky. The water was running, the sink nearly overflowing. Sondra walked over and turned the water off.

"Don't look at it, Eleanor. Don't do this to yourself. It's over. Let it go. He's dead, Eleanor. Can't you bury this too? At least try? He can't hurt you now. Not anymore. Not ever."

"I won't be able to see the moon," she said simply, still staring out the window.

"I know. But it's still there."

"You just don't understand," she said, as tears slid down her face.

None of them would ever understand. How could they? When her mother died, Eleanor had been eleven, but she could remember her clearly. The last few months of her life, her mother knew she was dying, and she tried to cram a lifetime of mothering into those short months. The last thing she ever said to her was "Eleanor, be a good girl." And Eleanor tried.

Papa found solace in the whiskey, but only at night. During the day, he kept the large farm running, profitably most years. He continued to serve as deacon at First Baptist Church, kept up his duties with the Masonic Lodge and maintained his public persona as all-around pillar of the community. Eleanor found her solace in Miz Mamie, the large-framed Black woman who had been in their house as long as she could remember. Many times, especially in the Summer, she would bring her niece, Naomi, with her. Eleanor and Naomi, a year older, always played together, while Miz Mamie went about running the house. When Eleanor was twelve, already tall for her age, her breasts began to bud. Miz Mamie took her shopping for her first bra. A year later, when her menses came, Miz Mamie was the one who showed her what to do. Miz Mamie had become her mama. Sometimes, Eleanor slipped up and called her 'Mama.'

Toward the end of that year, when her period didn't come on time, Miz Mamie asked her whether she had been letting any little boys fool with her. Although Eleanor didn't understand what she meant, she said no. Later, when Naomi explained to her what Miz Mamie meant, she did understand. Naomi felt betrayed when Eleanor refused to tell her about her boyfriend. Naomi had told her about hers. Eleanor did tell her mama. Miz Mamie just hugged her and rocked her, and cried.

Miz Mamie usually went home after dinner. That night, she stayed and saw Eleanor to bed. When they thought she was asleep, Eleanor heard their voices from downstairs. She had never heard Miz Mamie use that tone of voice with Papa. She knew something was terribly wrong.

"Mr. Tyler, you ought to be a ashamed of yo' self. She's just a child. You acting like some po' white mountain trash."

"I know. I know. It won't happen again, Mamie. I promise. I need your help with this tho'. You know what to do, don't you?"

"Yeah, I know what to do. I'm going to the authorities about you—what you doing to that child. And all these grown women throwing theyselves at you, too. You know it ain't right, Mr. Tyler."

"Now you just wait a minute. You go down there in town, telling folk about this. Who do you think they going to believe, you or me? And after all I've done for you. I'll have the sheriff put your black ass in jail." Papa was shouting. "I can get someone just like you to take care of this house. But who's going to take care of Naomi? You thought about that? Huh?" Then his voice softened, almost begging. "Just take care of this for me. I'll make it worth it to you. Please, Mamie."

"I don't want your money. Money won't make this right. I'll do it, but not for the money. I'll do it for the child. You gonna burn in Hell, Mr. Tyler."

When Eleanor heard the front door close, she pretended she was asleep. It didn't matter. He passed by her door. Papa never came in her room when the moon was full. She thought that the big bright moon, outside the window by her bed, was God's eye watching over her. While His eye was on her, nothing bad happened. She never understood why—when He slowly turned away. She tried to be good, like her mother told her to. She studied hard, made straight A's. She went to Sunday School and Church. She read her Bible and prayed. But nothing she did kept Him from turning away from her—or him from coming to her room.

A couple of weeks later, Miz Mamie took Eleanor to the strange woman's house, across the railroad tracks, near her own. The house had a smell she would never forget. The woman had her lie on the kitchen table, and violated her in much the same way as he did. Miz Mamie took her back to the farm, put her to bed, and stayed the night with her. Eleanor had never been so sick in her life. Miz Mamie did what she could to break the fever, but none of it worked. When the White doctor came two days later, Papa stood by the corner bookshelf that held her doll collection, a worried look on his face. Dr. Abrams gave her a shot, and gave Miz Mamie instructions about the pills before he left. By the time she recovered, the moon was growing full.

When He turned His eye away again, Papa didn't come to her room, and Eleanor thought it was over, that she was safe. She would have been happy, except she missed Naomi. Miz Mamie didn't bring her anymore.

When he started coming to her room again, Eleanor accepted it with resignation. She loved Papa—and hated him. She seethed at the smell of the whiskey, the feel of his hot, moist breath on her ear, the ugly grunting sounds he made. She showed no reaction other than to ball her fists stiffly at her side, and turn her face to stare out the window, vainly searching for Him. Except when it rained. Then she would cry.

When she told Miz Mamie it was happening again, Eleanor didn't understand why she couldn't do anything about it. She would just hug her and cry. Miz Mamie looked worried all the time. Finally she suggested that Eleanor tell her White teacher about it. When she did, Eleanor accepted the usual punishment meted out for lying, and never said a word about it again. Eleanor finally understood. They wouldn't believe Miz Mamie because she was a Negro. They wouldn't believe her because she was a child. No one who could help her would; and the one who would help her, couldn't. She would have to help herself. And she did—from then on. She buried herself in her books with a vengeance, finishing at the top of the class—a year early—and left for college.

Eleanor never saw Papa again—not even when he died. She made the arrangements by telephone, long-distance, with the local funeral director. She didn't care what the townspeople said. None of them had helped her when she needed it. She didn't need their help now. She'd done a pretty good job of helping herself.

She had a lawyer handle the sale of the farm and settlement of the estate. It came to a nice sum, but there wasn't enough money in the whole world to absolve it. She put a lot of the money in her company—and a good portion in her therapist's purse. The only time she went back to the town was when her mama died. Eleanor made sure Miz Mamie was put away in grand style. Papa and she both owed her that. She and Naomi hugged each other, and cried together like sisters, at the gravesite. Miz Mamie had been Mama to both motherless children.

Sondra saw the tears rolling down Eleanor's cheeks. She hugged her and kept saying, "It's still there. Baby, don't cry."

Finally, Sondra took her upstairs and put her in the bed. She laid beside her until she was sure Eleanor had fallen into a deep sleep.

TEN

From their seats on the covered deck, Ike and Jones watched the lightning flashes, each one seeming closer. Jones re-filled their glasses.

"That knife in the den. Where'd you get that?" Ike asked.

"I brought it back with me."

"You were in Nam?" Ike asked, looking at Jones in surprise. "Well, I'll be damned. When?"

"A long time ago."

"Me too. Drafted?"

"Volunteered."

"Not me. Why would you do a fool thing like that?!"

"I don't know, now. Maybe I believed it was the right thing to do. Maybe because I had been steeped in all that patriotism. Probably just rebellion against my father. My father had planned my whole life out for me. When I finished college, I was to come home, go into his business, eventually take it over. I wasn't sure I wanted to do that, but I didn't really have any other plan. I just had to do something on my own. Establish my independence from him. Don't ask me why I didn't buy an old VW bus and go cross country, like a lot of my friends. Or spend a year touring Europe—on his money. Not me. I joined the Army." Jones laughed and shook his head. "He nearly had a heart attack."

"I'll bet he did," Ike said chuckling.

"Did all he could to keep me from going. Pulled all the strings he could. I was gone before he could stop me. I don't regret it now. I got another whole education."

"You were just a wall-eyed fool," Ike said, still chuckling.

As they talked, they discovered Ike arrived in Viet Nam not long after Jones left. They spoke freely about the toll it had taken on each of them. In all those years, this was the first time either of them had been able to talk about it. Both of them, having chosen such isolating lives, were unaware of the movement that had finally grown up to support the veterans that America had refused to honor. On returning, they each had their own experiences that told them the sacrifice of their innocence and youth had no value. One had chosen to go, believing it was the right thing to do; the other had no choice, knowing it was wrong. Afterwards, one had no one to talk to about it; the other refused to talk to anyone about it. As the rain began to fall, a bond was formed that would never be broken.

Finally, Jones asked, "Wonder what's taking your woman so long."

"She's not my woman—yet," Ike said, with a mischievous smile. "We'd better go check on them."

The kitchen was clean when they went in the house. They found Sondra sitting on the couch staring at the fireplace.

"I put her to bed. Upstairs. Hope that was OK," Sondra said

to Jones.

"Sure. No problem."

"It's the weather," she said, trying to explain. "The rain. It always affects her."

"Should I go check on her?" Jones asked hopefully.

"No. She'll be OK after a while. When the rain stops, I'll get her up and we'll go on back."

"Doesn't look like it's gonna let up for a while. And it's dark now. You don't have to go back tonight. I don't think you'll be able to, even if you took my boat," Jones told her.

"Well of course we do. Angela will be worried about us. I hate to think of her over there by herself. I wish I could call her. Do you have a phone here?"

"Sure." Jones brought the telephone to her.

She called her cellular phone and frowned when she got no answer.

"I'll call Donnell over at the house and have him go check on her," Ike volunteered. He got no answer either.

As the force of the rain grew stronger, they both sat on the couch, their brows furrowed like worried parents waiting up for a child past curfew.

Jones didn't want them to leave. He returned from the kitchen with a bottle of wine, glasses and a wooden box.

"Since we only have three, we can't play bridge. You play poker?"

Ike did. Sondra didn't.

"We'll teach you," Jones said.

In the end, maybe it was beginner's luck, or maybe it was the lawyer training. Sondra ended up with most of the chips.

"I'm out. I give," Jones said. The second bottle was empty.

"Doesn't look like the rain is going to let up. You can't try to cross the lake tonight. You have to stay here. There's another bedroom down that hallway."

Jones saw the look on Sondra's face, and went to the closet. When he returned, he set the extra linen on the couch. It was for them to work out. He said "Goodnight," and went up the stairs.

Jones stood in the bedroom doorway, not sure what to do now. The occasional lightning flashes illuminated Eleanor, as she lay on her back, with her arm covering her eyes. Finally, he picked up the blanket at the foot of the bed and spread it over her. Then he stretched out on the bed on his back next to her, pulling one side of the blanket over himself. When the thunder sounded, she jumped and fidgeted, but didn't wake. She looked so vulnerable, he finally eased his arm under her neck. In her fitful sleep, she turned her body toward him and snuggled up against him. All through the night, as the storm's ferocity grew, she continued to jump and start with each clap of thunder. He held her and rubbed his hand over her head and down her neck, to settle her. When the sound of the thunder trailed off into the distance, she nestled close against him. The morning found them that way.

After Jones left, they each tried to place their calls again. Still no answer. After an awkward moment, Sondra said, "We may as well turn in."

"No point in messing up all these sheets for one night. We can share the bedroom."

"Jones obviously doesn't mind," Sondra said pointedly.

"You can take the bedroom. I'll sleep on the couch." She began spreading the sheets on it.

"No. If it has to be that way, you take the bedroom."

She did. No sooner than she had undressed and settled in the bed, she heard a knock on the door. She sat up, her back against the headboard, and pulled the cover around her, clamping it with her arms folded across her breasts. The door opened and she saw Ike, leaning against the doorframe, smiling. He was shirtless and she could see the tight pants were unbuttoned at the waist.

"I don't have a pillow."

As his eyes moved from her bare shoulders to the foot of the bed, Sondra was acutely aware of the pants and shirt she'd folded and laid there.

"I won't even touch you," he said sweetly. "That is, unless you want me to . . ."

She raised up, holding the cover about her with one hand, and threw the pillow at him with the other.

"Goodnight," she said emphatically.

"It won't be as good a night as it *could* be, this way," he said.

The nerve of him! How dare he say such a thing to her! She flopped over on her stomach and pulled the cover almost over her head.

After a long time, she heard the squeaking of the door hinges.

As the storm raged outside the patio door, another storm raged within her. She didn't like being out of control. She felt trapped. By the storm. By the sheriff. By worry. Maybe she should have kept Jones from going upstairs. She had expected Eleanor to come stomping down the stairs, and was surprised that she hadn't. She worried about Angela. She hated to think of her alone in this storm. The wind was probably rocking the RV.

Why wouldn't she answer the phone? Sondra knew it was plugged in. She sat up and looked around the room for a phone. She thought about the one in the den and toyed with the idea of going to use it. Maybe he would be sleep. But what if he wasn't? She didn't want to do anything that he might interpret as an invitation. She thought about the silly smile on his face as he stood in the doorway. How could he think a woman like her would allow a stranger to share her bed. She had only known him a few days. She thought he was probably used to having his way with the women. She had to admit, he *was* good looking, and had a body most men his age would kill for. She rarely paid much attention to men's bodies. The ones she was around were always in dress suits or uniforms.

She imagined him in a suit. Olive green would look good against his deep brown skin. He was tall and muscular, but not so much so that he would look cramped in a suit. The pants would probably be a little snug around his thighs. She shivered when she thought about his thighs touching hers the day before at the lake. She could still feel the strength in them. It seemed innocent enough, but she was sure he had another purpose than just teaching her to fish. He seemed to never miss an opportunity to touch her, even if he had to create one. He was so pushy. No, not really pushy, he just kept up a steady pressure. Still, she found it flattering, in a way.

Sondra was surrounded by men all day—deputies, police-men, attorneys. Some were pushy, some cloyingly sweet, most trying to flatter her to get their way—a ruling in their favor, a higher bond, a lower bond, a release card for a jailed client. Rarely was it aimed at her personally—as a woman. Only a couple of times. Once a White one, new to town. Maybe there were no women judges where he came from. She assumed a seasoned lawyer had spoken to him, since the next time he appeared in her court, he had a sheepish look on his face. She pretended it hadn't happened. Everybody's entitled to one mistake.

The other one was Andrew Simmons. There were few Black attorneys, and those her age were married. She had dated him for a while, but had broken it off earlier in the year. Andrew had been a good escort—at first. It was nice to have someone to talk with who understood what she was talking about. Michael had been an architect, and although they politely listened to each other, neither understood enough about the other's work to really get it. Even though she had heard the coffee shop gossip, from her secretary, Josie, as usual, about Andrew's pending divorce, she had been surprised when he had invited her to the Metropolitan Black Lawyers Christmas party. She actually enjoyed herself, and was glad she'd let Angela talk her into going. She invited him to escort her to the Link's annual gala, before it occurred to her his estranged wife might also attend. Mercifully, she didn't, but the thought caused Sondra to be distant and professional with him all evening. She didn't need all those wagging tongues and themsays. She had to be careful about her image. As the relationship continued, she was receptive to his kisses—when the girls weren't home. She couldn't go farther than that, for a while. It seemed Michael was staring at her from every wall. It was his house. He had designed it and built it. Andrew grew impatient.

After the Law Day Banquet in May, when she asked him not to paw her in public, he was insulted and pouted all the way home. She supposed she *could* have chosen her words more carefully. Sondra knew Andrew had not enjoyed the Banquet. He seemed jealous of all the attention paid her. What did he expect? She was a judge. They were all lawyers. It was a professional function. She wondered if he thought she should be sitting at the table beside him, mooning over him like a teen-ager? She knew he had ambition. He had talked of one day running for a judgeship. He was certainly smart and polished enough. More Black men were needed on the bench. She was happy to give what help she could. But when she steered him to meet some of the lawyers from the top civil firms, the ones with money and influence, he acted aloof and distant. He kept putting his arm around her possessively. She was embarrassed—and pissed. Finally she gave up and asked him to take her home.

It grew worse. When he drank more than he should—and those times increased in frequency—he would turn mean, uncommunicative, and brooding. Then he began to accuse her of having 'robe-itis.' No one had accused her of that, not even Michael. But she *did* think about what he said. She had been on the bench for a while, and it was a common judicial malady. She didn't see it, but maybe when you had it, you *couldn't* see it. She had delicately inquired of her bailiff and secretary. They worked closely with her, and were both regulars in the coffee shop where that sort of thing was discussed. They assured her there had been no change in her behavior or in the talk about her there. Besides, she had teenagers—a sure antidote to pomposity—to keep her humble. Like that time when Natalie got arrested on traffic tickets. That kind of news travelled at the speed of light down in the coffee shop and the corridors outside the courtrooms.

Still, since it was an issue for Andrew, she began to watch her speech and behavior around him. She was careful to always start even the simplest request with "Would you mind" or "What do you think." Although she complied with his incessant demands that she 'go put some lipstick on your face', she was non-committal to his request that she 'grow her hair out'. Even the time they made love, it felt to her more like a power struggle, an effort to conquer. They hadn't made love. Andrew had had sex. For Sondra, it was nothing like the sweet melding it had been with Michael. That night, she'd stared at the ceiling, listening to Andrew's snoring, and wondered for the thousanth time, why God had taken Michael from her. Why had He left her to raise her girls alone? And now that they were gone too, was she to be alone the rest of her life? Or did she have to pay for the good years by subjecting herself to this, so that she wouldn't be?

In the end, tiptoeing around his insecurity, became too tiring, too much hassle. She had enough other trouble to worry about. Natalie was wearing her hair in some weird style and was talking about piercing her nose. Sondra didn't care for the street-wise boy Tiffany had hanging around the house, usually with his feet up on the thick glass coffee table. She suspected he was raiding her bar, too. Maybe that was better than drugs. Maybe. She thought she saw him playing the same power games with Tiffany that Andrew played with her. Sondra was really disturbed when she saw Tiffany's behavior with him mimicking her own. She made up her mind. Her first duty was to her children.

At first, Andrew was infuriated, then unrelenting. She tried to ignore his banging on her beveled glass front door in the middle of the night, and the angry messages he left on her machine. She wished she had given him her private number, so Josie didn't give her those curious looks when she brought the pile of messages. Andrew knew Sondra didn't want her personal business exposed that way. It was just another power trip for him—manipulation. It wasn't about love, it was about dominance. He just couldn't begin to understand, she could not be dominated by anyone but herself. Finally, she had Josie call and summon him to her chambers. She calmly explained the entire situation to him—what he was doing to her, why she couldn't continue the relationship, the other pressures on her, the help she would continue to provide him—and the letter she would send to the grievance committee, if he didn't stop. After she finished, she escorted him to the door, just like the others.

"I know you're busy. Thank you for making the time to see me."

Then Sondra's thoughts wandered to the man she had given her private number, the one she met at the judicial conference in Nassau. He'd shadowed her the entire time. She enjoyed his company. Being a judge himself, he didn't seem threatened by her position. She'd let him touch her a little too much at the swimming party the last night. Afterwards he'd invited himself to her room for 'a little nightcap.' She mistook his meaning. When she resisted his sexual advances, he coolly handed her his business card. She mistook that as well, giving him hers, after she wrote her private number on the back. It took her nearly two weeks of waiting for his call, to figure out how naive she'd been. She shook the memory off. It was too painful.

This Ike was probably the same kind of cad. With those shining black eyes, the white smile under his moustache, riding around in his big noisy truck, he probably had half the women in the county waiting and watching their phones. She realized that in all their coming and going, he hadn't taken her to his real house. He probably had a wife tucked away there, while he was out galavanting with her, trying to get in her bed. Her anger at him grew. She felt like marching in the den, whopping him with her pillow and informing him that she was not that kind of woman. Then she thought how she'd been *acting* like that kind of woman, and the anger turned on her.

What else was he to think, her going off with him—a complete stranger? And worse, staying with him almost continuously for two days. Allowing him to put his hands all over her the way she had. Not once had she told him to keep his big hands to himself. What was making her act this way? Maybe this was what menopause was like, you just became somebody different—lost your mind. She'd heard of women who had. Maybe it was the safety of the distance from all the eyes that were usually watching her. Hell, maybe it was the full moon. Whatever it was, she was glad she had come to her senses. Tomorrow would be different. She'd go get her gun and talk to the others about cutting the trip short. Fuck that sheriff, he couldn't keep her here. She needed to go home. She finally fell asleep—as the rain slowed to a light pattering.

Ike lay on the couch with his hands behind his head, thinking about her. He couldn't remember ever having been taken with a woman this way. He remembered how Jackie used to ask him what he was waiting for. He could never answer. He realized now Sondra was the woman he'd been waiting for. He just couldn't understand why she wouldn't let him stay with her. It could have all been so perfect—the sound of the storm's fury, of the pine branches being whipped about, just enough wine to free them of their inhibitions. It would have been the perfect cap to the time they had spent together, and a perfect beginning for the rest of the week, for the rest of their lives. It had been two whole days. What was she waiting for? They didn't have time to play silly teenage games. They were both grown—real grown. Middle-aged even. Maybe. He didn't like the sound of it. But no matter what you called it, he had reached that age where he couldn't let any happiness pass him by, without at least trying to claim it. He was tempted to go in that room and make her. He would only have to *make* her at first. He was sure he could give her so much pleasure, she would thank him, for years.

He would close the door behind him, so as not to disturb the others. She would probably waken and turn over to tell him to get out. He would get on top of her and hold her down. Even though she was tall for a woman, and obviously in good shape, it would be no problem for him to subdue her. He could hold both of her hands over her head with one of his. He knew she was naked, so he'd only need one free hand—one finger really. He would cover her mouth with his own to keep her from calling out—until she no longer wanted to. He threw the sheet off and started up. As soon as he felt the cold tile under his feet, he came to himself. He didn't want it that way. He had never in his life forced a woman, and wouldn't start now. He lay back down, staring at the ceiling.

Most women would be flattered by his attention. Why wasn't she? Maybe she was concerned about what her friend would think about it. From what he had seen, and the little he had heard of their conversation, Eleanor had enough to think about other than Sondra's love life. Then he remembered how she and Eleanor were hugging. It seemed that she *had* stayed a long time in the bedroom with her, too. And Eleanor was talking about those books—about women loving themselves. Maybe Sondra didn't like men. No, she couldn't be that way; he remembered how she'd responded to him the day before at the lake. He absolutely wasn't mistaken about that. She couldn't be concerned about what Jones thought. She'd just met him, and after this week, would probably never see him again.

He liked Jones. They had a lot in common. He thought they could become fishing buddies. He owed Jones one. Jones went upstairs and faced the wrath of the she-devil, he thought, to give Ike the space he needed. He *had* insinuated he intended to make Sondra his woman. Then he chuckled at the thought that maybe he gave Jones too much credit; that maybe he had gone upstairs to make Eleanor *his* woman. If so, he sure was quiet about it. Ike hadn't heard a sound from the open loft, not even whispers.

Every now and then he *did* hear noise from the bedroom around the corner, through the door he'd not shut tight. He listened intently between the bursts of thunder, and was finally able to decipher the sound. Sondra was tossing and turning in the bed. And he kept hearing it all through the night. Maybe the storm was causing her to have a fitful sleep. Or, maybe she wasn't asleep at all. Maybe she was wrestling with herself—to keep from coming to him. He liked that thought, so he held on to it. A woman had needs, too. Any minute she would walk out that bedroom door and join him. He smiled. The couch would be too cramped for the both of them. He would make love to her on the floor. No, too cold. Looking up at the open loft, he decided he would carry her back to the bedroom. He was a patient man. He would wait for her. When the sky began to lighten, he was still waiting.

ELEVEN

Eleanor slowly opened her eyes. The sky was just beginning to lighten outside the patio door. The room was strange. She was disoriented. When she saw the man lying next to her, his arm under her neck, it all came back. Against the pillow, his gray hair looked silver in the early morning light. She jerked away from him and sat up, staring at him with a frown on her forehead. In a panic, she ran her hands over her body. She felt the rough texture of his shirt that she still wore. All the buttons were fastened. She felt for the button on the pants. It was fastened too. She pushed the blanket all the way down and looked anyway— just to be sure. When she looked back at him, he was awake and smiling his crooked smile.

"What are you doing here?!" she demanded.

"I live here. It's *my* room." Jones propped up on his elbow. A smile danced around his eyes.

"How did I…?"

"Sondra."

"Did you…?"

"No. I didn't. We didn't."

"Why? I mean, why not?" Then after a moment, "Thank you."

"Lie down. It's too early to get up. The sun's not even up."

She looked at him uncertainly, her head cocked to the side. She thought he was pretty strange for an axe-murderer on the make. When she laughed quietly, he looked puzzled.

"What?" he asked.

"Nothing."

Maybe she would tell him later. The chill in the room began to seep into her body. Slowly, she lay back down, his arm under her neck. He pulled the blanket back over her with his free arm. Feeling the warmth and comfort of his body next to her, she drifted back to sleep.

When Sondra woke, she was tired. More tired than when she had gone to bed. She was glad the storm had passed. All that was left, was the remnants dripping from the pine trees on the patio outside, and the resoluteness in her mind. Her clothes should be dry by now. She couldn't wait to put them on and leave this place. She planned out her day. As soon as they got to the other side of the lake, she would persuade Eleanor and Angela that they should go home. Then, she would go to town and get her gun, while they packed everything. Angela could do the un-hooking by herself, while she was gone. By the time she got back with her gun, they could take off. She would get home in time to wash all the linen, empty the fridge, and vacuum the RV. Maybe she would even go in to work tomorrow. There was always something to do there. Then she realized that plan wouldn't work—she didn't have a car. She'd have to borrow that man's truck. Hell no! She re-worked the plan. She would persuade them to leave. She and Angela would unhook, while Eleanor packed up. She'd drive the motorhome through town to get her gun, on the way out. That would work, she thought, nodding her head.

She listened. Didn't hear any sounds. It was still early. She didn't want to put Jones' clothes on, just to go across the hall to the bathroom. She stuck her head out the door. All she could see was his bare feet and one leg sticking out of the sheet, where he was prone on the couch. Must be asleep. Good. She could just tiptoe across that short distance. As she eased through the bathroom door, she heard, "Good Morning. Sleep well?"

Damn! she thought, and slammed the door. She hurriedly put on her own clothes. They were rough-dried, wrinkled, but she didn't care. She grabbed the washcloth and washed her face, then ran it over her teeth. Now what? The others must not be up, else he wouldn't be lounging on the couch, half-naked, leering at her. She didn't want to be alone with him. It was too early for Eleanor to be up. Where was Jones? Surely a man like him would be an early riser. Maybe he was in the kitchen—she hoped making coffee. She just wasn't any good without her coffee. She listened. Still no sounds, other than the dripping from the trees. She sure as hell wasn't going to be trapped in this bathroom until Eleanor got up. She had to have her coffee. She'd just make enough noise to wake them up. She ran her fingers through her short hair to fluff it, threw her chin up and walked out.

"I waited for you. All night," Ike said, smiling devilishly.

Sondra gave him a withering look, and walked past him to the kitchen. She found what she needed and put the pot on. Now what? No newspaper to read. She hated being out of her routine. She hated being here. She made as much noise as she could, getting the cup and saucer. Then listened. Nothing. She couldn't believe Eleanor let that man sleep with her. He was nice and all, but Sondra wouldn't have been surprised to have found his broken body on the tile floor in front of the fireplace, where Eleanor had tossed him over the railing. She laughed to herself at the vision. Eleanor was sure going to have to explain this to her—after all she had put her through last night. What was taking this coffee so long? Sondra drummed her fingernails on the counter impatiently, ready to get on with her day.

"You were in here so long, I thought you'd have breakfast going by now," Ike said, perching on the bar stool across the counter from her.

"Don't you have a shirt?" she snapped. She wanted to slap that mischievous grin off his face.

"Give me a cup of coffee, woman. At least."

She looked at the coffee pot. It was finally full. She filled her cup, took it over by the sink and looked out the window. She would just ignore him. She couldn't get over his nerve.

"I guess you're just mean—'til you get your good morning kiss. Guess I'll just have to come over there and give it to you, so I can get my coffee."

Sondra turned and looked at him to see if he was for real. The look on his face didn't help her decide. She got another cup and saucer down, filled it, and pushed it toward him across the counter. She wanted to throw it on him. Instead, she went back to her cup by the window. She felt his eyes following her every movement. It made her uncomfortable, but she forced herself to be still. Finally she had to say something.

"Wonder what's taking Eleanor so long? I'm ready to go," Sondra said, almost to herself, nervously tapping her nail on the countertop.

"Doesn't she usually sleep 'til noon? That's what you said."

"Well, not today. I'm going home today."

"Home? You mean across the lake?"

"No. I mean *home*. I've had enough of this."

"But I thought you were going to be here 'til Saturday."

"I've changed my mind. I'm going home today," she said emphatically.

"Well, if I'd known that . . ."

"What?!" she snapped.

"Well, things just would have been different. That's all."

"What things?"

"You know. Last night."

She cut her eyes at him. The grin faded.

"What about your gun?"

"Don't you worry about my gun. I'll get it today, on my way out."

"But Billy told you not to leave," he said, searching to find a reason.

Sondra almost exploded.

"He can't tell *me* what to do. I'll leave when I'm good and damned ready. And I'm ready today. Now!"

"Shush. Keep your voice down. You'll wake them up."

"I *intend* to wake them up. I don't know what Eleanor is thinking about."

"I do." The grin was back.

In exasperation, Sondra stomped to the doorway into the den and called up at the loft.

"Eleanor! Eleanor, come on. It's time to go!"

"Now why'd you go and do that? It's early. Leave them alone."

"Eleanor!"

Eleanor heard her name, and shifted against him. Reflexively, he pulled her closer. When she heard her name again, they both came to. Jones pressed his lips to her forehead.

"Sounds like you're being summoned."

She pulled away from him, reluctantly this time.

"Guess we'd better go down," she said sleepily.

"Don't go. Not yet. There's a little red bird I want you to see. I've been feeding him. He usually comes out there on the deck this time of morning."

"Do you like birds too? Aren't they beautiful? So free. How do you know it's a him?" she asked him, teasing.

Before he could answer, they heard Sondra calling again.

"Guess you'd better go see what she wants. If you're really interested in birds, I'll show you my bird book later."

When Eleanor found her way to the kitchen, she was wearing Jones' pants and shirt that she'd slept in. Hers were still in a wet bundle by the couch, where she'd left them the night before.

"I'm glad you're finally up. We're ready to go. We were just waiting for you," Sondra said.

She saw Eleanor lethargically look at the clock—7:45— then at Ike, dressed only in the too-small pants, then back at her.

"Ya'll hurry up and put your clothes on," Sondra urged.

"But, mine are still wet," Eleanor responded slowly, then

yawning.

"They'll dry by the time we get to the other side. Just put them on. They can't be *that* wet."

"It's bad enough, you getting me up at the crack of dawn. Now you want me to put on wet clothes. I don't *think* so," Eleanor said, slowly pouring herself a cup of coffee. She took the coffee to the table behind Ike and sat down.

"OK. Wear those. You can leave them with him," Sondra said, motioning toward Ike with her head. "Hurry up and drink your coffee. Better yet, we can make another pot when we get to the RV."

"What's all this hurry-hurry stuff? It's only Monday. What had you planned to do today?"

"Well, I wanted to talk to you about that. I thought we would go home today."

She saw Eleanor look curiously from her—to Ike—and back.

"Home? You mean Houston?"

"Yes, home. See, if we leave by ten, we'd have the whole day ahead of us when we get back," Sondra said brightly.

"The whole day? To do what?" Eleanor asked, a frown furrowing on her face. Then after another sip of coffee, "No."

"No?! No, what?" Sondra demanded, her voice rising.

"We're not going today," Eleanor said firmly.

Sondra could see Ike watching her, trying to suppress the big grin breaking out under his moustache. She wanted to throttle both of them.

"What's all this about going home?" Jones asked, from the door. "You just got here. I want to show you around the island today. It'll really be pretty after all that rain last night. Everything will be fresh and clean. A little muddy maybe. But the sun's shining now. It'll be nice. Then we can have lunch on the deck over my bedroom. You can see the entire lake from there. It's a beautiful view."

"I'd love to see the island. Let's eat a little something first," Eleanor said, smiling at him.

"Sondra, I'll take you across the lake, if you want," Ike interjected sweetly, the grin now turned mischievous, smug.

"No. Thank you. I'll just wait until Eleanor's ready to go."

She was not about to get in that little boat with him by herself. She snatched the phone off its hook on the wall and dialed her number. There was still no answer.

"Let's go take the tour now. We can eat when we get back," Sondra announced.

They were all starved when they returned. Sondra quickly set about making sandwiches. She wanted to get this over with, so they could get back across the lake. This was throwing her behind schedule. Eleanor didn't seem to be in a hurry at all. Sondra had noticed how Jones had taken her hand, to help her over the muddy places. And how Eleanor had almost blushed when he lifted her over one. She'd nearly stopped in her tracks, when she realized, in all the years they'd been friends, she had never seen Eleanor with a man. Sondra wouldn't have imagined that Eleanor would act this way. Like a school girl almost. Sondra thought it was cute. She knew when she told Angela, she would rib Eleanor unmercifully. Sondra wasn't even angry with Eleanor anymore. She *was* still angry with Ike, and every time he reached for her, ostensibly to help her over a water puddle, she would jerk away. She would rather get her tennis muddy, than have him touch her.

They took the sandwiches upstairs to the deck. It really *was* beautiful—and serene. The green pine needles glistened in the sunlight. It was quiet, except for the occasional squawk of a bird in the distance and the intermittent breeze swishing through the pine branches. Sondra could see the entire lake. There were houses on large tracts of land, along one side of the lake. Some were large and obviously occupied. Others were smaller and apparently vacation homes. On the other side of the lake, there were a number of motorhomes and trailers nestled among the trees. She knew it must have been the state park she had seen on her map, when Eleanor had first told her where they were going. She didn't see any of the condo developments that were so prevalent on the other lakes she'd visited. Their absence probably explained the lack of activity on the lake. The lake was too far from the interstate highway to foster that kind of development.

Turning back, she could see her own motorhome from where she sat. She knew Jones had been watching them, when she saw the binoculars on the table. She picked them up and looked through them at her RV. She was startled to see a man standing by the door. Then she saw the car with the lights on top. She sat bolt upright and handed the binoculars to Ike.

"Look! I'm gonna call Angela."

This time Angela answered.

"God, am I glad you called! You won't believe this! That sheriff is outside. He says he needs to come in and look around. What should I do? I'm scared."

"Look for what? What does he want?" Sondra asked.

"I don't know. He sounds serious."

"Did he say he had a warrant?"

"I don't know." Angela's voice was breaking.

"Angela, ask him if he has a search warrant."

Sondra tapped her foot nervously, waiting.

"He said he didn't, but he would get one—if I don't let him in. What should I do?" Angela was crying.

"Tell him to go get it. And don't let him in unless he shows you a warrant through the window. Make him give you a copy, and make sure it's signed. I'm coming now."

She hung up and turned to Jones.

"I need to use your boat. It's an emergency."

"Do you know how to drive it?"

She heard Ike talking into the telephone he'd taken from her hand.

"Donnell. Where've you been?! Never mind. Go over to that RV right now and stay with Angela. There's some kind of trouble. I'll meet you there."

As they all crossed the lake in Jones' boat, Ike watched Sondra sitting tall and erect on the benchseat in the bow. When he caught a glimpse of her face, he couldn't read it. She no longer looked frightened, as she did when she first placed the call. It struck him that she appeared calm and determined. Jones had the throttle wide open, and the front end of the boat underneath her was rising and falling hard against the waves. She didn't seem disturbed by it. The wind whipped her short hair backwards, as she led into it with her chin. He was glad he'd changed into his own clothes. He didn't want to look ridiculous in the too-small clothes, when he confronted Billy.

Ike couldn't figure why Billy was doing this. He knew in his soul, it had more to do with him than Sondra. Nearly thirty years had passed. He'd moved on. He couldn't understand why Billy wouldn't. Sports and girls were surely all-consuming for high school boys, but they were in their forties—old enough to be fathers, even grandfathers.

There *had* been that business of the two of them being named co-captains of the basketball team. Lee High School had never had co-captains before, and Billy had felt he deserved the honor alone. Ike *knew* he would have been the captain at Dunbar, and should have been the captain at Lee. The other players, Black and White, were torn, each feeling loyalty to their own. But all of them knew that Ike was their ticket to the Finals. In its entire history, Pine Branch's Lee had never been farther than the regional competition. Lee's coach had been wise to forego the customary team vote. That would have been nothing but divisive. They needed unity, if they were to take advantage of the opportunity to get to Finals.

Maybe the coach had done it that way to appease the still-separate communities that were being forced together, one feeling the greater burden—having lost its school. When Dunbar was closed and used as a storage building, the more recent trophies were taken to the Black church. The older trophies and other memorabilia were packed away in the former coach's garage, while the Black community raised money for a permanent display—and memorial. The School Board had refused their request for a display in the trophy case at Lee. Ike and Billy had forged an uneasy truce, both having to bear the burden neither of them had created.

With Laura Washington, it had been more personal. Ike had

grown up with Laura. They attended the same school and church. When they reached junior-high age, and the boys and girls began eyeing each other, he didn't even think about her in that way. They had always been competitors—for the highest grade at school, and the ribbons in Sunday School. Sometimes she won, sometimes he did. Besides, he knew she was too prudish—and too carefully watched—for what he had on his mind then. He went after the girls who were as interested in experimenting as he was. Of course, they were not the girls he would later take to the chaperoned dances at Dunbar. Laura was *that* kind of girl. They'd continued their competition when they were forced to attend Lee, even though the circle of competitors had widened.

When he first began to hear the whispering about the White boy talking to her, Ike couldn't decide how he felt about it. It wasn't like she was really *his* girl, although both sets of parents would have been pleased. On the other hand, he felt protective of his territory. The big blond boy could have his pick of the White girls, even the ones who made eyes at Ike—when they were certain no one was looking. Muhdea had schooled him about them, and Ike kept them at a polite distance. So why did Billy think he could just take one of their jewels? Why didn't he do like some of the other White boys, cross the tracks under the cover of darkness, to learn with the ones who were willing to teach? Ike confronted Laura about what he was hearing. She told him it wasn't his business and he could just go on back to his 'other girls.' When Billy came to the evening services at his church, Ike would sit with his arms folded, glaring at them.

Around the Courthouse square, the domino table down on the cuts, in the barber shops and beauty shops—on both sides of the railroad tracks—the talk grew louder, when word got out Billy had asked Laura to the senior prom. Now that was just going too far. Both communities felt insulted, angry, and fearful. The Washingtons and the Evans solved the problem for everybody. Laura and Ike obeyed their parents, did their duty, and went to the prom together—both pretending it had been their idea.

Over the Summer, the folks settled down—on both sides of the track. The White folk forgave Billy his youthful transgression, and accepted him back into the fold. The Black folk proudly looked on Ike as their hero—not only for his exploits on the court, and his acceptance to a prestigious college, but for saving their Honor. Ike and Laura, long accustomed to being competitors, had no one to turn to except each other. No one else could understand how heavy the role of savior was. If things had been different, they might have returned to Pine Branch with their degrees, after a while married each other, and taken their place as community leaders. When he left for the Army and she left for Fisk University, they promised to keep in touch. One letter each was all there had been. From her letter, he gathered she was enjoying college, and busy with its social functions. He'd been busy trying to stay alive. She had already married by the time he thought about contacting her again.

As they neared the shore, Sondra was relieved to see Donnell's car. She stood and jumped onto the shore, before the wake that caught up with them had spent itself. She ran to the RV, where she found Donnell comforting Angela.

"What happened? What'd he say?"

The others came in and filled up the RV, sitting and standing where space allowed.

"Donnell dropped me off this morning. I was taking a nap when the sheriff knocked on the door and asked for you. I told him you weren't here. Then he said he wanted to come in and look around. I told him to come back later, when ya'll were back. But he said he needed to come in right then. He started jerking on the door. You should have seen his face. I was scared," she said, her voice trembling.

"What did he say he was looking for?" Ike asked, his brow furrowed.

"He wouldn't tell me. He just kept saying I had to let him in."

"You should have called me at the house," Donnell said.

"I didn't know the number. I was so scared I didn't think to call the operator. Anyway, Sondra called about that time. When I asked him about the warrant, he turned *real* red in the face. Said he was going to get one and would be back."

"He doesn't have probable cause for a warrant. I wish I had been here. I'll be waiting when he comes back," Sondra said, stewing.

"He can't think you have anything to do with the murder," Jones said. "Why would you have called him that night? You could have driven away. This is crazy. We need to have each other's phone numbers for sure. We'll *all* be here when he comes back." He looked to the other men. They nodded.

After a while, they all went outside to wait.

"How long does it take to get a warrant?" Angela asked Sondra, as they settled into chairs.

"Til the end of time, in this case," she scoffed.

"Just driving time—to Judge Green's," Ike interjected. "This time of day, if he's not in the Courthouse, he'll be across the street at Trudy's cafe. Green'll sign anything Billy puts in front of him. I don't know how ya'll do things down in Houston, but here they do things their own way."

While tense silence surrounded them, Sondra absorbed what Ike had said. She'd heard some of the questions asked by a couple of the rural judges, at the judge schools she'd was required to attend annually. She could tell some of them had a different understanding of the law. Perkins wouldn't be able to get a judge in her entire county to sign a search warrant on what he had. He already had her gun. What did he want?

"I *knew* I was right. He's not coming back. He couldn't get the search warrant. He can't face me. I'm going up there," Sondra said, rising from her chair.

"Don't do that." Ike said. "No good can come of that. What would you say to him? If Judge Green wouldn't sign a warrant for him to search your place, Billy'll sure be pissed. He's not going to give you that gun now. Not 'til he gets over it."

"Well, if that's the case, there's no need for us to stay here. If we had left this morning like *I* wanted, none of this would have happened," Sondra said pointedly, toward Ike and Eleanor. "If we start packing now, we can still get to Houston before dark."

"Sondra, you can't leave," Ike said.

"What do you mean, I can't leave! You sound like your friend. I guess you're my boss now, too," Sondra said defiantly, her hands on her hips.

"No. That's not it. But don't you think that would make it look like you were running? Maybe had something to hide? At least stay 'til tomorrow. Maybe it'll blow over by then," Ike said, trying to sound soothing.

By the way she crimped her mouth to the side and folded her arms across her chest, he could tell she was thinking about what he'd said. The long, angry sigh was the sign he'd won the battle—for now. There was truth in what he said, but his real reasons were more personal.

"Why don't we all go over to my place for the night?" Jones asked.

"That sounds good to me," Eleanor said. "It doesn't look like he's coming back anyway. We can deal with this tomorrow. You were going to show me your bird book."

"I am *not* going to leave my RV. I wouldn't put it past that skunk to break in." She kicked her foot at the ground, stirring up a little cloud of red dust.

"You don't think he'd really do that, do you, Sondra? I mean, he's the sheriff. He has to go by the law," Angela spoke up, wide-eyed.

"Humph" Sondra said, thinking of how naive Angela was, and of a couple of rogue cops back home that she knew would— in a heartbeat.

Angela looked frightened again, then determined.

"I'll stay with you. He'll have to deal with us both. Course, you don't have your itty-bitty gun now, but we can handle him," Angela said, trying to humor Sondra. It didn't work.

"Humph."

"Well, I'll stay too. I can see the book later," Eleanor said, accepting and resigned, rather than eager.

"Then, let's go find some dry wood, so we can have a fire when it gets dark," Jones said to Eleanor, reaching for her hand.

"Good idea. Anything is better than just sitting around here waiting." She took his hand, and followed him toward the woods.

"Let's go help," Angela said.

"I don't think they need our help," Sondra said, shaking her head and sighing.

Angela turned and looked into the woods after them, then back to Sondra, puzzled. Had she missed something? Had she really seen Eleanor take his hand? Weird, she thought. Then it struck her—she'd never seen Eleanor with a man before. A big grin broke out on her face. Sondra crimped her mouth and rolled her eyes.

"Did either of you see which direction the boat came from?" Ike asked.

Angela and Sondra thought for a minute. Sondra shook her head.

"It was coming sort of straight into the shore, but maybe from that way," Angela said, pointing to the left. "I was in this chair, sort of angled toward your place, and Eleanor was in that chair, facing the other way. She saw it first. So must have been from that direction. Yes, that's it. Jones had left in that direction, and when Eleanor saw the boat, she thought it was him returning."

Ike mentally roamed along the lakeshore in the direction Angela had pointed. He knew the adjacent land was vacant, except for the small garage building. The next two tracts had vacation homes, and would be unoccupied this time of year. Farther, three had homes on them and permanent residents. A couple of vacant tracts, and so on.

"Donnell, let's ride up the road," Ike said, heading toward the car.

"Sure. Ya'll tell Jones not to leave before we get back."

"I don't think you have to worry about that," Angela said laughing. "I'm going in and finish my nap."

Shortly after Ike and Donnell drove off, Sondra went inside to join Angela. She hadn't slept well last night, and a nap sounded good to her too. She was sure Eleanor and Jones wouldn't mind. Angela was lying on her back in the upper bed, hands under her head, staring at the ceiling.

"Thought you were going to take a nap? What're you thinking about?"

"Nothing," Angela replied.

"Nothing sure looks serious. It's Quinton, isn't it? You made the right decision. Don't go back over that. Even if you took him back, what would you have, except a man who you *know* will play around on you. You deserve better than that."

"You don't understand. It was all a misunderstanding. He explained it to me."

"Explained what? When?"

"Thursday. He told me the whole story. He's going through a divorce. In New York. It's almost over. He's given her everything. They're just fighting over the kids now. She doesn't want him to see them."

"Why couldn't he tell you that before?"

"I knew you wouldn't understand. I shouldn't have told you. You never did like him." Angela huffed onto her stomach.

Sondra watched her out of the corner of her eye, as she reached in the overhead cabinet and got two of the crystal glasses. After she'd filled them, she handed Angela one, and sat in the chair, propping her feet on the couch opposite her.

"I admit, it sounds like a line to me. But it's plausible, I suppose. What do I know? Do *you* believe him?"

"Yes. Of course. Why would he lie?"

"Why wouldn't he tell the truth in the beginning, is the question."

"He loves me, Sondra. And I love him too. I've never met a man so perfect for me. There're so few decent men to choose from, at my age. I can't lose him. What kind of woman would I be, to turn my back on him when he's down."

"Well, Angela, if it's really love, it'll wait until he's free. Just don't see him 'til then."

"For Christ sake, Sondra, I have to work with the man everyday! How can I not see him!"

"I didn't mean in that way," Sondra said calmly.

"You don't believe him, do you?"

"It really doesn't matter what I think. There is an easy way to know though," Sondra said. She didn't think Angela was convinced either, else she wouldn't have agreed to the trip.

"I have a friend from law school. A judge in New York. Used to practice family law there before. She can find out whether a divorce has been filed, and what the status is. I can call her as soon as we get back. But only if you want me to. Do you?"

After a long pause, Angela nodded.

"What about Donnell? He seems like a nice fellow. You two have been spending a lot of time together."

"Only because you—and now Eleanor apparently—have been so occupied. What's Ike like? You like him, don't you?"

"The man is either sex-starved, or sex-crazy. Either way, I have no use for him."

"Oh, Sondra. You're the one who's sex-starved. Why don't

you just enjoy yourself, for a change. This is the nineties. You don't have to marry every man you have sex with."

"I *know* that. Anyway, he's probably got a wife, too. Up at his house."

"I didn't see one when I was up there last night. Or the night before. I don't believe a woman lives there."

"What were you doing up there?" Sondra asked, surprised.

"Donnell took me up there to use Ike's computer. Turns out, he knows a lot about computers. We worked on my project. I don't think the problem is in my program. I never did. I think it's in the data. He showed me a place it may be going off. We got it to print out the problem data. Made a lot of progress—'til the lights went out. We were going to work on it again this afternoon—'til all this shit happened."

"Is he sex-crazy like his brother?"

"I wouldn't know. He hasn't come on to me. I told him about Quinton."

"I can't believe you! You told him everything?!"

"Of course not. Just that I had somebody. He's been a real gentleman."

Angela didn't tell her that she'd noticed him checking her out. Or that she'd done a little checking out herself. There was a knock, then the door opened.

"I think we got enough wood to last a week piled up outside," Eleanor said.

"Did ya'll hear the siren a while ago?" Jones asked. "We were up by the road. That sheriff went by here like the devil was after him. Wonder what's up. Where're the guys?"

"Where're we going?" Donnell asked as he turned right, as

Ike had pointed, onto the road.

"Thought we'd look around at some of the vacant houses near here. That boat didn't just come from nowhere. It must have come from this direction. We were outside all that time Friday. I don't believe it could have passed us and neither of us saw it. You know, it's pissing me off—what Billy's doing. But even more, it's what he isn't doing. It seems to me he would be asking more questions. It's like he isn't investigating it. He's just bothering Sondra, to pick at me. He knows she didn't kill that boy. He thinks she's my woman."

"Well, isn't she?" Donnell asked with a sly grin.

"Not yet," Ike answered, with his own.

"I don't believe that. And after a cozy night on the island? You trying to tell me the ladies bunked together?"

"I'm just giving her some line, letting her run. That's all. I told you how to do it. Works every time. Wait. Turn in here. What about Angela?"

"What about her?"

"Don't give me that. We called the house—and the RV. Where *were* ya'll last night? Over at the Mansion? I've been intending to have a phone put in over there."

"No. We went by Trudy's Cafe, then up to the house. We worked on your computer. She's got an interesting project going."

"Yeah, right," Ike said, smiling derisively. "Why didn't you answer the phone, then? It was late when we called. Pull over. Stop. Let's look around."

They got out and walked around the vacant house, Ike trying both the locked doors, down to the boat tied at the shore, and back. There was nothing unusual.

"I meant to tell you. That storm last night knocked the power out. Maybe it affected the phone. It didn't ring. By the way, what are we looking for?"

"I don't know. Come on. Let's go. Drive right through there to that next house."

"Hell no. This ain't no jeep, in case you hadn't noticed. I'll drive around the road."

"Okay. So you're telling me you just worked on a project all night?"

"No. Just 'til the lights went out, and we lost the connection."

"Then what?" Ike asked, grinning.

"Then nothing. We talked a while, then went to bed. No point in driving in that rain." Then seeing Ike's raised eyebrows, "She slept in my old room, and I slept in yours. I took her back to the RV this morning. It's not what you think. She's a nice girl. Besides, I don't think she's interested in me."

"Bullshit. I'm your brother. You can tell me. I know, you're just giving her some line."

"Maybe," Donnell said, as he turned into the next drive.

The house was unfinished. The outer walls and roof were intact, but it was obviously in the construction phase. And Donnell figured from the condition of the lumber laying around, it was a long phase. Maybe the builder had run out of money. He noticed the door wasn't shut tight when they walked up to it.

"Don't touch the door," he told Ike. "Let's look in the windows first."

Through the cloudy window, the interior appeared in disarray. There were stacks of sheetrock flats, pieces of lumber, several 5-gallon buckets, some saw horses, a couple of mat-tresses, and lots of empty soda cans and glass cylinders strewn about.

"Come on. Let's go in. Don't touch anything. Whose place is this?" Donnell asked, as he pushed the door open with his elbow.

"Don't know. Nobody from around here."

"Looks like somebody's been here recently. Know what those are?"

Ike picked up one of the cylinders and examined it.

"Some kind of pipe? Not for weed. Too small. Crack?"

Donnell nodded.

"I've heard about that stuff, but I thought it was just in the city."

"It's everywhere. Probably comes here from Houston. Any idea who would be bringing it?"

"No. But you know what, a couple of times I had the boys over, Derrick didn't come. They said he'd gone to Houston with some friends. I couldn't imagine why Delores would let him go. He was too young. Course, he did just about what he wanted to anyway. You don't think . . ."

"Maybe. A lot of times, they use the younger kids. If they get caught, there's hardly any penalty. Uh oh. Look here."

Ike followed Donnell around into another room and saw the blood.

"You'd better call Billy to come out here. Looks like this may be where they killed him."

Ike and Donnell were leaning against the sportscar, when Billy came speeding up the road, lights flashing.

TWELVE

Derrick's funeral was at 11:00. Ike was up earlier than usual. He had to get some of the things done around the ranch he'd put off lately, trying to court Sondra. He laughed at the thought of himself 'courting.' It sounded so old-fashioned. He'd have to ask some of his Scouts what the kids called it these days. He was certain she was the woman for him. It obviously was going to take a little time to persuade her that he was the man for her. He planned to spend as much time with her as he could, doing just that.

She even *looked* like the woman he'd been dreaming about. She wasn't so much pretty or beautiful, as she was handsome. Although her age didn't matter to him, he knew she must be close to his, by the age of her children. He liked a woman with some color to her, and hers was perfect—the same shade as Muhdea. She had the kind of body he liked too, full and rounded, like he thought a woman should be, but trim and firm, like she believed in taking care of herself. She had muscular legs for a woman, and hairy. He loved that. Made him want to touch her all over. But, it was more than the physical. Jackie had been all of that. She had probably been the most attractive woman in town. It wasn't enough for him. Sondra obviously was smart and had a variety of interests. He needed a woman with some mental challenge. Jackie hadn't been that. Her incessant talk about soap operas nearly drove him crazy. She had no interest at all in his business. Maybe Jackie had been as frustrated in their relationship as he had been. Even if she had been willing to settle for less, he wasn't. He hoped she was happily married. She deserved it. She was a good person.

When he got back to the house, he woke Donnell up. Even though Donnell didn't know Derrick, he had said he wanted to attend the funeral. Maybe it was just to spend some time with Ike. They dressed and drove over to the church.

The church was packed. The melancholy organ music covered the hushed conversations and rustling of Sunday clothes. Ike and Donnell walked to the front of the church for the last view. The boy looked so young, just a kid. Ike batted back tears, as he shook his head, thinking how he would never have a chance to be a man. Ol' Man Johnson had done a good job. Derrick looked like he was sleeping peacefully. Between the mortician's skillful work, and the suit and shirt Ike had bought, there was no evidence of the cause of death to satisfy the curious and morbid.

All the Scouts were sitting together in their uniforms, in the front of the church behind two reserved pews. They had saved a place for Ike, and made room for Donnell. It looked like the whole high school had turned out. There was no protocol for their first acquaintance with out of sequence death. Most of the girls were crying, dabbing at their eyes with tissue, to keep their make-up from running. The boys shifted awkwardly in their seats, wearing looks of false bravado to cover their fear. Then there were the old folk, shaking their heads. They had sat here many times before—even for the sinners who didn't belong to the church, and who were certainly going to their Just Reward. But Derrick had grown up in the church, and his mama before him. The old folk remembered them both as little children.

The pallbearers—Derrick's basketball team and coach—followed the ministers into the church, and took their seats in front of the Scouts. Delores and Derrick's brothers and sisters followed them, sitting in the front pew. The youth choir sang. If Derrick's father came, he didn't sit with the family. The minister began the eulogy with 'Suffer the little children . . .' There were the usual resolutions from the church and the Sunday School class. Ike was proud that Bobby was able to get through the one from the Scouts without breaking down. Derrick had been Bobby's 'ace boon.'

When the young, heavy-set soloist started into Aretha's deep-throated version of *Amazing Grace*, Delores broke down first. As the mother's screams of grief vibrated through the sanctuary, Ike knew without looking, there was not a dry eye. Each one had their own reason, aside from Derrick. Some contemplated their own deaths, others re-visited the loss of a beloved. His own thoughts were about the sacrifice he had made. He wondered had he not, would he have sat in that front pew hearing Muhdea's screams for Donnell. As he reached for his own handkerchief, he thought he shouldn't let his boys see him cry. On the other hand, maybe they needed to see that a real man could cry. It didn't matter, he had no control over it.

Ike and Donnell returned from the graveside service, and shared dinner with the family in the church dining hall. Leaving, Ike told Delores to call him if she needed anything and hugged her. When they got outside, Bobby was standing by the truck.

"Mr. Ike. Can I get a ride?"

"Sure, Bobby. Hop in," Ike said, folding the seat forward. "You did good with the resolution. Why didn't you go with the others?"

"I need to talk to you."

As he pulled the truck onto the road, Ike asked, "What's up, Bobby?"

"Nothing. I'll, uh, tell you later."

In the rearview mirror, Ike saw the suspicious look on Bobby's face.

"It's OK. This is my brother, Donnell."

"Ya'll look just alike. You sure?" he asked, skeptically. "It's something serious."

Ike nodded.

"I heard Big Mike had Derrick killed, over his money."

"What money?"

"Derrick was selling that stuff for Big Mike. I thought you knew that. Anyway, Derrick told me he gave the money to his mama for the rent. Big Mike ended up with the money anyway. He owns that rat-trap house they live in. He didn't have to kill Derrick. He was my friend." Bobby angrily wiped the tears from his face.

"Have you told Sheriff Perkins about this?" Ike asked. He saw the boy's face close up.

"Ain't no point. That's why I'm telling you. You the only one who can do anything about it."

"Why can't you tell Perkins?" Donnell asked.

"I just can't. They may kill me, too. And you can't say I told."

"Don't worry. We won't tell. I'll do what I can," Ike said, as he pulled in front of Bobby's house and let him out.

When they were down the road a piece, Donnell asked, "What you think the boy meant, there'd be no point to tell Perkins? You think maybe Perkins knows something about this? About the drugs?"

"I don't know. He did seem kind of strange yesterday at that house, but I thought that was about me and Sondra. I've wondered for a long time why the law didn't do something about Big Mike, even before Billy was sheriff. I just don't know. I don't want to think about that today. I'll drop you off at the house. I've got a little fishing to do."

As Ike maneuvered the truck through the trees, he was shocked to see the empty space where the RV had been. The big smile fell from his face. He blinked his eyes and shook his head, not wanting to believe it. He let the truck coast until it was almost to the spot where the RV had been parked. Except for the fire ring, it was as though it had never been there. For one surreal moment, it seemed it had all been a dream. How could she do this?! And why? He knew she was angry at him, but didn't know why. Maybe he was trying to take her too fast. He could see how his approach might have led her to believe his interest in her was one-dimensional. He hadn't begun at the beginning. Hadn't told her how he felt. That was exactly what he'd planned to do today.

He thought he had persuaded her against leaving. If nothing else, he'd been certain she wouldn't leave without the gun. If he'd had an inkling that she was serious about it, he would have come by before the funeral—at sun-up even—to stop her. And those chores could have waited one more day. He didn't even know how to contact her, he thought dejectedly. He wondered where she lived. He imagined in a subdivision, just outside the loop. She had to have a place to park the RV. Remembering the contented look on her face that first morning, he knew she liked being outdoors. She probably had a little garden in her back yard. Vegetables, he mused, since she liked to cook. He wondered if she'd like living in his house on the hill. He knew just the spot where he would have turned over a garden plot for her. He sat a long time in the quiet of the truck, feeling empty. Thinking about how close he'd come, about what he'd lost.

Finally, he turned the truck around and drove toward the Mansion. He didn't want to have to talk to Donnell right now. Between the funeral, and her being gone, he was too wrung out. He just wanted to be alone.

Ike saw the two of them sitting at his picnic table, as he drove up the dusty road. A grin broke out on his face, when he recognized Eleanor. She hadn't left after all. He stopped the truck, and hopped down.

"Boy, am I glad to see you! I thought ya'll had left. I went to Derrick's funeral. Then when I went by over there, the RV was gone. Where is she? Where's Sondra?"

Eleanor saw the hopeful look on his face, and hated to tell him.

"I couldn't stop her. They left this morning."

"Why?" he asked. The grin had vanished.

"When she gets her head set on something, that's just it. There's no stopping her—Hell or high water."

"She left _you_?"

"Well, let's just say we, sort of, came to an agreement," she said laughing. "Course, we had one hell of a row first. I tried to talk her into staying—just a couple of days. We all had planned to be gone a week and had arranged for everything. It didn't make any sense to go back. I told her she should wait to get her gun back anyway. She said she would get it on her way out and…"

"Wait a minute. She didn't go up there fooling with Billy, did she?" Ike asked, turning to get in his truck.

"No. Thank God, she would still listen to _some_ reason. I promised her I'd get it for her, if she wouldn't go up there. That guy seems dangerous. And he seems to have a thing about her. Even she recognized that. When I refused to leave, she said she'd help me pack." Eleanor threw her head back and laughed. "And she did. I guess I'm as stubborn as she is. Once I said it, there was no turning back for me either. So I end up homeless and stranded."

"What about Angela?"

"Poor Angela. She didn't know what to do. She agreed with me, but she didn't want Sondra to go back alone. I really think she just wanted to go back to see this jerk that started this whole trip. Well, that set off another round. They were defending him. And after what he did to her! I couldn't believe it. They're both crazy. Jones was there, he can tell you—it wasn't pretty."

"It was something to see. All the screaming, the name-calling. Everything but hair pulling," Jones said, laughing with

Eleanor. "I tried to intervene, but they *all* let me know right away I wasn't in the circle. So I did all I could do—offered shelter to the homeless—and shut up."

"Sondra's nose has been out of joint ever since we were on the island. It must have been something *you* did. It's all your fault," Eleanor said in a mock accusation toward Ike.

"Who me? I didn't do anything."

"I don't understand it. She doesn't have anything to go back to. She'd canceled all her dockets for the week. And if she thinks any of those lawyers are going to volunteer to bring their clients to court early, just because she cut her trip short, she's nuts. I can just see her now, wandering around her courtroom in her black robe all by herself. I'll bet her bailiff won't even be there. You know, while the cat's away . . ."

"Wait a minute. Are you telling me Sondra's a judge?" Ike asked, puzzled.

"She didn't mention it, did she? She never does. She usually says she works for the government."

"That's exactly what she told me. I can't believe it," he said, shaking his head.

"She says people always start telling her about their legal problems, or they treat her like a Martian, if they know. You'd think she'd tell everybody she meets, hard as we worked to get her elected—the first time. Course, after she did the job for a while, the next election was easy. No one would challenge her. She's good at it."

"Well, I'll be damned. It never would have occurred to me. I thought judges had to be old," Ike said.

"But, you know, I'm getting a little worried. I think the job is getting to her. She doesn't seem to enjoy it. I'm afraid she won't run again. She wouldn't have any opposition this time either. The cops _and_ the lawyers like her, even though she's not cozy with either side. She's always talked about 'one of these days driving off into the sunset,' but she's been talking about it more often lately. Even talking about selling that gorgeous house, and living full-time in the motorhome. Seeing the country. She could probably afford to do it. The house is paid for. Michael left her pretty well fixed. Did she tell you about him?"

"She said he was killed in an accident," Ike said, absently, still stunned.

"Her girls are so smart. They both have full academic scholarships. And she lives frugally. That RV is about her only extravagance. Still, I can't see her doing it alone. By herself."

"You think she'd really do that?" Ike asked.

"I don't know. Angela sure can't pick up and go with her. She's just getting started. And even though I love our trips, I love my work. I wouldn't give it up for anything."

Ike saw the expression on Jones' face change, but couldn't read it.

"Ya'll want a beer? That's all I have out here."

"Sure. Just one. I want to take Eleanor over to the island while there's some light left. There's more to see than I could show you yesterday."

Ike returned with the bottles, and a glass for Eleanor.

"What time did she leave?"

"About 10:00 They ought to be home by now. I told her I would call and make sure they got there okay," Eleanor said.

Ike promised himself—again—to have the phone installed at the Mansion.

"By the way, we went over and brought your canoe back,"

Jones said. "It's still lashed to my boat. I didn't know where you wanted it. Never did find the oar."

"That's alright. I've got another one around here some-where. So, Eleanor, how long are you going to stay? How will you get back? Is she coming back to get you?" he asked, a twinge of hope in his voice.

"I don't know. I haven't thought it all through. This came on me rather suddenly, you know," she said, laughing.

"So what do ya'll plan to do?"

"I've got a speech to finish. Some birds to see. Otherwise, I plan to just BE—like my friend always says."

"I'm glad to hear you say ya'll are still friends. After what happened." Ike said.

"Of course." Eleanor looked at him surprised. "We'll *always* be friends, no matter what. Anyway, she may have called herself doing me a favor. She's like that." She smiled at Jones.

"Come on, Ike. Let's get your canoe. We've got to be going. Come over. Any time," Jones said.

Ike stood at the lake's edge, arms folded across his chest, watching them pull away from the shore. They felt like old friends, although he hadn't known either of them a week. They waved back at him from the boat, as they started across the lake.

Ike went about in a fog, doing his work in a perfunctory way. His heart wasn't in it. Even when he went by Big Jesse's pen, he didn't get the usual feeling of exhilaration and accomplishment. He tried to be good company to Donnell, but he couldn't get the woman off his mind. He saw that Donnell seemed restless too, almost agitated. Donnell spent a lot of his time at the computer and the fax machine he'd brought Ike the last time he was home.

Ike had to admit to himself that Donnell had been right. It had made a big difference in his business. He remembered how he'd resisted it at first. It was hard for him to let his baby brother teach him.

On Thursday, Ike found Donnell at his desk when he woke up. He wondered what was so important to have him up at that hour.

"I'm making coffee. Wanna cup?" Ike called from the kitchen.

"Yeah. I'll have a cup, maybe two."

"Whatcha doing?" Ike asked, handing him a cup.

"Nothing. Just something to do with my, uh, business. Say look, I know I said we could have the game this week-end. But I've got to go to Houston tomorrow. Can we do the game next week sometime?"

"Houston?" Ike thought a minute. "I'll ride with you."

Eleanor loved the feel of the wind blowing through her hair, as they rode back across the lake. The sound of the motor made any attempt at conversation futile, so she enjoyed the ride. Before this trip, she'd never been on a boat. The canoe was just fine with her, so quiet and slow. On the harried trip back from the island the day before, she discovered that it wasn't speed that she objected to, it was the threat of collision. It hadn't bothered her at all, racing across the lake at break-neck speed. There was nothing to run into, or to run into them. She thought she might even drive the boat before she left.

The big gray dogs were waiting on the dock, right where they'd left them when they had come for Ike's canoe. Jones handed her briefcase up to her, then her duffel-shaped tapestry bag. When Jones climbed onto the dock, Eleanor was stooped down, rubbing the dogs behind their ears. They were licking her on each side of her face. So much for them being good watch-dogs. At least they were obedient.

"Go. To the house," Jones commanded. Off they raced.

Inside, Jones told her to put her briefcase on the dining room table. He carried the big bag upstairs.

"Would you like to go for a walk?" he asked. "It's still light."

"I'd rather see your book. We can walk tomorrow. I need to call Sondra first though. I promised."

Jones returned with the book and laid it on the coffee table. He put some logs on the grate and stoked the fire up. When she finished her call, she walked over and picked the book up. It was a beautiful over-sized hardback with glossy pages, containing colorful pictures of various kinds of birds. It was organized by region of the state. On the page opposite each full-sized picture of a bird in its natural habitat, was a description of the bird, in some cases migratory pattern, its nesting and hunting habits, and so on. The bottom half of the page was a log to record sightings. Although there were scattered entries in all the sections, there were many entries in the section devoted to East Texas. His handwriting was bold and legible. She could tell from some of the dates, this was not a new hobby for him. The book got heavy in her hands, so she squatted and sat on the floor in front of the fireplace, with her back against the coffee table. They spent the better part of two hours poring over the book.

As it grew dark, they realized they hadn't eaten all day. Eleanor would have been satisfied with a salad, but he had no fresh vegetables. She suggested he should plant a garden. He said he'd thought about it. They put together a simple meal from the left-overs Sondra had cooked.

"I noticed your chess set on the end table. Do you want to play?" she asked.

"I used to be pretty good, but I haven't played since Philip went away. Don't get much company out here. I need the practice. I'm hoping he'll come home for Christmas vacation," he said, placing the board between them. "What would you like to drink?"

"Whatever."

"I have something I've been saving for a special occasion. I think you'll like it," he said, walking toward the kitchen.

Eleanor had set the board up, when Jones returned with a decanter and matching glasses. Eleanor hadn't played in a while, so they were about evenly matched. They played a couple of games as they sipped the cranberry liqueur.

"This is good. You seem to have a well-stocked bar, for a man who has no company," she said.

"I used to drink a lot. Too much. After Becky. . .I lost Becky. I wasn't crazy with it, but after I'd put Philip to bed, I would sit in front of this fireplace and drink myself to sleep. I was so lonesome for her, I guess. I didn't want to get in the bed by myself."

"What made you stop?" she asked.

"Philip. He was at the age he asked a lot of questions. I was drinking more and more. Sleeping later and later. Waking up hung over. One morning he asked me if my drinking kept me from having dreams about his mother, 'cause if so, he wanted some too. I quit that day. I don't believe I had another drink until the night I met you."

"You think that's a bad omen?" she asked.

"I'm not superstitious. I don't believe in omens."

"What do you believe in?"

"I believe life is what you make of it, for the most part. Sometimes things happen that you have no control over. . ." he trailed off, staring at the colorful flames in the fireplace.

"Yeah, I know what you mean," Eleanor answered, watching the flames, as she searched for the words. "Maybe life gives us each our own...I mean, a special..." She shook her head because the right word wouldn't come.

"Pain?"

"I was thinking 'burden,' but your word is just as good," she said, taking another sip, still staring at the dancing flames.

For a long time, they sat without speaking, the silence interrupted only by the sounds from the crackling fire and the nocturnal noises outside the glass wall.

"Then what? What do you do about it?" she asked.

"I don't know. I guess you do what you can."

"What did you do?"

Her bluntness made him steal a glance at her. The look on her face was not one of prying or idle curiosity, more searching for her own answer. He wondered if he answered her question truthfully, would she mock him. Think less of him. He took a chance.

"I hid." There. He'd said it. He'd thought it, wondered about it, then when it got too close, denied it. Now, for the first time, it was out in the open. He watched for her reaction.

"But you can't hide. It's inside you. You carry it with you, no matter where you go." She stared at the fire, and he wondered if she was responding to him, or to her own burden.

"I know. Now." He tried her bluntness on for size. "And

you?"

"I'm a fighter, I guess. But, maybe I just couldn't find a place to hide. You do what you can," she said, shrugging her shoulders.

He nodded, then went back to watching the fire with her. Sometime before it died down to glowing embers, he saw the glassiness in her eyes and the tightness in her lips. He knew she was fighting tears. He covered her hand with his. He wasn't certain whether he did it to give comfort or receive it. She responded by raising her fingers through his and clasping them tightly. A while later when her fingers relaxed, he knew without looking at her that she had won another round.

"I'm sleepy," Eleanor announced. "It's been a long day. Maybe it's the fresh country air. Where did you put my bag?"

"My room." He saw the uncertainty, the indecision, in her eyes, as they searched his. For a fleeting moment, he saw something else. Fear, maybe? Before he could identify it, it was gone. He longed to have the warmth and comfort of her body curled up next to him again. He didn't want to spend another night reaching for her, yearning for the smell of her, the feel of her skin and hair, only to be startled awake by her absence. Still, he didn't want her to be uneasy, and he certainly didn't want to invoke the return of her hostility. "I could sleep down here . . .?"

Eleanor crooked her head as she studied him. She had never felt about a man the way she felt about him. She trusted him. She'd spent so many years—a lifetime—not trusting anybody or anything, except herself, then Sondra and Angela. With them, it was soft, enveloping. This was different. It was there in his eyes. Hard, but yielding, cushioning. Something about his eyes, his face, made her think about the full moon. Protective. Comforting. She stood, then reached for his hand.

When Eleanor came from the bathroom in her nightshirt, the light was out, but the bright moonlight shone through the windows. Jones was already under the covers. She wasn't sure she was ready, but she'd come this far. No need in going coy now. She slipped under the covers and lay on her back. She felt Jones reach for her hand and entwine his fingers in hers. She waited. Was she supposed to do something? She adjusted her position, and waited. Where his hairy thigh touched hers, a tingling started that soon spread throughout her body. Finally, she loosened her fingers from his and placed the palm of his hand against her pelvis, where the fire she'd never felt before had started. When she turned her face toward him, he kissed it all over. Then he kissed her mouth—long, slow and deep. He smelled, and tasted, like cranberries. He moved his hand and turned on his side, slipping his hand underneath her hip, and with the other began caressing her breast. She panicked when she felt the hardness against her thigh. The fire died. Her arms were rigid by her side, fists balled up. She turned her face away.

"Is something wrong?" he asked, taking his hand away.

Then she saw it, through the window, in the clearing between the tall pines—the big moon, just past full. This time, it wasn't turning away. It seemed to be smiling at her. She watched it a long time—to be sure—before she turned her face back to him. He was waiting for her, searching her face. She reached up and ran her hand along his cheek and jaw, through the hair above his ears. When her fingers touched his lips, he kissed them softly. She ran her fingers up the back of his head, through his curly hair, and pulled him to her breast. They lay that way for a while. Then he tentatively touched his tongue to her nipple, and the fire caught again and flared. Eleanor pulled him hard against her breast. She could tell, by the feel of his mouth on her breasts, that he felt the same urgency she did. But he would go no farther than she led. She wrapped her leg around his, and he nestled against her on his side. When he kissed her mouth again, her body arched toward him. In one motion, he gently pushed her back and rolled on top of her. Tentatively, she ran her finger under the waistband at the back of his pajama pants. The hardness she felt rubbing on the inside of her thighs urged her to open her legs and lay them top of his. Her calves rubbed against the sides of his, in the same rhythm as his hands on her breasts, and his hips against hers. The flames threatened to engulf them both. He wrapped his arms around her and held her tighter and tighter, so tight she couldn't breathe. Suddenly, she felt his entire body relax, completely. He turned on his back and lay with his eyes closed, his arm across his forehead. The fire almost made her cry out, but she stifled it. As she stared at the ceiling, the tremors in her muscles subsided, and the flame slowly died.

Eleanor didn't know what to think. She had made so much of his having not taken advantage of her the other night. Maybe she had given him too much credit. Maybe he couldn't. That had not occurred to her before. But, why? He looked so virile. He was only fifty or so, she guessed. Maybe he, like she, had grown accustomed to pleasuring himself. And now, with her, he couldn't. But that didn't make any sense, considering her own response. What if it was something she had done? Eleanor felt the panic rising, when she thought he could tell—about her, about what happened, that she had been bad. Maybe something in the way she responded to him, told him. What could it have been? She couldn't evaluate it. She didn't know what normal was. The few experiences she had had other than *that*, were almost as abhorrent, and a long time ago. A couple of frat boys when she was in college. Even now, she had the same feelings about them. Her nose twitched as she remembered the same whiskey smell, the groping at her, the feeling that her pleasure was not important, the feeling of being used.

Eleanor beat herself for having acted so impulsively. Why had she let her friends leave her with a man she hardly knew? What could she do now? She couldn't call Sondra to come get her, as she'd offered. The ride was too long, and she didn't want to be captive—to have to explain. Not yet. There must be a bus route through the town. She would check on that first thing in the morning. The least he could do is take her to the station. He was a decent guy. Even knowing what he knew about her, he would do that. Looking at him out of the side of her eye, she could tell he was awake by the rhythm of his breathing. When she looked the other way, she could see the big moon. Its smile seemed to be mocking her, now.

The morning was no longer young, when Eleanor first stirred. Jones had been waiting for her to wake, enjoying the feel of her, curled up against him, her face against his neck. Before she was full awake, before she could do or say anything, he kissed her softly on her mouth. He felt her stretch, in that half-wake state, and kissed her deeply. He felt her take in a deep breath. He had put his arm over her while she slept. Now he pulled the full length of her body against him. It wasn't resistance he felt, more uncertainty. He understood, but it wasn't necessary. He hugged her to him and caressed the lingering tension away. He pushed one of his legs between hers—and she let him. This time the hardness didn't make her jump and pull away. She ran her hand through his hair, slowly massaging. He knew she was hearing the music. He heard it too. Together, they moved to the same tempo, the same sweet melody. As the final strains slowly faded away, they drifted into a peaceful sleep, completely satiated.

The next time Eleanor woke, she had a vague dream-like sense of having walked across a long bridge, of having emerged from a fog on the other side of a deep chasm. She felt like a woman, in a way she never had before. She luxuriated in the feeling. The house was quiet. Finally, she sat up and looked around the room, wondering where he was. When she saw the little bird on the table outside, she wanted to call out to Jones, but she didn't want to startle it. Eleanor *knew* it was a she. She watched the bird until she flew away. Then, she saw the wall above the desk. There were gaping bare spots. All of the pictures of the woman had been removed. She understood then. It hadn't been about her at all. She smiled, took a long stretch, then laid back down and waited for him.

THIRTEEN

Judge Ellis was on the bench Friday morning, as she had been since Wednesday. Since she had canceled her dockets for the week, she offered to take any overflow from the other judges. They were happy to oblige. This morning she had accepted the plea bargains for a long line of defendants before the morning break. That done, she started the first trial. It wasn't a particularly interesting case. The typical 'they didn't find the drugs *on* him' defense. This boy brought Derrick to mind. She wondered, if he hadn't been killed, how long it would have been before he stood in front of that Judge Green, his lawyer urging the same defense.

From time to time, Sondra scanned the spectator area. She always wanted to know who was in her courtroom. Several letters she'd received from prisoners she'd sentenced made her cautious. There was the usual cast of characters. A couple of lawyers, their clients and assorted family members, waiting their turn. She recognized a news reporter—must have been a slow news day. The elderly couple that always came on Friday seeking cheap entertainment was there. None of the crazies that she kept an eye out for. People were constantly coming and going. It wasn't your Perry Mason-type courtroom.

The man came in and sat in the back row. The olive green double-breasted suit was just like she'd imagined. Although she'd only seen Ike dressed in jeans, the man looked so much like him, her heart nearly skipped a beat. That was silly. What would he be doing here? She forced her attention back to the trial. After a moment she squinted toward the back of the room, just to make sure it wasn't him, but a couple had come in and sat where her view was blocked. She resisted the urge to lean over to see past them. Too obvious. The long-winded lawyer was droning on and on, as though his client was paying him by the word. She forced herself to pay attention. When she looked up again, the man was gone. She chided herself for even thinking about the farmer. It wasn't the first time, since she'd left Eleanor at the lake. Mercifully, the prosecutor asked for a few minutes recess. It was 11:15. She told them all to come back after lunch.

As she entered her chambers through the back door, unzipping her robe, the phone was ringing.

"There's a Mr. Evans to see you. He doesn't have an appointment. What should I tell him?" Josie asked, her voice full of questions.

"I'll see him. Show him in."

When Ike strode in, holding the big black Stetson hat in his hands, Sondra put on her best business face, and extended her hand.

He smiled at her, and ignored her outstretched hand.

"Good to see you again, Mr. Evans. What are you doing here? I mean, please have a seat. What can I do for you?" she asked pleasantly, sitting behind her desk. She wouldn't admit to herself that her heart was fluttering.

"I came to take you to lunch, *Judge* Ellis." He saw her eyes flicker at his emphasis of the word.

"You came all the way here to take me to lunch? Well, you should have called first. I already have lunch plans. I'm sorry. Maybe next time you're in town." She looked down at her hands clasped together on the desk to escape his steady gaze.

"A busy woman like you would have plans for lunch, and your secretary wouldn't know about it? I doubt it. Nice lady. She told me about a place near here, that the judge *really* likes," he said, controlling the mischievous grin beneath his moustache.

"I can't believe you would pressure Josie to give you personal information," she said indignantly. "On second thought, yes I can."

"I didn't pressure her. I just asked. Now, what's wrong with that?" he asked, innocently. "She's just looking out for you. She thought you would enjoy shrimp scampi more than the tuna sandwich you had her put in the fridge for you this morning. She *said* it was the judge's favorite dish."

Sondra couldn't help but smile and shake her head. She had to give it to him—he just kept up a steady pressure.

"Okay. You busted me. I do love scampi. But Josie can forget about a Christmas bonus," she said, getting her suit jacket from the coatrack.

November in Houston was warm and green. It could have been Spring, except it didn't smell like it. Ike wanted to take her hand and hold it as they walked to the restaurant, but it wasn't time yet. Sondra hadn't said anything to him on the walk from her office, in the elevator, and out of the courthouse. She acted almost like she wasn't with him. She only acknowledged his presence when, coming out of her office, they nearly bumped into the tall fellow on his way in.

"Oh, David," she said, clearly startled. "I mean, uh, Judge Goldstein. Did you need something?"

"Well. I can see you're leaving. It can wait," he said, slowly touching his fingertips together repeatedly as he stared at her. "Going to lunch?"

Ike wondered what their relationship was, that she was so flustered. When their eyes met and held, he could feel the man sizing him up—like a competitor—under the benign, pleasant exterior. Ike did his own quick assessment. About his age. Tall as he, not as muscular, but not an ounce of fat. Light blue oxford shirt, sleeves rolled up almost to the elbow, khaki pants, soft shoes—expensive preppie clothes. He'd have bet there was a double-breasted navy blazer hanging in the man's office. Clean-shaven, dimpled chin. Thin lips turned down at the corners, prominent nose, light brown eyes under bushy eyebrows. Broad forehead that blended into the prematurely-bald top, ringed by straight brown hair, neatly trimmed. Soft hands—accustomed to holding expensive pens and handling paper. Ike couldn't imagine those hands grabbing a bull by its horns, turning its head and wrestling it to the ground, or grasping another man by the throat and squeezing until no breath was left—or holding Sondra.

"Oh. Judge Goldstein, meet Isaac Evans."

Ike felt the tension, almost animosity, in Goldstein's hand when they shook.

"Pleasure to meet you, Mr. Evans," he said, with the same benign smile. But the deep furrow in his brow didn't reflect pleasure.

"I'll get with you later," Sondra said, smiling weakly at him as she started off down the hall. She looked back once. Ike noticed.

Ike could feel Goldstein watching them all the way to the elevator.

There was a long line at the restaurant. Since Ike had made reservations, the maitre d' showed them to a small corner booth right away. When the waiter came, Ike ordered two ice teas, shrimp scampi for her, prime rib—medium—for him.

"So what are you doing in Houston?" she asked.

"I told you. I came to take you to lunch."

"No, seriously."

"Seriously? My plans for the week were disrupted when a certain lady left me, all by myself, by the edge of the lake. She didn't even say goodbye. So I thought I'd find her and ask her why."

"It was for the best," she said, after a moment.

"Best for whom?"

"Look, if I'd stayed, there would have been trouble. More trouble than there already was."

"We could have handled it. You left a lot of unfinished business."

The waiter brought the food. Ike waited for her to respond. They ate in silence for a while. Finally, when it was obvious she wasn't going to respond, he continued his courting.

"Donnell had some business here, so I rode down with him. I'd planned to take you to dinner too, but it seems you have other plans. So now, I'll have to take you to a dance instead. That's OK with me. I hope you don't have a date, 'cause he's going to be real disappointed." His black eyes were shining.

Sondra was caught by surprise. She'd almost forgotten about the dance. She wondered how he knew about that. Josie! She was going to have to have a serious talk with that girl.

"But it's a formal affair," she protested.

"That's fine."

"I wasn't planning to stay long. Just put in an appearance. It's just business for me. I doubt you'd enjoy it."

Sondra was irritated at Josie for telling her business to a complete stranger, and at Ike for intruding in her life. She couldn't let him take her to the dance. What if he started pawing her in public, like Andrew? And what would he talk about— fishing?

"That's okay. What time should I pick you up?"

"Well, I don't think . . .What would you . . ." She gave up when she saw the determined look on his face. She decided she would only stay a few minutes, and be out of there before he could do anything to embarrass her.

"Nine. No, eight."

"I'll be there at eight."

The phone's ringing jarred Angela. She was deep in her program, trying to re-construct the steps she and Donnell had worked out. She'd left the disk in Ike's computer, planning to return the next day. In all the excitement of the storm, then their sudden departure, she had forgotten about it. She'd tried to call several times, but got no answer.

"Angela Reeves. Can I help you?" she said, absent-mindedly.

"Hey. What's going on?"

When she heard the masculine voice, her heart raced. She knew Quinton had gone to New York. She had called him yesterday morning and, Francis, his secretary, told her he wouldn't be back until Monday. Now, she had a moment of confusion, when she realized this voice, with the sweet Southern drawl, wasn't Quinton's.

"Excuse me?"

"This is Donnell. Remember me?"

"Of course, I remember you. I'm glad you called. I've been trying to reach you. You know I left my disk."

"Yes. I've been working with it. Found something interesting I want to show you. What time are you leaving? How about dinner?"

"Dinner? Where are you? Are you here in Houston?"

"I'm staying at the Ambassador. Do you know where it is?"

"Of course." Quinton's favorite restaurant was there.

"Why don't you meet me there? What's a good time?"

"Let's see, it's 5:30 now," she said looking at her watch. "How about 7:30?"

"I'll see you there."

Angela moved her little Miata in and out of the Friday evening traffic. She'd left work right after Donnell's call, and run home to change clothes and freshen her make-up. She'd dressed casually for work. It _was_ Friday, and besides Quinton was in New York. There was no one she had to impress. But the restaurant was too up-town for the jeans and Oilers sweatshirt she had worn to work. After rejecting several outfits, she put on the emerald green pantsuit. It was her favorite. Not only did the silky fabric feel good against her skin, but the rich green complimented her coloring—the golden undertone in her light brown hair, and the flecks of gold in her hazel eyes.

Angela was aware that she had taken more care than usual, more even than for her dates with Quinton. Digging deep in the drawer to find the eye shadow that she rarely wore, a twinge of guilt had nudged at her. Well, she was just going to get her disk. Thoughts of her week-end at the lake had drifted across her mind more often than she cared to admit. And Donnell. She'd spent so much time with him, she decided he couldn't be into drugs. She was almost ashamed of herself for having thought that about him. He was smart. She liked a smart man. And good-looking. And sweet. The sound of the horn behind her, jolted her back. What was she thinking about? She loved Quinton.

She had called him as soon as she got back to her house Tuesday. He came right over. As soon as she saw him, she melted in his arms. They made the sweetest love. Afterwards, lying in her big bed, he told her how worried he had been that she wasn't there when he called on the week-end, or in the office when he got back. Holding her close, he made her promise to never leave again without letting him know. Feeling so secure and protected, Angela knew she had been wrong to doubt him.

Wednesday, they had lunch together, and he persuaded her not to go back to the office. They spent the afternoon at the Museum of Natural Science and the Cockrell Butterfly Center in Hermann Park. He said it was in celebration of their 'fifth-month anniversary'. He was counting from the first time they'd made love. He was so thoughtful. Most men would not have remembered the date. She hadn't.

That night, he brought pizza, Chianti, and a movie. They only watched half of it. He made wild, passionate love to her, on the floor with the TV watching. Later, in bed, he talked of the time when he wouldn't have to go home in the middle of the night, of the place they would buy together. A condo. Neither of them had the time, or interest, to maintain a yard. They agreed on a color scheme. She was constantly amazed at how much they had in common. Their life together was going to be perfect—as soon as this divorce business was over with.

"Did you talk to your lawyer while you were in New York?"

"Yes," he answered flatly.

"What'd he say? How much longer?"

"We're going to court Friday morning. I'm leaving tomorrow."

Before she could ask her next question, he pulled her on top of him and let her have her way with him. Later, she didn't hear him leave.

Now, the twinge of guilt about Donnell was growing. If Quinton were in town, how would she explain her meeting him? Just business. But why dinner? At his hotel? She was just going to get her disk.

As the valet ran around to her door, she checked her face in the mirror one last time.

Donnell was waiting for her just outside the etched glass doors to the restaurant. He was smiling as she approached, and hugged her when she reached him. Well, they *had* been through a lot together. The restaurant was dark, candles on each table providing the only light. It must have been the most romantic setting in all of Houston. Even the 90-degree angle booth where they were seated seemed designed for romance. Angela wished Quinton was here with her—and that she had selected another place to meet Donnell.

"It was so sweet of you to come to Houston to bring me the disk."

"Oh, I did have some other business here. But I wanted to see *you* for sure."

"See me? About what?" she asked, intending to discourage what he was about to say by her business-like tone. She wanted to save them both the embarrassment. He knew she had a man—engaged in fact. Besides, Donnell lived across the country. And he was a security guard. They really had nothing in common except a pleasant week-end at the lake, and computers. He was too tall for her liking anyway. Tall men didn't fit, she thought, as the waiter brought the first course. Too awkward.

"Well, there are some things I want to show you about the program," he said, backing off, as though he could read her thoughts. "Maybe we can go by your house after dinner. You must have a computer there."

"Tomorrow would be better. At my office."

She could see him struggling to hide his disappointment.

"Oh, before I forget again, let me have the disk," she said sweetly.

"I left it in my room. Upstairs," he lied. "We can go up and get it after dinner."

"Oh, that's alright. You can bring it by my office tomorrow. It's near here. About 10:00. Is that okay?"

"If you say so," his disappointment more evident. Then, hopefully, "What about hitting some of the clubs? It's been a while since I've been to Houston. We both like to dance." He looked at her expectantly.

"No. Thanks, anyway. Sounds like fun, but I've had a long

day. A long week. I need to turn in early."

To hide the lie in her eyes, Angela wouldn't look at Donnell, keeping her gaze straight ahead at the tall palm plants by the door. He really did seem like a nice guy, but to go out with him would just be leading him on for nothing. When she saw Quinton walk in the restaurant, with his arm around Francis, she was stunned. What was he doing here—with her?! That bitch had told her he was in New York. There was no mistaking this for a business dinner. Quinton's hands were all over Francis. The maitre d' was leading them in the direction of Angela's table. When their eyes met, Quinton's face registered shock, and his hand fell from Francis' waist. Angela stared him straight in the eye, her face devoid of expression. As he neared her table, she leaned over, took hold of Donnell's chin, and pulled until his ear met her lips.

"Come on, let's go to your room. Now," she whispered. "Want to?"

Donnell was surprised—and confused.

"Sure. But . . ." He looked down at the steaming plates the waiter had just left on the table, then up at her, his whole face a question mark, only to see her scooting out of the booth. "Sure."

As Donnell stood, Angela slid her arm around his waist under his sportscoat. He tousled her curly hair before putting his around her shoulder. As they passed him, the maitre d' handed Donnell the check and he hurriedly signed it. Angela felt Quinton's eyes on them as they walked out.

The elevator was open when they got there. When they entered, Donnell pressed '19'. As soon as the elevator began rising, Angela took her arm from around his waist and pressed '5'.

"Why did you do that?" he asked, puzzled. "My room isn't on the fifth floor."

"I'm sorry. I changed my mind. I shouldn't have been so forward, inviting myself to your room. I don't know what came over me. Let's just meet tomorrow at the bank. At ten. Take the main street in front of the hotel, 'til you get to Travis. It's right there. Don't forget the disk."

The elevator stopped on five, and Angela started off. Donnell grabbed her arm, pulling her back.

"Hey, wait a minute. Where're you going?"

"I'm going home. Stop. You're hurting my arm."

She tried to pull her arm away, but he wouldn't release it.

"Nah, nah, nah. That's bullshit. You said you wanted to go to my room. That's what you're gonna do."

Donnell felt his fingers pressing into the flesh on her upper arm through the silky blouse. He remembered grabbing Stephanie's arm the same way that night almost four years ago.

The bouncy light-skinned cheerleader from New York had convinced him that she loved him as much as he loved her, although she'd not shown any interest in him the three years they'd traveled together with the team. He hadn't realized until later that her interest coincided with his making the starting line-up. After his injury, he hadn't expected her to sit around playing nursemaid. Nor did he expect she'd start spending all her time with her friends. He'd been surprised and hurt. The thing that galled him most was that one of her 'friends' was Dejuan, the player who replaced him in the line. Only Ike's voice in the back of his head kept him from smashing her face in right there in the corridor, when he caught her coming out of Dejuan's room. There was the same fear in her eyes then, that he saw in Angela's eyes now.

Even knowing that Angela wasn't like the women who had only been attracted to him because of his celebrity status, he wouldn't release his grip. He'd had enough of her coming on to him, then changing her mind. As the electronic tone signaled that the elevator had reached the nineteenth floor, he thought about the way he had treated her that night at 'the Point,' and wondered if he didn't deserve this. After he opened the door to his room, he pushed her down by both arms into a sitting position on the bed, then sat in the chair opposite her.

"What's up with you?" he demanded. "Why do you come on to me, then pull away, just when I get interested. This tease game you're playing is dangerous, little girl."

Angela wouldn't look at him. She had light eyes, and knew if she looked at him, he would be able to see all the way to her soul. No words would come when she tried to explain. She fought it as hard as she could, but the tears welled up in her eyes and spilled over.

Donnell didn't know what to do. He sat back in the chair, and watched her. He was relieved that the fear was no longer in her eyes. But, she kept crying. The racking sobs were so out of proportion to what had happened between them, that he didn't believe his behavior was the cause. He went in the bathroom, brought back the box of tissues, and sat next to her. He didn't know what else to do.

"What is it? Tell me." The soothing tone he used calmed her.

"I'm sorry," she whimpered, wiping her eyes with a tissue. "I shouldn't have dragged you into this. I'm really sorry."

"Into what?" he asked, putting his arm around her shoulder and pulling her against him. "You can tell me."

Angela didn't resist. She felt ridiculous, but she couldn't stop crying. His fingers rubbing the back of her neck were so comforting. He leaned back against the headboard, pulling her with him, and let her cry.

Finally, she collected herself and sat up.

"Remember I told you I was engaged? In the restaurant, my fiancé, Quinton, was there. With another woman. Sondra tried to tell me. I should have listened."

"So that's why we had to leave so suddenly? And I thought you were overcome by my charms. I told you, you're a mean little heifer," he chuckled, remembering her lips brushing against his ear. "Maybe it's not what you think. You should, at least, give him a chance to explain."

Angela shook her head, her mouth drawn in a determined line.

"What are you going to do?"

"I don't know. It's going to be hard, having to work with him. I'll have to get through the contract somehow. But with any luck, I can get it finished in a couple of weeks—maybe less."

"Is Quinton the guy from New York?"

She nodded.

"Is his last name Rawlins?"

"Yes. Why?" she asked, puzzled.

"Just wondered. Do you have a computer at your house?"

"Sure I do. Why?"

"The way you are now, you're not going to get any rest anyway. And you shouldn't be alone. We may as well look at that disk now. Anyway, I just remembered I have another appointment in the morning."

FOURTEEN

Sondra was *too* happy when the trial was over, and left the Courthouse right away. The dress she had planned to wear to the dance didn't seem right now, but she sure didn't have time to go shopping. On the drive home, she thought her way through all her closets, reminding herself that he hadn't seen any of her dresses. She finally settled on the long black beaded dress, with the matching jacket. The long sleeves would be perfect because it was usually too cold in the hotels for her. The dress's neck was high in the front, giving an sedate, even austere, look. The back neckline was cut to a deep V to the waist. Having small breasts at least had the advantage that she wouldn't have to wear a bra, she thought ruefully. Still, she wondered if it wasn't a little too much. Then she thought maybe she could be a little daring—at her age. On third thought, she would keep the jacket on.

She put her arms through the sleeves and let the dress slink down over her body. The dress fit closely, but not tight, in all the right places. The beading made it heavy, so it felt good too.

Not very judicial, she thought as she surveyed herself in the full-length mirror. Swinging her hips from side to side provocatively, she smiled as she thought 'sexy.' She turned around, still dancing and admired the back view. She straightened up, as the thought clashed with the asexual roles of widow, mother, and judge that had circumscribed her life for so long. Even in the privacy of her own bedroom, she quickly glanced around to make sure she hadn't been seen. Yes, she'd definitely keep the jacket on. She chided herself for having acted like a teenager with a first date, giddy even. What the hell, it had felt good while it lasted.

Ike rang her bell promptly at eight. She was ready. She had *been* ready, but she fought the urge to dash to the door. She waited until he rang again.

"You look beautiful. That dress was made for you," he said, his eyes roaming over her appreciatively.

"Thank you. Come in. You're looking sharp yourself. Where on earth did you get a tuxedo on such short notice?"

"I have connections," he said smiling.

"Josie, I'll bet. Would you like a drink?" she asked, trying not to blush under his gaze.

"No. Have you had dinner?"

"Dinner?" she asked, realizing she had been too excited to think about eating.

"You'd better not drink on an empty stomach. You want to go back to your favorite restaurant?"

"No, lunch was enough for one day. There are lots of places along the way," she said, picking up her jacket and purse.

Ike helped her into Donnell's car. When he pulled into the

parking lot at the Taco Bell, she laughed. She enjoyed the stares from the other customers. They both had very serious looks on their faces—he in his tux, she in the beaded gown—as though there was nothing unusual. She hadn't felt free to act a little silly in years. She loved it.

When they were close enough to hear the music from the combo Sondra turned loose his hand, and put on her business face. Ike followed her lead, understanding his role. She steered him to the table of her hostess and introduced him around. He made small talk with the others at the table—asking them questions about current events, and letting them talk about themselves. She was surprised at how well-read he was. He didn't mention fishing even once. When he took her to the dance floor, he held her like a very proper escort. After the number ended, he followed her around the ballroom, as she greeted the people she needed to see, and be seen by. He was attentive, but didn't intrude. All the fears she had about him embarrassing her, seemed petty and unwarranted now. She relaxed and enjoyed herself, staying much longer than she had intended. As the wine warmed her, she took the jacket off. She wanted him to hold her closer on the dance floor, to touch the bare place on her back, but he maintained a respectful distance.

They were at their table when she saw Andrew approaching. She stiffened when she saw the glassy look in his eye, knowing he had passed his limit. She'd seen that look before. Ike felt her reaction. Andrew swaggered up to Sondra and leaned over in her face. The smell of old whiskey on his breath made her draw back.

"So, Miss Judge. I can see what the *real* problem was. You

could have just told me the truth, instead of all that bullshit," he said derisively, leering at Sondra, slurring his words.

Sondra had heard the talk about Andrew's drinking problem, and the incidents that were making him a laughingstock. He looked bad, almost unkempt. She felt sorry for him, but not enough to subject herself to it. She could feel all eyes at the table on them. All the chatter had ceased. Should she tell him off, or try to humor him? Before she could respond, Ike was on his feet, slapping Andrew on his back and shaking his hand.

"Say man! It's been a long time. Good to see you. Let me buy you a drink."

Ike took the surprised Andrew by the elbow and walked him away from Sondra, toward the bar.

"What do you drink? My guess would be Scotch. Listen my man, we won't have a problem here, if you stay away from my woman."

Ike was smiling tightly, the tone in his voice that of an old chum. Both hid the dangerous glint in his narrowed eyes. Andrew squinted at him, but couldn't quite place him.

"*Your* woman! Humph! Did she tell you she *was* my woman?"

"Well, my friend, you blew your chance. What can I tell you?"

"That bitch . . ."

"Say, watch your mouth now. You won't enjoy the Scotch nearly as much, trying to drink through a busted lip."

By that time, they'd reached the bar.

"One Scotch, a bourbon and a white wine," Ike told the bartender.

"Do I know you?" Andrew asked, still trying to place him.

"Doesn't matter. Just don't forget me."

Ike picked up two of the drinks and shook the finger on one hand at Andrew.

"Remember now. We don't want to have a problem."

He left Andrew at the bar.

Ike set the drinks on their table, and immediately took Sondra onto the dance floor. He knew the others would be curious and trying to listen.

"Where do you know Andrew from?" she asked.

"What makes you think I know him? Never saw the man in my life before tonight," he said, his mischievous smile showing.

"But, you . . . I can't believe you," she said, shaking her head.

"I can't believe _you_—fooling around with a loser like him."

"Oh, Andrew's OK. He wasn't like this before. He's just going through a phase. He has a lot of problems."

"And you're defending him! Good thing I didn't punch him out, like I wanted to."

"That _is_ a good thing," she said, nodding and returning his smile.

"I told him not to bother my woman again—and I meant it."

"Your woman? I'm not your woman."

"Not yet."

Ike parked the car in the circular driveway in front of her house. He opened the car door and helped Sondra out. As she put the key in the door, she turned to him.

"Thank you so much. I _really_ had a good time. I usually don't enjoy those affairs, but this was fun," she said, not sure whether to extend her hand or peck him on the cheek.

"Me too. Before I go, I need to use your phone."

"Phone? Oh, sure. Come on in."

As Ike dialed a number on the telephone that she showed him in the kitchen, he took his jacket off and hung it around a chair back. Sondra noticed how the crisp white shirt accentuated the rich color of his skin.

"How about a cup of coffee?" he asked, then into the phone, "Room 1904, please."

She made half a pot of decaf, and got down mugs from the cabinet. While he carried on his conversation, he pulled the knot out of the bowtie and let it drape around his neck. He undid the button at his neck, as he placed another call. Shaking his head, he hung the phone up.

"Well, it looks like I've been evicted. Donnell has company. I *told* him we should have gotten a suite."

"So what are you going to do?" Sondra asked, as she handed him the steaming coffee cup.

"I don't know. The hotel doesn't have any other rooms. I checked. Apparently there's a big convention in town. Shriners or somebody. I guess we were lucky to get that room. Maybe I'll just sleep in Donnell's car."

She looked at him across the table. He *had* acted like a gentleman all night.

"Well, it's so late. I suppose you could stay in one of the girls' room upstairs."

"You sure it won't be any trouble?"

"Oh, no. The linen's clean. It'll be fine. I put Michael's clothes in the closet upstairs. I'm not sure you they'd be big enough for you. Maybe his robe."

"That's OK. My bag is in the car. I'll go get it."

As she watched him go toward the front door, she wondered if she'd been had.

When he returned with his bag, she showed him to the bedroom.

"This is a gorgeous house."

"Thank you. Michael was an architect. He designed it—all but the kitchen. I helped with that part."

"It's beautiful, but it's awful big. Don't you get lonesome here, by yourself?"

"Well, sometimes. I keep busy," she said with a wry smile. "Make yourself at home. The bath's through this door," she said, getting a towel and facecloth from the cabinet.

"You want me to help you out of your dress?"

She turned to face him with a hard stare. His face was all innocence.

"No thank you. I can manage. Good night," she said firmly, and walked down the stairs.

Sondra pushed aside the decorative pillows, climbed into bed, and lay on her back, thinking. This would be the second night she'd spent with him. Maybe she'd gotten the wrong impression that night on the island. This evening had turned out so well. He hadn't tried to put his hands on her the whole time, even when they were dancing, when she wanted him to. Almost like he was courting her. She laughed to think of herself 'courting'—at her age.

When she thought of him as a suitor, she thought of his hands first. Hands were more telling for her than faces. His were working hands. Big and strong—but well cared for. Like his body. He looked so good in the tuxedo. She had seen the other women looking at him, some slyly from under lowered lashes, and some openly. If he noticed, he didn't let on. He proved himself to be a good conversationalist. And the thing with Andrew—that was just amazing. She couldn't wait to tell Angela and Eleanor about that.

Sondra was glad Eleanor wasn't still pissed off with her. They had exchanged some pretty heated words at the lake. Eleanor's voice on the answering machine had sounded happy, in fact. Sondra wondered what the rest of her week had been like. And how she got back to Houston, after refusing her offer to come get her. She'd call her tomorrow and apologize, as soon as she thought she was up. That would be late morning, after she and Ike had had several leisurely cups of coffee, probably on the patio by the pool. Suddenly, she remembered the coffee pot—she'd left it on.

Sondra grabbed her robe and padded, bare foot, toward the kitchen. Sure enough, she saw the little red light from across the room. She flipped the kitchen light on. She jumped and put her hand over her heart at the sight of Ike sitting at the table smoking a cigarette, a cup of coffee in front of him.

"You scared me! What are you doing up?" she asked, catching her breath. "I didn't know you smoked."

"I don't smoke much. Only when I can't sleep. I hope you don't mind. I found this ashtray in the cabinet," he said apologetically.

"No. It's OK. It doesn't bother me. Michael smoked. I never did. It seemed stupid to me."

"Yeah. You're right," he said, crushing the cigarette. "You couldn't sleep either?" A little smile peeked through his moustache.

"No. I was sleep," she lied. "I dreamed I'd left the coffee pot on."

His black eyes were disbelieving and piercing, so she avoided them, looking lower. Where the top of his robe was open, his chest was muscular and smooth, nearly hairless. She wondered how it would feel to her fingertips.

"Come over here. By me," he said quietly, holding out his hand.

Thinking he had read her thoughts, Sondra abruptly turned and walked to the counter. She started rinsing her cup out, to pour another. He walked up behind her, putting both hands on her waist, and kissed her on the neck. Something that felt like electricity shot through her body. She jerked around to push him away. Anticipating her reaction, he caught her face with both his hands and drew her lips to his.

His kiss was sweet. Patient. After a moment she stopped pushing against him and her hands fell to her sides. His kiss became more insistent, probing. Even though her mind told her she shouldn't, she put her arms around his waist. He felt so good. Her hands were drawn up his back and rested on his shoulder blades. She felt his weight pressing her against the counter. Her fingers ached to touch his skin. She pulled the robe away from his shoulders and rested her fingers on them. When he nibbled her ear, then kissed her on the neck, she felt the molten lava beginning to rise and gripped his bare shoulders in reflex. He kissed her in the hollow of her neck, and she arched her back, pressing her breasts against his chest. She felt his arousal at the same time that she felt his fingers pull at the little buttons on her satin pajama top, then give up, and feel for the hem. His hand closed around her breast, the strong fingers massaging. Now, his kiss was insistent, urgent, summoning a long-buried response from deep inside her. Her fingernails dug into his warm flesh.

The sound of a thud and breaking glass outside her front door tore them apart.

"You hear that?" he asked.

She just blinked at him, trying to catch her breath. They both listened. There was silence.

He was reaching for her again, when they heard pounding on the door.

"You expecting somebody?" he asked.

She shook her head, still unable to speak.

"Don't move. I'll be right back."

Ike was at the front door, by the time she got to the living room. She could see a man's form through the beveled glass. When Ike opened the door, she saw Andrew, swaying and trying to maintain his balance.

"What are you doing here?!" Ike angrily demanded. "I thought I told you to stay away from my woman!"

"I just wanna talk to Sondra. This doesn't involve you."

"She doesn't have anything to say to you. Go on home— before I have to do something to you."

Andrew looked past Ike, to Sondra standing in the living room. Feeling self-conscious standing there in her pajamas, she pulled the thin satin robe around her, tying it at the waist.

"Well, ain't *this* cozy," he said derisively. His tone changed to whining. "Sondra. I need to talk to you, baby." He tried to look around Ike, blocking the door. "Move, dude."

The instant Andrew pushed him, Ike drew back and threw the first punch, connecting solidly with Andrew's face.

"Oh, my God!" Sondra screamed as she ran toward the door. When she reached it, she saw that the large clay planter had succumbed to the greater force of Andrew's Mercedes. The poodle bush was uprooted, lying atop the hood.

Andrew had staggered backwards against Donnell's car. There was blood on his nose and mouth. Ike pounced on him, riding him to the ground, landing blows on Andrew's face. She heard Ike saying, "I told you, man. I *told* you."

Sondra could see Andrew was helpless in his drunken state, trying to fend off the blows. She jumped on Ike's back, trying to hold his arm.

"Stop it! Ike, leave him alone! Ike!" Then, when she heard the siren, "Oh, shit! It's the police! I can't have the police coming to my house!"

The alarm in her voice called Ike back, his arm in mid-air poised for another blow. Ike grabbed Andrew and jerked him to a standing position. He dragged him into the house, shoved him down on the couch, his back to the door. He heard the car stop in front of the house, and the siren silence.

"Don't you move," he said, menacingly close to Andrew's face. "If you say one word, I'll finish you off before they can stop me."

Then he strode to the door, Sondra still on his heels. He pushed her behind him, and held his bloody hand behind the door. He took a deep breath to steady himself.

"Evening officers," Ike said pleasantly, as the two uniformed policemen approached the door.

"Your neighbors called. Said a car had crashed into your house."

"No, sir. Only the flower pot. Our son had a little accident. Teenager," he said, jerking his head toward the couch behind him. "That boy'll be grounded until he's 30. You know how kids are at that age"

"Yeah, I *do* know," the older cop said. "I've got one too. Can't wait 'til he's grown."

"Our insurance will take care of it. There's no problem. We appreciate your coming out."

"We'll just make a report. Good night, Mr. Ellis."

Ike closed the door and exhaled. When he saw the look on Sondra's face—fury and relief—he knew it was over for them, for that night.

"Go on upstairs. Sleep in that bed. I'll take care of your friend," he told her, motioning toward Andrew.

"But . . ."

"But, go on upstairs," he said firmly. "We'll be alright down here. I'll sleep in your room. He's OK."

Sondra could see Andrew was breathing, slumped over on the couch.

She marched up the stairs, looking at Ike standing in her den in his maroon robe, like he was the man of her house. Mr. Ellis, indeed! She wondered how long it would take for that 'report' to travel from the precinct station to the courthouse corridors. Probably by Monday. She was furious with Andrew for causing this mess. She should have insisted that the police take him to jail. Would serve him right, she thought, as she threw herself across the bed. Instead, he was in her house, probably bleeding on her white couch, and she was in her child's bed! If it hadn't been for him, she would probably be in her own bed now—with Ike.

The thought shook her to her core. She realized that was all Ike had been after, all the time. Playing his little courting game. And she had nearly fallen for it. She had thought Ike saved her from Andrew. Maybe it was Andrew who saved her from herself. Since the day she met the farmer, there had been nothing but disorder and upheaval in her life. First, the body; then that damned sheriff taking her gun; then the fight with Eleanor. Now this! She couldn't stand it. She fell into a fitful sleep, determined to regain control of her emotions—and her life.

Sondra awoke long before sun-up. When she descended the stairs, Andrew was gone. She frowned at the stain on her couch. Ike was at the kitchen table fully dressed, drinking coffee. He smiled at her. Her expression didn't change.

"Good morning. I made us some coffee. Hope it's the way you like it."

"I'm sure it'll be fine," she said coolly, as she walked by him, toward the coffee pot.

When he reached for her hand, she jerked it away. He looked at her puzzled.

"Why'd you do that?"

"Just don't touch me. You keep your hands to yourself!" she snapped, glaring at him.

He put his hands behind his head, fingers laced together, leaned back in the chair, and stared at her.

"You didn't seem to object to my touch last night."

Her eyes flickered. The thought of his hand on her breast caused her nipples to harden under the satin pajama top. She was glad the robe hid it from his sight.

"Well, I *should* have," she said, as she turned away from his amused gaze and went to the cabinet. She poured herself a cup of coffee, took a deep breath, and carried the cup to the table. As she sat across from him, he let the chair down and took a sip of coffee.

"Look, Ike. We need to talk. This isn't going to work. I'm glad I met you. And I had a nice time last night—at the dance. But we're from different worlds. We have nothing in common. There's nothing . . ."

"Our worlds aren't so different, Sondra," he said, leaning forward, his forearms on the table. "You're trapped in a job that controls your life 24-hours a day. I'm trapped too. I didn't realize until I met you, that I've been trapped by a decision I made years ago. But there's no need for either of us to live this way for the *rest* of our lives. We've been responsible. We did the things that had to be done. You for your girls, and me for Donnell and Muhdea. But when do *we* get a turn? We . . ."

"No, Ike. You don't understand. See . . ."

"Hush. Let me finish. We have enough in common. We both need somebody in our lives. You're bumping around in this big ol' house all alone, running yourself raggedy to all these functions that you don't enjoy. You're just running away from yourself. And me—I'm no better. I'm just running the ranch out of habit now. I keep myself busy, fooling with the Scouts, and anybody else that needs my help. Fishing. When I dropped out of school, I was so busy keeping everything going, and keeping Donnell out of trouble, I didn't have time to think about myself. God, that seems like a lifetime ago," he said, shaking his head. "The only thing I did for myself was to breed Big Jesse. He was my Daddy's dream, too. I know he would be as proud as I am— you should see him," he said, the pride showing in his voice. Then the smile turned to a frown.

"But now, there's nothing left. I could finish that last semester on my degree. But I don't care about it now, the way

I did for so long. I don't seem to care about much of anything any more. I need someone to share my life with. I need *you* Sondra." He took her hands in his and looked deep into her amaretto-colored eyes. "We can spend the next forty years learning the other things we have in common. We can travel. I know you like that. And I've always wanted to see the country. And when we've seen all we want of this one, we can go to Africa. Or the Caribbean. Or anywhere you want. How about . . ."

"Whoa cowboy," she said, jerking her hands back. "You're getting *way* ahead of yourself. Do you realize I've only known you for a week! And you think I'm going to give up my career, my house, my girls? And do what? Go traipsing off to the country with a man I barely know. Not hardly. I'll bet your little line works every time, to get you in some woman's bed. But not this time. Not mine."

"It's not a line, Sondra. It's the truth. And I'm not trying to get in your bed. I'm trying to get in your heart. And I will. When you're ready. It's just a matter of time."

"Time! I'll tell you what time it is. It's time for you to leave. Just close the door behind you."

Sondra stomped off to her room and slammed the door.

Ike smiled to himself, picking up his bag and throwing the garment bag with the tuxedo over his shoulder. He closed the beveled glass door, making sure it was locked. As he walked to the car in the darkness, he thought, "This is going to take a little time."

FIFTEEN

"We'll have to go in your car. Ike took mine," Donnell said, as they rode down in the elevator.

"Ike? Is he here too? Where is he?"

"This morning, he said he was going to the Courthouse. I haven't seen or heard from him since."

He and Angela shared knowing smiles. When the valet brought the little car, Donnell laughed, towering over it.

"And you said my car was small! I'm not sure I can fit in this thing. Maybe we should take a taxi. Plus, I don't usually let women drive me."

"Oh, you'll be alright. I'd let you drive, but you don't know where we're going. Besides, you don't drive a stick shift as well as I do," she said, giving him her pixie smile.

"Nice place," Donnell said, as they approached her back door from the carport. "Not very secure though for a young lady living alone. Next time, get a place with a garage."

"It's safe enough here. And quiet. Mostly older people. I

know all my neighbors, and we look out for each other. Make yourself at home. What kind of music do you like? Put on whatever you like, while I fix a snack. I'm sorry about dinner," she said, going to the kitchen.

From his survey of her music collection, Donnell concluded she had wide-ranging taste in music, but blues and jazz were dominant. They were his favorites too. He selected a CD by Kyle Turner. He'd read a blurb about him in a magazine as an 'up and coming' artist to watch for, but had never heard his music. The title, "Sincerely Yours", sounded like the right kind of background music. As soon as the sweet sounds of the jazz saxophone came on, he knew he had made a good choice. Donnell had the feeling he wouldn't be described as 'up and coming' for long.

"What would you like to drink?" she called from the kitchen.

"A soda would be great. Not a diet, though. How long have you lived here?" Donnell asked, walking around the living room. He guessed her decorating style would be called eclectic. It worked; was comfortable. The couch, glider rocker and matching ottoman were modern, but many of the other pieces were antiques. He admired the huge armoire, running his hand over the ornately-carved doors. It was a wonder she had gotten it through the front door. The top of it barely cleared the ceiling. The treadle sewing machine cabinet under the front window was like the one his mother had. It was flanked by two straight-backed chairs, with needlepoint-covered cushions. The top of it, covered with a lace doily, held picture frames of various sizes. He picked them up and looked at them, one by one. The people looked so much alike, he knew they were her family. He lingered on the one of the group done up in their Sunday best.

She apparently had two older brothers, who must have taken their height from the tall, light-skinned father. Angela, in two shoulder length bronze pigtails, had his coloring, but otherwise looked just like the petite brown-skinned mother, flashing the same pixie smile back at him from the photograph. This was the only photo in which Angela wore a dress. He concluded she had been quite a tom-boy.

"Almost three years," she answered. "We've never had any trouble around here. The old couple on that side—the Lignowsky's—have adopted me. They say I remind them of their granddaughter. It's funny though, because they never had children. Maybe they've gone 'round the bend. They're harmless, even if they have. They stay to themselves. Don't seem to have any friends. No one ever comes to see them."

Through the partially open mini-blinds, Donnell noticed the car that drove up and parked at the curb in front of the Lignowskys. He found it curious that the driver didn't get out.

Angela came in balancing a large tray. There were stacks of thinly-sliced beef, cheese and bread, little cups of mayo and mustard, utensils, napkins and soft drinks.

"OK. Let's get to work. Would you open those doors," she said, nodding to the armoire. "And pull on the rope."

"This is a beautiful piece."

"It belonged to my grama. All of these old pieces were hers. We were very close."

As he folded back the long doors, Donnell was surprised to see the computer. He had assumed she kept it in her bedroom. He pulled the silk braided rope and a narrow cantilevered worktable swung down and came to rest on one leg. Angela set the tray on it, and instructed him to pull the two chairs over, as she turned on the machine.

"It originally was used as a wardrobe, of course. After she died, my brothers brought it to me from New Orleans. I had the insides re-done to accommodate my computer. Now, when I'm working, I feel her spirit with me."

"You're lucky. I never knew my grandparents. They all died before I can remember."

Donnell took one of the chairs and inserted the disk. His hands flew over the keys. When what he was searching for appeared on the screen, he sat back to give her a better view. To Angela, it just looked like a listing of account numbers, dates and amounts. She scrolled through three screens of it, then turned to Donnell.

"So? What is this?"

"Remember when we were up at Ike's place, we had run the loop in your program, and were down-loading the problem data. This is what we got before we lost the power. You notice anything about it?"

"Well, let's see. All the amounts are nine thousand and something. And, a lot of the account numbers are repeated. Looks like it's not that many accounts."

"Five."

"So what does it mean?" she asked.

"I don't know yet. It looks like someone is being careful to avoid the $10,000 mark. You know banks are required to report to the IRS any transaction above that amount. And look at the dates. Somebody is moving a lot of money through these accounts. Can you find out who the account-holders are?"

"I'm pretty sure I can." Angela went to work, dialing into the bank's system, then inputting the account numbers. As the screen for each account came up, Angela saved it onto the disk.

"Print that," Donnell said, when she had all five. QJ Construction Company. QJ's Transport. QR Distributing, Inc. Jennifer's Fashions. And Rawjenn, Inc.

When the printing finished, they took the print-out and the almost empty tray to the dining room table. Looking at the print-out, Angela noticed that the address for all five accounts was the same post office box in New York. That, and the company names, told her who owned the accounts. She tried hard to keep the anger, disappointment, and sadness out of her face.

"What is it?" Donnell asked, searching her eyes.

"These are Quinton's accounts."

"Why do you think they're his?"

"Jennifer is his wife's name," she said quietly.

"Wife? But, I thought you said . . ."

"They were supposed to go to court today. In New York. For the final divorce."

"He obviously wasn't there. You think they did it without him?"

"No. I think it was a lie. It was all lies. He was just using me all the time."

As she said it, one hot tear fell down her cheek. Donnell pulled her against him and put his arms around her.

"Don't cry. He's not worth your tears. Plus it makes your nose turn red."

She giggled against his chest. She knew it was true.

"Don't worry. He'll get what he deserves. I'll see to that."

She leaned back and looked at him. "What do you mean? What can *you* do?"

"Don't you worry about it. I'll take care of him. You just stay away from him. His little house of cards is about to come tumbling down. He's not going to like it either. He may be dangerous. Desperate."

"Quinton?! Nah. He's not like that," she said, surprised. "He's a rat—obviously. And a liar, and some other things. But he's not dangerous."

"If you insist. At least promise me that you won't mention to him about what we've found out. Not one word," Donnell said, looking very serious.

"Oh alright. I promise."

"It's late. I think it's about time for me to go back to the hotel. Why don't you let me take your car. I'll bring it back first thing in the morning. Surely, Ike will show up by then."

"No. I'll take you back. I don't mind."

"But it's too late for you to be out by yourself. And it's a long drive back."

"How do you think I've managed all these years before I met you?" she asked, laughing.

"Alright, Ms. Liberated. I guess if you and your girlfriends can go wandering all over the countryside by yourselves, you can get back home by yourself. Still, I don't like it."

"Think about it this way. If we hadn't, I'd have never met you," she said smiling smugly, as she picked up her purse and keys.

"Yeah, I thought about that already. Maybe I just don't want you to meet anybody else. By the way, let me keep that disk. I'll bring it back tomorrow."

"I don't know . . ."

"Didn't I bring it all the way from Pine Branch?"

"Okay. But tomorrow for sure. I still have work to do," she

said handing him the disk. She flipped off the lights as they went out the back door.

"I'll even let you drive," she said, tossing him the keys. "Let's see if you can find your way back to the hotel."

"That won't be a problem. I'm extremely observant. It's my job," he said, as he started the car. He didn't tell her about the car that had been parked out front. The driver had slouched down in the seat. He'd thought, maybe it was just somebody sleeping off a drunk, but he had noted the license number anyway. The car was gone when he pulled out of the driveway.

"So what's it like being a security guard? What kind of building do you work in? Have you ever been shot at?"

Donnell laughed out loud. He'd forgotten her remark that night they went to the Point. Then, he'd been so intent on his prey, he'd let it pass.

"No. I've never been shot at—except by Sondra. But several of my employees have been. I own a security company. I specialize in sports arenas. Mostly in the Northeast. Lately, I've been venturing into computer security—evaluating security, actually. Other companies hire me to break into their systems, then tell them how to prevent someone else from doing it. Your bank ought to hire me. Their security is so weak, a 6th-grader could access their system. If you still want to meet in the morning, I'll show you a few measures you can put in your program that will help some. But make them pay you extra for it."

"I think I owe you an apology. I thought . . ."

"You don't owe me anything. I'm used to it. Many people underestimate Black men—sometimes even Black women." He winked at her as he said it. "A lot of times, in my business, I use that to my advantage."

Angela looked properly chastised.

"So, did you use it to your advantage with me?"

"Of course not. I wouldn't take advantage of you. I like you, and my horse likes you. You're alright, Sleepyhead." He pulled the little car in front of the hotel, parked just past the front doors, and killed the motor.

Angela liked the thought of being liked. She needed it—now especially.

"Why don't you come up to my room? Let me take you home in the morning." When he saw the look on her face, he said, "No funny business. I promise. I just don't want you to drive all that way back by yourself, this time of night. I'm worried about you."

"No. Thanks anyway. I'll be alright. Besides, what about your brother?"

Donnell laughed. "He went fishing—for Sondra. I swear he's been mooning behind that woman ever since ya'll left. I doubt he'll be here tonight. But even if he is, we'll just kick him out. He'll manage."

Angela laughed at the prospect. "Go on. Get out. I'm going home. I'll see you in the morning."

Reluctantly, Donnell struggled from under the wheel and walked around to the other side to open her door. He took her hand and helped her out.

"Isn't there *anything* I can say, or do, to keep you from leaving?"

Angela shook her head.

"Not even this?"

Donnell leaned over, took her face in his hands and pressed

his lips to hers, in a chaste kiss. She was so surprised, in reflex she grabbed his hands. Before she could exert any strength against them, he gave her another kiss—this one not so chaste. She felt the strength melting away. She relaxed and enjoyed his kiss, returning it. Finally she broke away from him, firmly pulling his hands to his sides.

"I *know* I have to go now," she said, breathing heavily through her pixie smile. "Let's make that noon tomorrow. At the bank. Don't forget the disk."

Angela hurried around to the other side of the car, and got in. Her hands were shaking so, she had a hard time turning the key in the ignition. She hoped he didn't notice.

Donnell watched the little car roar off down the curved driveway, then turn onto the main thoroughfare. As he turned and walked through the hotel doors, he wondered if he could still click his heels in the air. He could hardly wait until noon.

Ike wasn't in the room. Donnell smiled to himself as he thought, 'must have reeled her in.' He picked up the phone and dialed in his card number for the long-distance call.

"Hey. This is Donnell." He looked at his watch. "Yeah, I guess it would be four o'clock there. Sorry 'bout that, but *some* of us are working. Listen I need you to check something out. I need everything you can find on a Quinton and Jennifer Rawlins, New York." . . . "No, R-A-W-L-I-N-S. Fax it here to Jimison's office as soon as you can. Oh, and another thing—I need the registration of a red Porsche, license LTD-978. If it's not registered in Texas, try New York." . . . "I'll be in Jimison's office first thing in the morning. That'll be nine, your time. Have it there then. I'm sending you some data too. You will definitely find it interesting. Get back to me ASAP." . . . "Pine Branch? Oh, yeah, I've got something on that too, but it's small-time stuff. Jimison can handle it out of the office here in Houston. It can wait. Let's catch a bigger fish first." . . . "Yeah, OK. See ya."

All the way home, Angela thought about Donnell. His kiss was sweet. She would have expected him to be furious at her for the way she'd acted. She was ashamed of herself for that little stunt she'd pulled in the restaurant. She was glad he understood. Still, she shouldn't have misused him in that way—especially for that jerk. When she thought of Quinton, a sneer came on her face. She was glad she had done it. She hoped it ruined his little dinner with Francis. She was angry with herself for being such a fool for him—a bigger fool even than she or Sondra had thought. The man was totally devious. He could sho' nuff kiss her ass now. And there were still a few good men around. Donnell proved that, in lots of little ways—and some big ones too. They *had* gotten off to a rocky start, but he had made up for it. He could have done anything to her in that hotel room, but he hadn't. He could have insisted on staying the night at her condo, but he hadn't even suggested it. She wondered why no woman had snapped him up. Women were pretty aggressive these days. Maybe that's why she always seemed to end up with the jerks. She hadn't been raised to chase men, so she was at a disadvantage. She giggled aloud, hearing her Mama's voice saying, 'It's the *man's* job to chase the woman—and kill the bugs.' From the way Donnell had subdued Sondra and taken her gun, Angela was certain he would kill the bugs. She laughed at the vision of all of them rolling around on the ground in the red dirt and pine needles. She thought of him riding Ike's big black horse—tall and strong. Like a warrior. There was a warrior look on his face when he came to rescue her from that sheriff. Every thought she had of Donnell brought a smile to her face. That was the kind of man she needed. One who would make her smile.

Angela was still smiling when she opened her back door. The repeat button must have been pushed on the CD player—Kyle Turner was still playing when she turned the light on in her living room. She turned the CD off, and was heading to her bedroom when the doorbell rang. She knitted her brow, wondering who would be at her door at this hour.

Anger exploded within her when she saw Quinton's face through the peephole. She undid the locks and jerked the door open.

"What the hell are you doing here?! Where's Francis?" Her eyes were flashing, her hands on her hips.

"Where's your man?" he smirked, leaning against the doorframe.

"That's none of your business. Nothing I do is any of your business anymore. So just take your ass on away from here."

She almost lost her balance when he shoved past her, closed the door and strolled into her living room.

"Who is he? How long have you been seeing him?"

"Ain't none of that your damn business. Get out of my house. Now!"

Quinton calmly walked over to the armoire, looking at the computer.

"I'll leave when I'm ready. So tell me, An-ge-<u>la,</u> were you with that dude when I couldn't find you last week-end?"

"Get out!"

"What did you two do all night? Play computer games? I saw

you, you know."

"You've been spying on me?" she asked, incredulously. "I would have thought you'd have your hands full with Francis."

"You should at least close your blinds when you're going to play around on me."

"Play around on *you*! You really *do* have a lot of nerve. Get out!"

He strolled over to the table.

"Oh, and I see you fixed him a little supper. Isn't that sweet," he said, as he fingered a slice of the hardening bread. There was a strange look on his face, when he looked back up at her. "Did you give him a little after-dinner treat, An-ge-<u>la</u>?"

Angela didn't respond, her mouth set, her arms folded across her breasts.

"Well, let's just see," he said, as he sidled into the hallway. He leaned against the doorway and peeped into her bedroom. "Smart girl. You know I'd have to hurt you about giving my stuff away."

"Your what! You must be crazy!"

"I am crazy, An-ge-<u>la</u>. Crazy about you."

"Oh, give me a break," she said exasperated. "Why don't you just go on—back to Francis, or to your wife, or any damn where you want—other than here?!"

"Nice girls don't use profanity, An-ge-<u>la</u>," he said condescendingly.

"And you ain't my daddy, Mr. Mother Fucker," she said defiantly, her chin jutting out.

Quinton walked over to Angela and tried to put his arm around her.

"You're so cute when you're mad. Come on, let's make up.

I forgive you. Kiss me."

She jerked away from him in disgust, causing him to almost fall. He caught himself on the table and gave her a sneery smile.

"I like it like that too, An-ge-<u>la</u>. You know I'm used to fighting for what I want. And I *always* get what I want."

Angela hadn't seen this side of Quinton. Fear was creeping up on her, pushing the anger aside. To keep him from seeing it, she averted her eyes down to the table. She saw the printout. His hand was almost touching it. She must have looked startled, because he followed her eyes. She saw the frown on his face as he read the words. Just as she reached for the paper, he jerked it off the table and held it out of her reach, his eyes scanning the page. His eyes narrowed when he looked back at her.

"Where did you get this? What are you doing with this?" he demanded.

Angela didn't say anything, just blinked her eyes.

"I'm talking to you. Where did you get this?" His voice was louder, angry.

Angela didn't know what to say. She had promised Donnell. His warning came back to her.

"I was just, uh, doing a test run. Uh. For the conversion. And then…then this just printed out. I don't know what it is," she blurted out.

It seemed to her his arm was moving in slow motion. It felt and sounded like lightning had struck her, when his palm connected with her face. She fell sideways from the momentum of the blow, sprawling over the back of the couch. She shook her head to clear it, and gathering herself up, scrambled for the front door. He moved to block her way.

"You showed this to your boyfriend, didn't you? This is

what you were doing huddled over your computer, wasn't it?" he demanded, waving the paper in the air.

"No. He didn't see it." she said, getting to her feet. "We were just playing games."

"Who is he, Angela? Is he a cop?" Quinton demanded.

"No. No. He's from out of town. We went to school together. He's just a friend." She felt the side of her face swelling and touched it with her hand. The anger at him slapping her, wrestled with her fear of the look on his face. Desperate and dangerous— just as Donnell had said.

"And he's coming back. For breakfast. So why don't you leave," she said, sounding more assured than she felt.

"Coming here? When? What time?"

Her mouth was crimped tight, her eyes little slits.

Quinton was angered even more by her defiance. He slapped her again, and caught her by the back of her blouse jerking her back before she could fall, her weight tearing it. He shoved her toward the kitchen.

"Call him. Tell him plans have changed. Tell him you'll get back to him later."

"I don't know the number," she said petulantly.

"Bitch, don't make me hit you again," he said menacingly, his hand drawn back.

"OK, OK," she said, reaching for the phone book. She closed the book before Quinton could see, and dialed the number.

"Room 1904, please." She was relieved to hear Donnell's sleepy voice answer.

"Hi. This is Angela. Listen, about breakfast. Don't come back over here. I've got other plans. I'll call you later." Then she thrust the receiver at Quinton. "Now are you satisfied?"

Donnell sat up on the edge of the bed and shook his head. "Angela? Angela?" When he heard the phone disconnect, he held the receiver out and looked at it, as though it could answer his question. He was sure they hadn't discussed breakfast. He wondered if this was some little game she was playing, but decided they were past that. Maybe it had been a dream. As he rubbed his eyes, an uneasy feeling crept over him. He knew for certain they were to meet at the bank, not her house. He didn't know her home number. There was a number for A. R. Reeves in the phone book. It was the right street. When he dialed, there was no answer. He knew then, his instincts were correct. Angela was in trouble. He shouldn't have left her. He dressed in a flash, left a note for Ike with the address, and was on the elevator in a matter of minutes. He couldn't believe his luck when he saw the taxi through the front doors of the hotel. He jerked the door to the cab open, flashing his badge, and pulled the driver out.

"You can go for the ride, or stay here 'til I get back. You choose," he said, climbing into the driver's seat.

The cabbie said something in a language Donnell didn't understand, and dove into the back seat, just as the big yellow car screeched off. Donnell drove like a madman, speeding and running red lights. Where was a cop when you needed one? He could hear Angela saying, 'Now are you satisfied?' He knew who she was talking to. He pulled up behind her Miata, threw the gear shift into Park, and jumped out while the car was still rocking from the sudden stop. He banged on the back door, calling her name. He frantically tried the knob. He ran around to the front door and tried that one. He could see through the front window—the lights were on—the place was a mess. He ran back around to the back door. It had glass panes in it and would be easy to break in. When he reached the door, he heard the thick-accented voice.

"Stop right there, young man."

He looked around and saw the old man pointing the gun at him with his palsied hands.

"Mr. Lignowsky, don't shoot. My name is Donnell Evans. A friend of Angela's. If you have a key, get it. Otherwise I'm going to break in. Angela is in some kind of trouble."

The old man looked puzzled, as he peered into Donnell's eyes.

"Our Angela? Trouble?" he mumbled. Then finally, "Yes, we have key."

The old man yelled something Donnell didn't understand back toward his door. Mrs. Lignowsky came out, looking worried, and handed the key to Donnell. The old man followed him into Angela's kitchen, nervously running his fingers through the shock of white hair. His eyes widened as they entered the dining area. The tray had been knocked over onto the floor, and they had to step around the food and utensils. Donnell searched the bedroom and bathroom, but no Angela. When he came back into the living area, the old man was standing in front of the armoire, shaking his head.

"Such a shame. We tell Angela. That Quinton. He no good for her. No love in his eyes for her. He did this bad thing. We hear noise, bumping, glass breaking. We see his car. I get gun. Then car is gone."

"Red car?" Donnell asked.

"Red. Yes. Fancy car. Mr. Fancy. Me and my wife, we call

him that. Fancy car, fancy clothes."

Donnell saw the picture frames laying about on the floor, the glass broken, stepped on. The soapstone statuette from the coffee table had been thrown through the screen on the computer. The cantilevered table hung crooked—it's leg broken. It appeared to Donnell that these were not random acts of vandalism, but were calculated to hurt Angela. Anger rose in him until it reached an intensity that at least matched Quinton's. It was personal for him now. When he got his hands on Quinton, he would hurt him more than he had hurt Angela. He looked back at the computer and remembered the print-out. He could see it was not on the table, but walked over to it and looked all around and under it. Now he knew the why.

"Do you know where he lives, Mr. Lignowsky?"

The old man shook his head. Donnell grabbed the phone book from atop the refrigerator, and riffled through the pages. There was no listing for Quinton Rawlins. He frantically searched the drawers and cabinets, until he found her address book in the night stand drawer. There was no listing for him under R. Under Q, he found a Quenton, a Quinton and a Quinn. He knew the right one, by the little hearts drawn around it. There was a phone number, and street number, but no street name. He tore the page out and stuffed it in his pocket. He sat on the bed and dialed the hotel number, while he flipped the pages in her book. There was no answer in his room. He found the number he was looking for and dialed it.

"Sondra. Let me speak to Ike. Now!" ..."Gone? How long's he been gone?" ..."Where does Quinton live?" ..."I don't have time to answer a bunch of questions. I'm at Angela's. He's torn her place up and taken her somewhere. Can you find out his address?"..."Hurry. Call me back. I'll be waiting." He hung the phone up.

Waiting, it seemed like an eternity. He could hear the Lignowsky's speaking to each other in a foreign language— soothing tones—comforting each other. In the dining area, Donnell saw they had cleaned up the food and utensils. Mrs. Lignowsky was replacing the cushions on the sofa. She shrieked, then began talking rapidly in the foreign tongue while crossing herself with one hand. Donnell ran over and took the pillow she was clutching to her breast. Seeing the blood on it made his own blood boil. The jingling of the phone kept him from exploding. He ran and snatched it off the wall in the kitchen.

"Yeah? Sondra? Oh."... "Woodhollow? 4516? Got that." ... "How do I get there from here?"... "Bout how far?"... "Thanks man. Thank Sondra for me." Donnell looked up to see Ike walking through the back door with a puzzled look on his face. "Nah. Thanks man, but I've got all the help I need."

As he hung up the phone, he said to Ike, "Come on. Let's go." He turned back to the Lignowskys on his way out the door. "Call the police. We'll be back."

As he passed the big cab, he saw the cabbie peeking up from the floor in the back seat. He stopped and handed him a card. "You can go. Take this to the Federal Building. Sixth floor. Ask for Jimison. He'll take care of your bill."

Donnell sped off, tires screeching, as Ike closed his door.

"Tell me. What's up?" Ike asked.

"Her ex-boyfriend. Involved in something—probably money-laundering. She found out. You saw what he did to her place. There was blood. He's got her. He hurt her, Ike. I'm gonna kill him."

Ike saw the murderous look in his eyes, and believed him.

"Now, Donnell. Listen . . ."

"Listen, bullshit! I'm gonna kill him, I'm telling ya! In fact, hand me that holster under your seat." Donnell was taking angry, shallow breaths, in and out. Ike thought he looked like an angry bull.

"Holster? What are you doing, carrying a gun around? You don't need a gun."

"Gimme the damn gun, man," Donnell yelled. He was gripping the steering wheel and driving like a maniac. Ike had to hold on to keep from being thrown about.

"No," Ike said firmly. "You need to get a grip on yourself. You always were a hot-head. I thought you'd have grown out of it by now. You've got yourself all worked up over this girl—like she's your wife or something. I thought you said you weren't even interested in her."

"I said I didn't think she was interested in *me*. But that's all changed. He's a dead man, Ike. I'm telling you."

"OK, OK. Just calm down. Take a deep breath."

"But . . ."

"Just *do* it! NOW!"

Donnell took a long, deep breath. He and Ike had been through this so many times before, it was a conditioned response. He could hear Ike's voice from the basketball court, "You can't win *anything*, with your emotions running all over you. You have to be in control!"

"Another!" Ike demanded. "Once more." As Donnell got in the rhythm, Ike saw the tension in his jaw releasing, his grip on the steering wheel easing.

"Alright. That's better. Now, let's go get this dude," Ike said with a satisfied look on his face.

Donnell pulled into the large complex, cruising, his eyes searching for the red Porsche. He told Ike to look for 4516. The sky was just beginning to lighten into morning gray.

"Here we go. 4504. Keep going. It's going to be on this side. 4508. Keep on. 4512."

Donnell stopped the car in front of 4514, and turned to Ike.

"Give me the gun, Ike."

Ike didn't move. "No. If you're all that determined to kill him, then do it with your bare hands. You'll enjoy it more. Cleaner too. I showed you how to do it. Remember?"

Donnell nodded, and got out of the car. They approached the door together. Donnell braced himself to break the door down with his shoulder. Ike held his palm up at him, and eased the knob with the other hand. It opened. Ike gave him a wry smile and a nod. Donnell pushed the door open wider, leaning back into the corner, waiting. After a moment he stepped into the sparsely-furnished living room, his eyes scouring the room. He could hear rustling and drawers shutting, from across the room, down the hall. He saw movement out of the corner of his eye. His head riveted in that direction. Angela was on the floor in the adjoining dining room, in a sitting position, her back against the wall. Grey duct tape was wound around her head, covering her mouth, and around her ankles. Her hands were behind her back. Seeing her black and blue face—one eye swollen shut—caused the anger to explode inside him. She jerked her head forward and trying to signal him with her good eye. He pointed to her, for Ike behind him, and headed toward the hallway, his head set like a bull about to charge.

Quinton was removing clothes from his dresser and throwing them into open suitcases on the bed, when Donnell rounded the corner. Their eyes met in the mirror. Quinton startled when he saw Donnell coming toward him, then opened the top drawer and reached inside. Donnell threw his full weight against him, slamming the drawer against his hand, and at the same time, grabbing him around his neck. He jerked him backwards away from the dresser, and heard the heavy metal object clattering inside the drawer, as Quinton dropped the gun. Donnell punched him in the back, twice, so hard each blow lifted him off the floor. Then, Donnell felt the air rush out of him, as Quinton jabbed his elbow into his stomach and broke the hold around his neck. Quinton spun around and delivered a kick to the stomach, knocking Donnell backwards atop the suitcases on the bed, then crouched in a karate-like stance. Donnell started up from the bed, growling and clenching his teeth. Quinton spun around again. This time, his foot connected with Donnell's jaw. Donnell fell back on the bed, as Quinton crouched again. The pain was greater than anything he had experienced, even on the rough play of the professional basketball court. The blind anger was overtaking him. He was about to rise again when he heard Ike's warning in his head. Donnell realized he had underestimated his foe. Although the man was smaller in stature, he had obviously been trained in some kind of martial arts. Donnell's fighting style was more that of a street brawler. He took the three deep breaths, watching Quinton's brown eyes. Now in control of himself, he faked a rising. This time when Quinton spun around, Donnell caught his ankle with both hands and jerked hard. Quinton hit the floor on his back. Donnell leaped on him, straddling him, pinning Quinton's hands under his knees. He held him by the collar with his left hand and pounded his big fist into his face repeatedly. Donnell could feel the skin tearing and bones breaking under his knuckles. He didn't care. Mr. Fancy wouldn't look so fancy when he finished with him. Angela's swollen face appeared in his mind. He swung his fist against the side of Quinton's head. The diamond stud earring ripped the skin on Donnell's knuckles. Blood spurted out from the broken eardrum. Donnell saw the blood on Angela's sofa pillow. He changed hands on Quinton's collar and began hitting him with the other fist. As he drew back again, he felt a strong grip on his wrist, and heard a soft, deep voice.

"That's enough, son. That's enough."

Donnell pulled hard against the restraint, but the huge man standing behind him easily held him. He felt his arm being twisted behind his back and his body being pulled backwards into a standing position, by the grip around his chest.

"Go see about your girl, son. She's hurt bad. Leave this one to me."

Donnell slowly stopped fighting against the hold as he recognized the voice. It was the one on the phone that had given him Quinton's address. He felt the hold on him being released.

"I sent for an ambulance. From the looks of this fella, we may need two," he chuckled softly.

Donnell turned and looked into the face of Lt. Kirk Maxwell, then nodded his thanks, before going to Angela.

Ike was folding his pocketknife and putting it in his pocket when Donnell knelt beside Angela. Ike had taken the tape from around her wrists and ankles, but had only slit the tape around her head. As Donnell slowly eased it away from her mouth and cheek, she winced. He didn't try to pull it farther. He tried not to let the emotion show in his face when he saw her swollen lips. He touched two fingers to his lips, then touched hers as softly as a whisper. She blinked her good eye, and tried to smile through the busted lip.

The paramedic tapped him on the back. Donnell looked up, then backed away from her so they could do their work, never taking his eyes from hers. He felt her pain, as they eased her onto the stretcher. He heard Maxwell's voice from the other room.

"You're under arrest for aggravated kidnapping and attempted murder. You have the right to remain silent. If you give up that right . . ."

Donnell followed them out and climbed in the ambulance behind the stretcher, sitting in the little jumpseat. He held Angela's hand to his lips all the way to Mercy Hospital.

SIXTEEN

Mercy Hospital was one of those tall, glass-sheathed struc-
tures that exemplified the reigning architecture in Houston and
the other cities of the New South. In the morning light, it looked
more like a sleek, modern office building than a hospital. The
large waiting area was full, but not crowded and chaotic, as it
would be at the county hospital in the aftermath of Friday night.
Ike sat on the long padded bench in front of the windowed wall,
watching Donnell pace back and forth. Ike made no attempt to
stop him. Every man had to deal with fear in his own way, he
thought, as he turned the brim of the big black hat round and
round in his hands, an inch at a time.

The double doors swung open and Sondra strode through.
Ike stood up and started to meet her, searching her face. Before
he reached her, the door opened again, and Eleanor walked in,
Jones right behind her. All their faces bore the same worried
frowns. Sondra walked past Ike to Donnell and hugged him,
stopping his pacing.

"How is she?"

"Don't know. They said they'd come tell me something. But it's been a long time."

"What happened?" she asked, taking his hands and pulling him down on the bench where Ike had been sitting. Ike shook Jones' hand—they didn't need any words. Eleanor sat on the other side of Donnell. Sondra turned his hand over and examined the broken skin on his knuckles, as Donnell explained what had happened.

"Did Maxwell show up in time?" she asked.

Donnell nodded.

"He always does," she said, satisfied.

The other door opened and the ER doctor came out, in his greens, the mask hanging down around his neck.

"Donnell?" he asked hesitantly, scanning the group. They all stood.

"That's me. I'm Donnell," he said anxiously. "What is it? How is she? Is she OK?"

The doctor held up his hands to calm him.

"She's going to be OK. She'll be in a lot of pain for a few days. We can't give her anything for it but aspirin or ibuprofen, because of the head trauma. The x-rays showed nothing is broken, but there are several cracked ribs. Her face took the worst of it, but we don't think there'll be any permanent damage. Nothing that requires immediate surgery, anyway. She's asking for you. Come with me. You can't stay long," he admonished.

The rest of the group heaved a sigh, in unison, as they watched Donnell follow the doctor through the doors that said 'No Admittance.'

Ike watched Sondra out of the corner of his eye, squeezing her hands together, one thumb rubbing the other palm. He walked over and put both his arms around her. He felt her go limp against his chest, then felt the wetness soaking through his shirt. He closed his eyes, enjoying the feel of her. When he looked up, his eyes met Jones'. Ike cocked his head, and mouthed, "Not yet." Then he smiled.

Donnell had to hold himself still, when he saw Angela, under the glare of the bright lights. Her face was more swollen than before, the other eye almost closed now. She looked so small and helpless, lying on the table, the tube running out of her arm to a bag above her head. Where the hospital gown wasn't pulled under her, he could see the wide banding wrapped around her chest. He walked over to her and stood, looking down at her. When he took her limp hand in his, she opened her eye a little, and strained to see him. She whispered his name through her swollen lips and tried to smile, before drifting back to sleep. He held her hand until the doctor came back.

"They'll be moving her to a room now. You'll have to leave," he said in his official doctor voice.

"I'm not leaving her," Donnell said, matter-of-factly.

"There's nothing you can do. These kinds of injuries just take time. What she needs now is to be still. Her doctor's been notified and should be here soon to take over. I've put her under 48-hour observation, but he could change that. You can talk to him when he gets here, but you need to leave now."

"I'm not leaving," Donnell repeated.

As the doctor stared at Donnell's resolute face, he heard his name on the paging system. He had other battles to fight, other injuries to heal, lives to save. He turned and walked away.

The orderly pushed Angela's gurney through the doors to the waiting room, Donnell walking beside her. The others formed a procession, following them down the hall. In the elevator, Eleanor and Sondra got their first look at Angela's face. They were both reduced to tears, and hugged each other for comfort. When they reached the room, the orderly tried to move Angela to the bed, Donnell stopped him.

"Don't touch her. I'll do it." The orderly looked skeptical, but didn't argue with the big man. He'd worked a double shift, for the third time this week. He had a woman he loved too.

"OK. But don't tell anybody. You could get me fired. And brother, I *needs* my job."

As Donnell eased her body onto the bed, the pain brought her out of the sleep. When she looked up into his face, she relaxed. The nurse came in, took vital signs, checked her pupils, asked her her name and where she was. She seemed satisfied with the answers, making notes on the chart before leaving.

When her doctor came an hour later, Angela was embarrassed, and turned her face away from him. He'd been her doctor since she first moved to Houston. Over the years, he'd seen parts of her she hadn't even seen. It wasn't modesty. She was embarrassed. This wasn't a virus or a rash—something that just befell one in the course of living. Her injuries were the result of a choice she'd made. She felt guilty.

"Can't you do something?" Donnell demanded. "She's hurting. And they keep waking her up. And asking her stupid questions."

"We have to do that. We're looking for signs of brain injury. She's just going to have to weather this," he said, in the lilting accent of the islands that he'd left years ago.

Dr. Richards had seen more than his share of domestic violence victims. Even if he hadn't known from the chart, he knew from the look on Donnell's face, that he was not responsible for this. The batterers usually looked at him, out of hooded eyes, as though he was the enemy. Not so much concern for the woman, as fear of arrest for themselves, or shame at having been caught in such an unmanly act—asking only about how soon she could be released. He decided Donnell must be one of her brothers.

"I'll keep her for observation, perhaps as long as 48 hours. We'll see tomorrow."

Late in the afternoon, Sondra came in the room and touched Donnell on the shoulder. "Go," she said firmly. "Get something to eat. We'll stay 'til you get back." She and Eleanor took up the vigil.

Donnell went with the men to the basement cafeteria. He ate, but didn't taste the food. He could feel Ike watching him.

"I'm glad you didn't kill him," Ike said finally.

"I'm not," Donnell replied bitterly. "You saw what he did to her. He'd better hope they don't let his ass out of jail."

Ike kept his counsel. He didn't tell Donnell that Quinton had been brought to the same hospital—that he was on the floor above Angela, under guard, and in much worse condition.

As night fell, the other four left, promising to return in the morning. Ike walked with Sondra to her car. Neither of them knew what to say.

"She should have listened to us," Sondra said finally. "I *knew* he was no good. But I had no idea he would do something like this."

"You couldn't have known."

"I'd love for his case to end up in my court!"

"Wouldn't there be something kind of wrong about that?"

"Yep. But, I might risk a sanction from the Judicial Conduct Commission to get the chance to send that bastard away," she snorted.

"No you wouldn't. I know you'd do the right thing."

When they reached her car, and she unlocked the door, Ike bent over and kissed her on the cheek.

"You get some rest. I'll see you here in the morning." He watched her drive away, thinking things were going to work out.

Donnell stayed with Angela, holding her hand through the night, listening to her shallow breathing. When she stirred, he talked to her softly, close to her ear. At sunrise, Ike peeked his head in the door and motioned for Donnell to come out.

"How's she doing?"

"She slept, off and on," Donnell answered, the tiredness showing in his voice. "The nurses came in every hour and woke her up."

"Here. I brought your shaving kit and a clean shirt from the hotel. There's a lavatory down the hall."

"I'm OK."

"Go and get yourself cleaned up a little. You look like you've been in a fight, and then stayed up all night. You don't want to scare the girl," he said with a crooked smile.

Sondra maneuvered the Explorer through the ever-present Houston traffic. Although she was not in a hurry, she was anxious. She had spent the night trying to sort out her thoughts, with little success. So much had happened, and in such a short time. It was all jumbled up in her head, and she hated that feeling. Each time she made up her mind about Ike, the 'But Sisters', she called them, would come dancing onto the stage. They were the handmaidens of her enemy—Indecision—and did his dirty work for him. She despised him so much, she'd almost rather suffer a wrong decision, than his presence. Before, he had only attacked her at work. But lately he'd sicced the But Sisters on her at all hours—and with a vengeance. This morning, they were in rare form.

When she'd think that she'd only known Ike a short time, one of them would twirl around and whisper, "But how long is long enough, sweetie?" She'd decide to put him out of her mind, and another would execute a flawless pirouette and smirk, "But you can't, can you?" She'd tell herself that getting involved with him was only asking for trouble. He's a farmer. You're a lawyer. Nothing in common. "But you need to get off that high-horse, sista girl, before you fall off." She'd vow to never let him touch her again, and the first would get in her face, "But who are you saving yourself for, honey?" She chided herself for having indulged herself those few moments of pleasure in his arms, and the meanest one hissed, "But you *know* you liked it." If he would just go away, she could get on with . . ."But, with what?" one of them tossed over her shoulder, trailing the others off-stage.

Sondra was exhausted from the dueling. She was glad when they took their leave. Except her old enemy was there, staring at her victoriously from the edge of the curtain. In frustration she stomped on the emergency brake, then slammed the door. She marched toward the hospital, determined.

Sondra just nodded to Ike's "Good morning. Sleep well?"

"Any news?" she asked Donnell.

"Not yet. Doctor should be around soon."

As if summoned, Dr. Richards entered the room and shooed them out. When he came out, he spoke to Donnell.

"There are no signs of brain injury so far. The rest is just going to take time. She'll be sore for a while, maybe a couple of weeks, maybe longer. I'll discharge her tomorrow, unless something unexpected comes up. She's going to need someone to stay with her three to four days, to observe. To make sure there's no unusual behavior, blurred vision, disorientation, etc. Is her mother coming?"

"I'll be staying with her. What should I do if there're any signs?"

"Call me right away."

Eleanor and Jones arrived just in time to hear the news. When the doctor left, they all huddled in the hall, and worked out a plan. Eleanor and Sondra would go to Angela's house. Jones volunteered to ride with Ike to check them out of the hotel, and return the tuxedo. They'd all meet back at the hospital. Donnell declined their offer to bring food for him.

Angela was struggling to get out of the bed, when Donnell returned.

"Don't try to get up. The doctor said for you to stay still. What do you want? I'll get it for you."

She lay back, exhausted and groggy, and turned her face away from him. He pulled the chair back to the bedside.

"You hungry? I'll get you something to eat. The food in the cafeteria ain't half bad," he said, trying to sound cheerful. She didn't respond.

"Does it hurt?"

She said nothing.

"Do you want the nurse?"

Still nothing.

He sat back in the chair, sighed and stared helplessly at his hands in his lap.

After a long moment, she mumbled, "Does it look as bad as it feels?"

He could see it hurt her to talk. He pursed his lips, then tightened them. He didn't know how she'd react to the truth. Finally, he settled on the lie.

"No. Not at all."

"Get me a mirror."

He grimaced, then pretended to look around. "There's no mirror in here."

"Then help me up. There's one in the bathroom," she said, struggling up on her elbows.

"No! Don't get up. Hang on. I'll find something." He rummaged in his shaving kit, and found nothing suitable. The lady at the nurse's station gave him a puzzled look, as she handed him her compact. He opened it and put it in Angela's free hand. He couldn't read her expression as she held it this way and that, looking through one eye. She snapped the compact shut, and handed it back to him. The tears seeped out of the sides of her swollen eyes and ran down to the pillow. Conscious of her injured ribs, he resisted the urge to gather her up in his arms. Instead, he took her hand in both of his and pressed it to his lips.

"It doesn't matter. It'll go away."

She was quiet for so long, he wondered if she'd heard him.

"Did they get him?" she finally asked, in a whisper.

"*I* got him."

"Did you hurt him?"

"I hurt him as bad as I could. I would have *killed* that bastard, if Sondra's friend hadn't stopped me."

"Thank you."

When she didn't say anymore for a while, he realized she'd fallen back asleep.

In the afternoon, Eleanor and Sondra returned with clothes for Angela, and food for Donnell insisting that he eat. Ike and Jones weren't far behind. The nurses came at regular intervals, checking her pupils and vital signs, and asking the questions. Angela lay still. Donnell stood watch.

In the waiting room, Eleanor sat with Jones, holding his hand and watching her friends. Ike's eyes followed Sondra's every move. Sondra pretended to ignore him, but Eleanor knew she was fidgeting. She smiled and shook her head. She didn't understand why Sondra was fighting it so hard. It was plain as day the man was gone behind her. It was all in his eyes. And he didn't seem like the kind to give up easily. As evening approached, Eleanor decided he needed a little help. She suggested they go out for dinner.

Ye Olde English Pub was swathed in dark red leather and soft lighting. Sondra would have preferred a table, but only the booth was available in the non-smoking section. She stared at the menu, and refused to allow Eleanor to draw her into the conversation. Eleanor and Jones ordered first, when the waitress came. She turned to their side of the booth, and Ike ordered the scampi for her, steak for himself, before Sondra could speak. She closed her mouth, and shot a sideways look at his innocent-looking smile. That had been her choice anyway—to hell with cholesterol. But she was offended that he would take liberties. The But Sisters were cackling off-stage, "But he's just being thoughtful, honey."

"Jones is gonna give me a ride back to Pine Branch tomorrow," Ike said.

"Oh, really. What time are ya'll leaving?" Sondra shifted her body in the booth to break the contact between their thighs. She was certain he was doing it on purpose, and she was angry with her body for responding with little twitters, arcing across her pelvis. While the waitress set the plates down, she felt him pressing against her again.

"We'll help Donnell get Angela settled in first," Jones said. "When is her family coming from New Orleans?"

"She doesn't want them to know. Forbid us to call them," Eleanor said. "You know, her Dad felt the same way about Quinton that we did. That should have told her something. All the folks who love her didn't like him."

"Maybe he was doing something for her none of ya'll could do," Ike said, watching for Sondra's reaction over the glass of iced tea he was sipping.

"Yeah, and look where it got her," she huffed.

As he ate the last bits, Ike fought to keep the amusement off his face. He knew that the look on her face, and what she was feeling, were in conflict. She had only picked at her plate.

"It's not always that way," he said, innocently.

"Ya'll about ready to go?" she snapped.

Donnell was balancing a square of squiggly green jello on the spoon, trying to feed Angela, when they arrived back at the hospital.

"Too bad it's not Halloween. I could get some good use out of this face," she said, trying to make a joke, through her swollen lips.

In anticipation of discharge the next morning, the nurse came in to remove the catheter, and sent them out. When she finished, she nicely encouraged them to leave. They all promised to, after their goodbyes—except Donnell.

Before leaving, Sondra told Angela she would come by on her lunch break the next day. Eleanor said it would be closing time before she could come—she was short-handed at the store. They both thought she would be in good hands with Donnell. Angela sleepily promised to rest.

In the parking lot, Eleanor and Jones were bidding them good night, when Jones asked Ike, "Where will you be in the morning? Where should I pick you up?"

Ike looked at Sondra with raised eyebrows. She turned her head and walked away.

"I don't know. I'll call you," he said, with a shrug.

Ike caught up with her, walking to her car.

"Hold on. Let me walk you to your car so the bogeyman won't get you."

"Thanks anyway, but I'll be fine. I'm not scared of the bogeyman."

Undeterred, he walked beside her. As she unlocked her car door, he took her by the shoulders and turned her around to face him.

"Why, Sondra?" he asked, looking deep into her eyes.

"Why, what?" she asked, avoiding his.

"Why are you acting like this? Treating me like this?"

"We've been over all this. There's no point."

"The point is, I need you. And you need a man in your life. I'm going to be that man, Sondra—when you're ready."

"Let's get this straight. I don't *need* a man. And I especially don't need *you*. In fact, I'll be glad when you leave," she said, jutting her chin out to make her point.

He chuckled, to hide the sting of her remark.

"Girl, you gonna miss me. You gonna miss this." He took her face in his hands and kissed her so hard, it took her breath away. She grabbed his arms and tried to push him away. He pulled her hard against him, his arms encircling her waist. What little resistance she offered, ceased when he tickled her lips with the tip of his tongue. She felt his nature rising—and hers too. She slowly shook her head from side to side, partly to tell him to stop, and partly to tell him not to. She turned her face to the side to break his spell. He kissed there too, nibbling at her ear, gently sucking her lobe, drawing her farther into it. When she leaned her head back to take it from him, he kissed her neck in the exposed hollow. She felt the hardness in her nipples where they touched his chest. The tension in her pelvis made her palm itch for the other thumb, but all she could do was ball her fists and rake her nails across her palms. "Put your arms around me," he whispered against her ear, then moved back to her lips. This time they were willing—her lips and her arms.

The sound of voices, approaching, jerked Sondra back from the brink of passion. She pushed him away and looked up to see the group of three, almost even with them. Her ears and cheeks burned violently, when she recognized the woman. She hurriedly turned and got in her car, hoping the other judge's clerk didn't recognize her. She heard Ike's knocking on the window, and pressed the button to roll it down.

"Wait here. I'll get my bag out of Donnell's car," he said, smiling—and unaware.

"No, Ike. Don't do that," she said quietly, her voice husky, as she stared straight ahead.

"What?" The sharpness in his voice made her turn to look at him. She saw his smile dissipate into a frown. As his eyes narrowed into slits, the anger in his face made her draw back. He took three deep breaths before he spoke.

"Alright Sondra. I'll tell you what. When you're ready, you call *me*. I'll be waiting." He turned and walked toward the hospital.

The bustle of activity that accompanied the changing of the nurses' shift at seven, woke Ike. He'd dreamed of Sondra all night, and was disoriented to find himself sprawled on the cramped loveseat in the waiting room. He'd used his rolled-up jacket for a pillow. He found the nurses' lounge and poured coffee into two paper cups. When Ike got to Angela's room, Donnell looked as worn out as he felt. Donnell looked surprised to see him, but didn't ask any questions. Ike was relieved.

Ike walked to the window and stared out at the traffic, plodding toward the work-week, in every direction. The gray misty morning matched his mood. He wondered if any of those specks were Sondra. Why would she want to start, and end, every day that way? He could never live in the city. The man-made glass spires were no match for the beauty and majesty of the pine trees. The constant noise, the bodies jostling against him, would be grating, would keep him from feeling God. He remembered trying to make the new preacher understand why he never attended services—that he didn't have to be in the church to feel God. He felt Him while riding his big mower around the church grounds every other Saturday, or driving Miz Nita to church on Sunday, and the other old ladies who wouldn't have had a way. He wondered if they got there yesterday morning. He leaned his forearm against the glass and forlornly rested his forehead on his arm. He shook his head. No matter how much he wanted her—needed her—he couldn't leave. But she could.

He remembered her descriptions of her travels. Not once did she mention the cities—not Phoenix, nor Los Angeles nor San Francisco, not even Atlanta. Only the quiet, connected places. His mood was broken when he heard Donnell say "Morning, Sleepyhead."

When Dr. Richards came in, Ike went to the phone booth down the hall. He dialed the number. When he heard "Judge Ellis' office", he hung up. He'd said he would wait—and he would. He dialed Eleanor's number and told Jones to pick him up at the hospital.

Donnell opened the back door and let Angela go in ahead of him. It was good that her friends had straightened the place up. Everything appeared to be in order. When he returned from the car with his bag and the sack with her clothes and medicines, Angela was standing in front of the photograph collection. He watched, as she fingered each one, then rearranged them. She opened the doors to the armoire and stared at the damage for a long time before the tears came. He walked over, closed the doors, and pulled her to the couch. In the safety of his arms, she wept openly, bitterly. He petted and rubbed her back until her body stopped racking from the sobs.

"I'll bet your nose is *really* red now."

"It'll make a nice contrast to the very drab, black and blue. The fashion statement of the season," she snickered. He laughed with her.

A little after noon, Angela jumped at the sound of the doorbell. Donnell let Sondra in. She handed him the bag of burgers and fries, and went to gingerly hug Angela.

"It looks a lot better today. You feel OK?"

"Yeah. It only hurts when I move—or breathe."

"I hope you can eat real food. I know how you love the greasy stuff. I got you the spicy fries. Come on over to the table. By the way Donnell, Maxwell wants to talk to you," she said as he came in, laden with plates, glasses filled with ice, and sodas.

"Give me his number. I'll call him."

"He said you really whupped up on our Mr. Rawlins. And we thank you," she said with a mock curtsy. "Quinton thinks you're a cop. He's up there at the hospital mouthing off—rather gumming off—about police brutality," she said laughing. "I spoke with the magistrate. Not in my official capacity, of course. Just an ordinary citizen concerned about the safety of the community. I think $500,000 is a fair bond for a man of Mr. Rawlins' means. His lawyer's livid, running around red-faced, trying to find a judge to hold a bond reduction hearing. He'll get one before the week's out, I'm sure. It'll probably be reduced—to $490,000." Donnell laughed heartily along with her.

"I hope he *gets* out," he said, looking at the scab that had formed on his balled-up fist.

"I don't," Angela said quietly. Sondra and Donnell sobered.

"You don't have to worry about him getting out. I had Ike take that disk to a friend of mine at the Federal Building. Those federal boys don't play. They're probably getting a warrant right now," he said, looking at his watch. "Rawlins won't even get a bond *at all* from the federal magistrate. You won't have to worry about seeing him for a long time."

"What about my disk? I still have work to do."

"I'll pick it up tomorrow. They'll make a copy."

"Where *is* Ike?" Sondra asked, trying to sound nonchalant. "I thought he'd be here. I brought him a burger."

"He and Jones went back this morning. Pretty early. Didn't he call you?"

"Oh, I was probably on the bench," she mumbled, trying to hide her disappointment. "Speaking of bench, I need to get going. I'll be late for my afternoon docket. Don't get up Angela. If you need anything, call me."

Angela jumped again when the doorbell rang. The Lignowsky's stood there, smiling through the worried looks on their faces.

"We brought you some special dessert. I make it myself, just for you." Then Mrs. Lignowsky looked sheepish, handing the dish to Donnell. "Of course, you must share with your friend. He'll like too. We go now. You should get your rest," she said, patting Angela's hand, just like her grama used to.

At the door, Mr. Lignowsky took both Angela's hands in his, smiling at her. He pulled her closer, so he could whisper in her ear. "Your big friend. He has the shining eyes for you. He's the one, Little Angela."

After they left, Angela went through the sack from the hospital. Without a second thought, she dropped her beautiful pantsuit in the trash can. Even if it could be repaired, she would never be able to wear it again. It would only hang in her closet, reminding her. She took the pills and climbed in her bed. She longed to curl up in her usual sleeping position, but the stabbing pain in her chest stretched her out, flat on her back.

Hours later, when she awakened, she heard Eleanor's voice. She and Donnell were talking in hushed tones in the living room. She tried to get up, but it hurt. She called out to Eleanor.

Eleanor had brought movies and dinner. Sitting on the bed with her legs crossed under her, she told Angela all about her time at the lake—watching the birds, her driving the boat around the lake until it ran out of gas, exploring the island, her discovery of sexual pleasure. When she told the part about them skinny-dipping, Angela clasped her hand over her mouth in feigned shock, and they both broke down in a giggling fit. Donnell knocked on the door.

"I hate to break up the pajama party, but it's time for my patient to eat," he said, as he set the tray on Angela's lap. Eleanor only stayed long enough to watch one of the movies with them. When she left, Donnell gave Angela the pills.

After he'd straightened up the kitchen and put everything away, Donnell returned to the bedroom to put another movie on. He saw Angela standing in front of the mirror, a strange expression on her face.

"What are you thinking?"

"How much I want to take a hot, hot, shower." She had the strong urge to wash away the awful thing Quinton had done to her, to scrub everywhere he had ever touched her. But the pain in her chest wouldn't allow her to move that much. Although the spandex banding was removable, Dr. Richards had told her not to remove it at all for a couple of days.

"I might be able to help you with that. Can you pretend that I'm a nurse?" Donnell asked.

"You sure don't look like any of the nurses I had at the hospital," she giggled. "But I could try. Why?"

"I'll be right back."

He brought two large bowls of warm water and sat them on the floor by the bed. He helped her sit on the edge of the bed. With the soapy cloth, he washed her face, neck and ears, then wiped the soap off with the cloth from the bowl with the clear water.

"Can you unbutton your blouse?"

"My blouse?"

"I'm the nurse, remember," he said. He worked the buttons and pulled the sleeves off her arms. From a kneeling position, he washed each arm with the soapy cloth, then rinsed them off with the other cloth. He hesitated at her breasts. He quickly wiped them with the rinse cloth, looking in her eyes, to avoid looking at her protruding nipples.

"What do you want to sleep in?" he asked. He brought back the pajamas she wanted from the dresser, and helped her into the top.

"Now lay back." When she hesitated, he said "I'm the nurse. Just close your eyes and pretend. This will only take a minute." She complied. He unfastened the button and zipper on her pants.

"Raise your hips a little. That's alright, I'll do it." He pulled the pants and panties down and eased them off her legs. Then the socks.

"Stick your feet out."

"This feels silly," she said, giggling nervously.

"OK, put them down," he said, after he'd washed and rinsed her feet and lower legs. He got back on his knees and began wiping on her thighs. That was when he began to have trouble with the nurse bit. He could get his mind to buy into it, but his body would have no part of it. Hard as he tried, he couldn't take his eyes off the little triangle. The hair was cut short, nearly the same color as her skin. It looked almost like down.

"Get ready. I'm going to turn you over," he said, his voice husky. He pushed the pajama top up, and started the soapy cloth where the binding ended, in the hollow of her back. He moved it down over the firm mounds of her buttocks. He wanted to throw the cloth aside and massage them with his hands, but he reminded himself that he was the nurse. And it worked—for a minute—while he wiped the soap off her back. But when he got to the mounds, his hands moved slower than a nurse's would. Even after he had rinsed them, the heady smell of the jasmine soap lingered. He leaned over and rubbed his cheek against hers. The moan made him draw back—unsure whether it was his or hers.

"OK. Get ready. Back over," he said, his voice cracking.

Again, in the front, he started where the binding ended. He soaped her abdomen, and braced himself, as he spread her legs slightly. He pulled his cloth-covered finger up through the opening. He rinsed in the same order, lingering too long there. This time he couldn't stop himself. He dropped the cloth into the bowl. He knew that all he had to do was stand up and go empty the bowls. Instead, his fascination with her hairless appearance held him on his knees. He rubbed his fingers upward through the short hairs. He knew the moan was hers, when he gently rubbed his thumb into the V.

He had never been in this position before—to observe. He was entranced by her reaction, as he gently rubbed his thumb up and down. He wondered what she would do if he kissed her there. He'd come of age listening to the locker-room lore that Black men didn't do that. And he never had. But he did it anyway—quickly. He wondered if his moustache tickled her lips, the way her little hairs tickled his. When he kissed her again, he touched her with his tongue, and saw the shiver in her hips.

Curiosity prodded him. He wanted to see what it looked like. He had felt the pleasure of that part of a woman's body—many times. But he'd never actually seen it. Circling her ankles with his hands, he gently placed her feet flat on the bed, on either side of him. The resistance in her knees, the reluctance to bend, and the tension in her thighs, suggested her uncertainty. The fleshy down-covered lips parted to reveal another set of thinner ones, guarding the passage. When he kissed her again, then ran his tongue across them, her thighs clamped against the sides of his head. He pushed them aside enough for him to breathe—and to see. The next time, he probed deeper into the salty softness. As he stroked the insides of her thighs, and underneath, to relax her, he wondered about the little protrusion of flesh at the top of the thin lips. When he flicked the tip of his tongue over it, he felt her stiffen all over, then heard her call his name. He licked it, like a tiny ice cream cone. He could tell she liked that by the little sounds she made. So he licked it some more. Then he closed his lips around it and sucked it. He felt her thighs relax under his hands, as she spread them wide open for him, thrusting her hips at him. She seemed to enjoy it so much, he couldn't figure why he wasn't supposed to do it. He wondered what Ike would think if he could see him, with his head between her legs. Maybe he could teach big brother about something, other than computers. Then he thought, maybe Ike already knew.

The little knob of flesh appeared to grow. When he drew his tongue up through her lips and stopped at that place, it felt larger. He felt her trying to rise higher and knew that would hurt her, so he put one hand on each side of her hips, and held her still against the bed. Her pleasure was heightened by the restraint. Hearing her whisper his name softly, raised sensations in his body that overrode his curiosity. He kept licking, and tickling her lips with his, until he felt her hips straining against his hands, trying to meet his now-eager tongue. The sucking intensified her reaction. As her hands stroked his head, he felt himself being engulfed in her passion. His fingers dug into the softness of her backside, and he pulled her to him. He squeezed her in the same rhythm he felt his toes squeezing inside his shoes. He felt it coming, and had no power to stop it. She stiffened, then her body jolted with repeated spasms. As his own subsided, he laid his head on her abdomen, overwhelmed by a sense of fulfillment. The last thing he remembered was the softness of her fingers stroking the side of his face.

SEVENTEEN

Sondra didn't hear from Ike all week. She didn't expect to—well, maybe just a little. Instead of her usual occasional scanning of the courtroom, she found herself looking up every time the courtroom door opened. It was distracting—she wouldn't admit disappointing. The paperwork was stacking up on her desk. There was even a pile on the floor by Friday. She had earned the reputation of keeping current on her paperwork. This week, however, she just stared at it and couldn't force herself to open one file. She even thought at one point of taking a stack of it home, but she had an iron-clad rule against that. If she had wanted to work all day _and_ all night, she could have kept her law practice—and made more money. In the courtroom, she was no more focused. The lawyers kept having to repeat their objections, even when she was looking right at them. She decided the dismal weather was keeping her from concentrating. It had turned cold. She hated cold. And it rained all week. At the end of the week, the only thing she had accomplished was sending off the Motion to Recover Property. She had not forgotten about her gun.

Sondra's life had settled back down, just like she'd wanted.

All was quiet. The house was still clean. She had her routine back. Now, she began to wonder what it was she liked about it. As she drank her coffee in the morning, her eyes wandered to the chair where he had sat. She held the newspaper up to block the view, but nothing in the paper interested her. Her eyes went over the words, absorbing nothing. Maybe a slight change in the routine was what she needed. She took the paper and coffee with her to the couch. Bending over the paper spread on the low glass coffee table was uncomfortable. And drinking her coffee from that position was awkward. She went back to the kitchen table.

Thursday, she thought about calling him. Just to say they shouldn't leave it the way they had—angry and undecided. She saw his mischievous smile—the arrogant SOB would misinterpret the call. Forget it!

Ike was certain she would call. Not the first day, though. Too soon. She'd need a little time for it to sink in. He rode the big black Arabian all over the ranch, making sure things had been taken care of in his absence. He wondered if Sondra could ride. If not, he'd teach her. The phone was ringing when he got to the back door of the house. He nearly knocked over the kitchen table getting to it. He rubbed the bruised place on his thigh, while he answered the rancher from Oklahoma, inquiring about Big Jesse's services. The disappointment in his voice was so evident, the man upped his offer.

The next day, he stayed close to the house. He carried the portable phone with him, making sure not to get beyond its range. The only call was from Donnell, saying he and Angela wanted to stay at the Mansion for a few days. Ike wanted to go over and make sure things would be comfortable for them, but it was beyond the range of the phone. He called the phone company and arranged to finally have the phone installed.

That night, he sat in the floor and unpacked the box, with the answering machine Donnell had sent him last Christmas. At the time, he had thought it frivolous and silly. Anybody that really wanted to reach him, would call back. He chain-smoked, as he followed the instructions for recording his greeting. "Sondra. I've been waiting for you to call. Stay by the phone. I'll call you back as soon as I get in." He laughed at himself, when he thought how the Oklahoma rancher would have reacted. In the end, he settled for "This is the Evans Cattle Co. Leave your name and number and we'll return your call." It took nearly an hour to get it right, so that his voice sounded just like he wanted her to hear it. At sunrise, he drove to the store and dialed his number from the pay phone—just to make sure it worked. The light was blinking when he got home—with his call. When he checked in at mid-morning, there were no messages. Again at lunchtime, no message. He decided she wouldn't call him from work anyway, so he headed off to the Mansion.

Angela and Donnell were sitting by the lake when he drove up. Most of the swelling in her face had gone away. There was a dark blue half-moon under one eye. She was a spunky little girl. Just what Donnell needed, he thought.

"Looks like ya'll are all settled in over here."

"Yeah. Angela was so jumpy and nervous at her house, I thought a little time away from it would do her good. We were going up to the house in a little bit to use the computer. She wants to work on her program. Is that OK?"

"You know it is. Course, if you wanted to, you could bring

it down here."

"Til Friday, maybe? I've got to take her back to the doctor Friday. But I—we may come back Saturday."

"You want to go get the computer now?"

"Nah. We're just going to relax today. I'll come up there later and get it.

Just before sundown, Ike helped Donnell load the computer and printer in his car.

"I'll ride with you down to the road. I forgot to bring the mail in," Ike said. He was lonesome. He didn't want Donnell to leave, but didn't ask him to stay since he knew Angela was waiting.

Donnell's eyes followed the old yellow Cadillac as it rumbled by, just before he reached the end of the driveway. He didn't mention it to Ike. Donnell knew whose it was. It was headed in the direction of the Point, so he also knew what was up.

"I'll call my boys tonight about the game. During the day or at night? You know we've got lights."

"Four or so would be good. That'll give me plenty of time to get back and rested up for it," he said as he pulled the car to a stop, short of the cattle guard.

"Can Angela cook? We could grill some burgers and . . ."

He stopped mid-sentence as he saw the beige pick-up go by.

"Did you see that?" Ike asked.

"The sheriff?"

"Bobby. That looked like Bobby with him."

"All I could see was, it was a Black kid."

"I'm pretty sure it was Bobby. Wonder where they're going? Away from town?"

"Get the mail. I'll give you a ride back up to the house."

When Ike got back in the car, his brow was furrowed, and he was shaking his head.

"You got a minute? Go that way," he said, pointing left. "I want to check something out. Remember that first house we went to? Go there."

Donnell stopped the car next to the house and turned off the headlights. Even behind the cloud-covered sky, there was no moon. It was dark, as only dark can be, in the woods on the new moon.

"Now what? There's nobody here."

Ike saw the light from the abandoned house through the woods.

"If I'm not back in ten minutes, come get me," Ike said, getting out of the car.

Donnell rolled the window down while he reached under the seat for the Glock semi automatic pistol. It was his new model. It was smaller than his old one, and although it only held nine rounds, the magazine from his larger gun was interchangeable. He liked it because it made a compact package in the ankle holster. Remembering that it had taken him some time to get used to it, he changed his mind. If Ike actually had to use it, he wouldn't have time to get adjusted.

"Hey. Here. Take this. It's loaded," he said, handing the other Glock that he kept in the glove compartment to Ike, through the window.

The sight of the gun brought a new level of seriousness to the mission for Ike. What was he planning to do when he got there, if he was correct? He realized he didn't have a plan. He didn't even know what to expect. What if it wasn't the sheriff who was there? What if the place was full of crack smokers. He'd read about how crazy that stuff made people. Ike stared at the gun a minute before taking it and tucking it into his waistband. "Ten minutes," he said, as he walked away from the car.

The shoreline was cleared all along the lake. Ike took that path, staying close to the edge of the woods. When he reached the clearing where the house sat, he bent down and sneaked up to the side of the house. He had been right, he thought, when he saw the beige pickup. He didn't recognize the old Cadillac. Angry voices pierced the quiet of the night. He eased up to the window and peeked in. He could see Billy through the door to the other room, where the light was on. Even in the quiet of the night, he couldn't make out what was being said. He eased around to the other side of the house. Through that window he could see all three of them. Bobby stood next to the red-faced Billy, with his hands cuffed behind his back. His eyes were bugging out, wildly looking from one man to the other.

"I don't give a damn about that. You can't kill this kid! You said you wanted to scare him. Now I was going along with that. Shut him up. But you're going too far. Have you lost your mind?!"

"He ain't gonna shut up. Can't your big stupid ass see that?!"

"What did you call me?! Boy, don't you forget I'm the sheriff!"

"I ain't forgot it. You ain't gonna forget it either—in the same cell with me. I *been* down. I can handle it. But I don't think you can. You know what they do to cops in the joint."

"This is all your fault. I told you. Just keep that shit over across the tracks. On your side of town. And there wouldn't be any trouble. Next thing I know, a body's turning up at the lake.

The nice folk all around the lake calling me, worried, and scared. I've been puffing a lot of smoke up around it, but now I know you killed that other kid. I'm taking you in right now. Put your hands behind your back and turn around."

"You 'bout a stupid mother-fucker. You ain't taking me nowhere. Big Joe Crowley ain't gonna let you fuck up his money that way. You ain't runnin' nuthin'. I been making Big Joe rich since you wuz wet behind the ears. He can get another big dumb White boy to be sheriff. Easy. I'm a little harder to replace. He done fucked you, and you don't even know it. Just like that last boy. He tried to get all self-righteous—like you. You ain't even heard from him since you took over. He just took all the money Mr. Crowley had me put in an account for him down at the bank, and left town. Every two weeks, I take Big Joe his money, I put some money in the sheriff's account. What I do with mine ain't nobody's business but mine," he said smugly. "I been doing it for years. Ain't nothing changed."

Billy thought about the bank statements that he'd thrown in the drawer without opening. He usually had a good idea how much money he had. His wants were few, he'd inherited the house, and he never had any trouble living on his salary. He figured if he ever overdrew his account, the bank would hold him 'til the county payday. He _was_ the sheriff. Now it was clear he should have been more careful—about a lot of things.

He could hear Joe Crowley's gravelly voice, "Don't bother the niggers, if they don't bother you. Long as they keep to their side of the tracks." He knew at the time he should have said something, at least corrected his language. But Big Joe was an old man—and his biggest backer—so he'd let it pass. Billy realized he'd been doing that all his life. Letting things pass—

when he should have stood up for what he knew was right. The last time he had taken a stand for what he thought was right, all the people he'd known his entire life had turned against him, even his own parents. The powerful forces of isolation and ridicule had overpowered his sense of rightness, had dragged him back into line.

"Now, I'm gonna take care of this little problem. And you and me, we can get back to business as usual," the man said, pulling the big gun out.

Billy stepped in front of the boy.

"You gonna shoot me too?" he asked, as the man took aim.

"If I have to," he said matter-of-factly. "Don't be no hero. See, that'll work just fine for me. You and the kid shoot each other. Fact is, it's even better that way. They'll figure one of you killed the other kid too. I get away clean. Been nice knowing you, Sheriff."

Billy was desperately grasping for his weapon when he heard the three shots in rapid succession. The big man fell forward and slammed to the floor, revealing the shooter. Donnell stood in the doorway, his gun still trained on Big Mike as he lay on the floor.

The scent of pine filled her office, when Sondra came off the bench at mid-morning Monday. The large basket had been placed on her desk where she couldn't miss it. The card was unsigned, contained no message, only the florist's name imprinted on it. She sensed that its arrival had already caused much speculation among the staff, when Josie immediately came in with the phone messages. She usually waited until Sondra asked for them. Sondra shrugged her shoulders at Josie's knowing smile. The basket was of sturdy willow, rustic looking, even with the hot pink ribbon woven around and tied in a bow. It was full of fresh pine cones. Sondra was glad he hadn't sent flowers.

The next day Sondra moved the basket to the table in the corner. Having it on her desk was too distracting. It had made her think about him, instead of the paperwork that she was plowing through, between hearings. All week the basket kept drawing her eye. She thought about throwing it out, but it *did* make the office smell good.

David, however, had wrinkled his nose at what he felt was an invasion of his territory.

"What *is* that smell?"

"It's pine. Don't you love it?"

"It stinks. Throw it out," he said, in a pout.

Their relationship had been strained since her trip to the lake. They lunched together out of habit, but few words passed between them. He had been short with her, and she returned it. It bothered her. She missed the closeness they'd had. She remembered the way he had looked at her, that day with Ike. She knew him well enough to have seen the helplessness and anger, underneath the pleasant smile. Whenever they were together, the question was in his eyes, but he didn't ask. And she didn't give him an answer. There was no answer to give. Or that should be given. Why should she explain—like a mistress who had strayed. It stunned her to realize she had been his mistress. That they had been lovers all along—they just hadn't had sex. The strain between them and the sadness in their eyes were the only outward manifestation possible of their breaking up. There could be no shouting, no recriminations, begging, or wailing. There was nothing they could say. She couldn't even tell him about the gun—not at least until she got it back. It wouldn't be long now.

The notice of hearing had arrived from the Pine County court clerk in the mail. It would be in two weeks. She was grateful the hearing was set on a Friday—the slowest day at her own court. She could juggle her docket around and still have plenty of time to drive down for the three o'clock setting. The thought of taking the RV and staying the week-end was enticing, but she really didn't want to do it by herself. Angela was going to D.C. and Sondra didn't know when she'd return. As for Eleanor—it was Jones, Jones, Jones. Even the lure of the full moon wouldn't drag her away from him. So, she'd drive the Explorer down instead and drive back that evening. She speculated the hearing wouldn't take more than thirty minutes. Even with the change from daylight savings time, she wouldn't be on the road long after dark.

As the week wore on, Sondra felt her life coming back together. Either the pine cones were losing their scent, or she had become inured to it. By Friday, the paperwork was almost back under control. There was only one stack left, and she could easily manage that on Monday. The tiredness descended on her as she arrived home. She tossed a salad and sat on the couch to watch the evening news, and then whatever mindless drivel Friday night TV held. When the phone rang, she thought it might be him. She resisted the urge to run to it. She picked it up on the fourth ring, just before the answering machine would have. It was the girls. How did she feel about them going skiing in Colorado for Thanksgiving?

"Of course, that would be fine." . . . "Oh, don't worry about me. I'll go to Mom and Dad's." . . . "Have fun. Send me a postcard."

When she hung up, she hoped she had sounded upbeat enough, had hidden the hurt and sadness she felt. This would be the first holiday she wouldn't have them with her. She'd just taken for granted they would be home. She was looking forward to seeing them, to them all drinking hot chocolate on her big bed late at night like they used to, to them telling her about their lives at the university. They'd just have to save that for the Christmas holidays. Then it occurred to her—they might not come home for Christmas either.

Somewhere in the back of her mind, she had always known they would leave one day—make their own lives. That day always seemed so much farther off. She remembered the article about the 'empty nest syndrome' she'd skimmed in the dentist's waiting room. She had thought that it didn't apply to her, maybe to some middle-aged housewife. Looking around at the big beautiful house, for the first time in her life, she felt lonesome. She heard him saying "You're bumping around in this big ol' house all alone . . ." As the tears fell over her lids, ran down her face, then dropped in her lap, she realized she hadn't cried since Michael died. She'd been too busy. Now she had time.

The ringing of the doorbell brought her out of the depths of self-pity. She had no idea who it could be, probably somebody lost. She wiped her eyes with the heels of her hands, then wiped her hands on her pants. The smile on the delivery boy's face turned serious and sympathetic when she opened the door and he saw hers. He handed her the box, and before he left said, "I'll bet he's real sorry ma'am. He's trying to make up. This was a special order. They had me running all over Houston looking for it. I know you'll like it."

As she closed the door, she thought about what the boy said. Sweet kid. Trying to be consoling. How could he know he was so wrong. It wasn't Ike making her cry. He'd made her smile, he'd made her angry, he'd made her feel passion, but he didn't make her cry.

Sondra sat the box on the kitchen table, and poured herself a glass of wine. She thought about not opening the box until tomorrow—she hadn't finished her crying. But her curiosity got the best of her. It was wrapped in shiny hot pink paper. No bow or ribbon, only the gold rectangle sticker, embossed with the company name. Even so, she *knew* it was from him. The size of the box gave her no clue as to its contents. Too large for a book. Too small and square for clothing. A hat? But why would he give her a hat? She pulled the paper from around the box, broke the tape around the edges with her fingernail, and opened it. When she pulled the wads of tissue out, and found another box wrapped in shiny hot pink paper, she sat back in the chair and laughed aloud. She took a sip of wine, pulled the paper off, and removed more wads of tissue, and found another box—wrapped in hot pink paper. She enjoyed this little game. Her anticipation was growing. She tore the paper off and opened the smaller box. More wads of tissue, then the gray velvet of the little hinged box. She felt uneasy, but couldn't keep herself from opening it. A little gold pine cone, exacting in every detail, sat gleaming on a bed of gray velvet. She pulled at it with her forefinger and thumb. It was attached to a thin gold ring. She tried to put it on her right hand. It didn't fit. She pulled off the ring with the big diamond from her left hand and tried it. It fit perfectly. She held her hand up and admired it. She laid her hand on the table, then shook her head. Without looking at it, she took it off, set it back in the box, and put her ring back on.

It was unusual for her to be on the freeway this time of day. The traffic wasn't so bad. There were lots of cars—all exceeding the speed limit—but none of the stop-and-go she was accustomed to, going to and from work. From the loop, she headed north on Interstate 45. Mile by mile, the subdivisions became more scattered, the lots larger, the realtor signs less numerous. She hadn't realized how far out the city had grown.

Once the city was behind her, anxious thoughts began crowding her mind. Although she had spent half her life in courtrooms, she had never been a witness. How would she react if the state's attorney put her on the witness stand? She wasn't used to being questioned. She'd have to be careful not to appear…what? Maybe she should have hired an attorney to handle this. The old saw about 'having a fool for a client' came to mind Would they swear her in? That was a formality from which judges were usually excused. She didn't care about that. She would tell the truth, oath or no. Then she remembered they wouldn't know she was a judge. And she wouldn't tell them. It wasn't relevant. She was entitled to have her property back, regardless of her occupation—hell, even if she didn't have an occupation.

Sondra exited and turned on the first of the farm-to-market roads that would carry her to her gun. She hadn't heard from Ike since she sent the letter, and hadn't expected to. She absolutely would not call him. She knew it would give him the wrong impression. But she had good home-training, and every gift had to be acknowledged. She wouldn't admit that it was easier for her than calling—she had complete control in the writing. The letter had been as bland as she could make it, thanking him for his thoughtfulness, for teaching her how to fish, and for taking her to the dance. She tried to keep it upbeat and arms' length. Not too long, not too curt, but final. She wasted three pages of her good stationery before she got it right. Since she didn't know his address, she had sent it to him general delivery, in care of Evans Cattle Company. She knew, in a town that small, the postman would deliver it, even without an address. She didn't know why she didn't send the ring back. Maybe that would seem insulting and ungrateful. She suspected they would see each other again. From the way Angela and Donnell were carrying on, she and Ike might even be attendants together in a wedding, she thought with a smile. Her letter was designed to set the tone. They could be friends, but no more. Since she had made up her mind, the But Sisters hadn't even been bothering her. Every now and then, she thought she saw her old foe, smirking from behind the curtain. But she knew she had him bested, because he was holding sista girls in check.

This courthouse definitely wasn't the prettiest she'd seen, but it _was_ old. That counted for something. Inside, it had the same feel as most she'd been in. The white plastered walls held years and years of tears. When she thought about it, the only happy things that happened in courthouses were marriages and adoptions. The part she dealt with held tears.

At 2:45, Sondra walked up the wide, creaking stairs to the second floor. Her three o'clock hearing was posted on the docket outside the courtroom. This one was in marked contrast to her own. Quiet, with little movement. Almost like church. Same sad bunch of people though—mostly poor, judging by their dress. Sitting in the spectator section felt strange to her. Even before she was a judge, she always sat in front of the bar. Judge Green seemed to be on some schedule, other than the one posted outside. She sat patiently, almost feeling the weight of the gun in her purse. She was shocked that most of the defendants had no attorney. She noticed that the judge and prosecutor were on such friendly terms, it seemed they were on the same side. Finally he called her case. She rose and approached the bench.

."Good afternoon, Your Honor," she said respectfully. "I'm Sondra Ellis, the petitioner. I'm here to ask the Court to order the sheriff to return my property."

"Well, where's the sheriff?" he demanded, peering down at her.

"I don't know, Your Honor," she answered, wondering why the hell he thought she was supposed to know. In her busy court, the absence of the state's witness would be a gimme—petition granted, case closed, next.

"Well, you just have a seat, little lady. He'll be along in a while. I'll just call the next case."

Sondra forced the calm on herself. This 'little lady' shit was too much, but she knew she was out of her territory.

"Perhaps, Your Honor, the absence of the state's witness indicates that there is no opposition to my motion," Sondra said evenly, trying hard to sound sweet and non-threatening.

Judge Green studied her over his half-glasses. "Just have a seat, ma'am," he said, the impatience in his voice barely disguised.

Sondra was furious, but obeyed. After coming all this way, she had to keep her eyes on the prize. She could file a complaint with the Commission on Judicial Conduct later—*after* she got her gun.

After the next case, she approached. "Your Honor?"

He motioned her back to her seat, flicking his wrist at her like she was a child. She seethed. When the last case was over, she approached again. Judge Green was flipping pages in the file.

"Well, little lady, it looks like ain't nobody contesting this. So, I'll have to order your property returned," he said, sounding disappointed, as he signed the order. "What exactly do you need a gun for?"

"Thank you, Your Honor," she said, ignoring his question. "I'd like a certified copy of your order for the Sheriff's Department."

"Certified? Naw, just go on down there and tell Billy I said for him to give you the gun."

Sondra was speechless. Hell, if she'd had any idea that was all it would have taken... Oh well, it seemed Ike was correct—they did do things their own way.

When she pushed the door open, Billy was standing just where he had stood the last time she saw him. He seemed to be waiting for her. The gun was on the counter.

"Afternoon, Ms. Ellis."

"Sheriff Perkins," she said nodding. "The judge said to tell you to give me my gun." She felt silly saying it, like delivering a message from daddy to a misbehaving sibling.

Billy nodded to the gun. She refused to pick it up, holding out her hand instead. Finally, he picked it up and laid it in her palm. Sondra was satisfied. That was all she had wanted in the first place. She put the gun in her purse and walked out.

EIGHTEEN

Sondra saw the big black truck before she saw him. Ike was leaning against her Explorer. She wouldn't be able to avoid him, and she wasn't sure she wanted to. It was almost like seeing an old friend. She fought a smile as she walked toward him.

"Billy give you the gun?"

"Yep," she said, nodding and patting the purse hanging from her shoulder.

"Can I take you to dinner? To celebrate."

"Thanks, but I need to get on back. It's already after five o'clock. I don't like driving after dark."

"It's gonna be dark in thirty minutes anyway. C'mon. I can't get you shrimp, but at least you won't have to drive back on an empty stomach."

The look on his face was so determined, she couldn't turn him down. Besides, he was right—it would be dark anyway. And she *was* hungry.

Walking through the door he held open for her, Sondra thought that Trudy's Cafe was probably the nicest Pine Branch had to offer. He ordered fried catfish platters for both of them. This time, she didn't object to his forwardness.

Ike leaned forward, elbows on the table, fingers laced together pressed against his mouth. He stared at her, drinking her in. He was so glad to see her. No matter how hard he had tried to push her out of his mind, she had been in his thoughts constantly. He'd been so tempted to call her, it had taken every bit of strength he had to resist. Only Donnell saved him from giving in, when he had called to let him know he and Angela were going to D.C. for a week. They'd agreed he could set the game with his Scouts up for the next Saturday, around four. He mentioned, almost in passing, that Sondra was coming for the hearing. Ike had counted each hour.

"Got your letter."

"Good. Figured you would." She wouldn't look at him, remembering, almost embarrassed at how terse the letter had been. Instead, she fiddled with the cheap metal fork and knife on the table. She wished he would stop staring at her. Realizing she was fidgeting, she placed both her hands flat on the edge of the table to stop herself. When she saw him staring at the big diamond sparkling on her finger, she put her hands in her lap. She couldn't think of anything to say. Every time she glanced up, he was still staring. She thought she saw the mischievous smile, hiding behind his hands.

Finally he asked, "What did you think of our Judge Green?"

She shook her head and rolled her eyes, a slight smile on her face. The anger had left when she got her gun.

"You were right. They sure have their own way. It was a lot more informal than I was expecting."

"Chances are, we could have worked all that out before—if

you hadn't left."

She looked down again. "Well…it's all worked out now." She hated to admit he was probably right again. She wondered how it would have turned out, if she had stayed. She winced when she thought maybe that awful thing wouldn't have happened to Angela.

"Did you know Angela went to D.C. with your brother?" she asked, looking up at him.

He nodded.

"You know when they're coming back?"

"Tomorrow. He's gonna play a game with my Scouts at the Mansion around four. You oughta come."

The waitress brought the plates. Sondra ate as though she hadn't eaten all day. In fact, she hadn't. The food was good, and she was glad he'd persuaded her to stay. Otherwise, hunger would have driven her to stop at some fast food place on the road. She would have made a mess in her car, trying to balance a plastic-tasting burger and fries in her lap as she drove. She hated eating on the road, and the way it made her car smell. This was so much more civil. She sipped the beer. Although it was not her preferred beverage, she liked it when it was really cold. This one had ice crystals floating in it. It fit with the atmosphere of the country cafe, George Jones tunes playing on the jukebox. The navy suit she wore had been perfect for the courtroom. She always wore it, with the high-collared white blouse, when she had serious business. Here, she felt out of place in it. Everybody wore jeans.

The waitress cleared the plates away and brought them each another frosted mug. Outside the window next to their table, the street lights flickered on all around the courthouse square. There was no traffic. Occasionally, a car or a pick-up truck would go by.

"Your courthouse isn't much to look at during the day, but it's almost pretty at night, with the lights around it," she said.

Ike looked out the window. "I'd never thought about it, a courthouse being pretty."

"Oh, some of them are gorgeous. I always go by one, if I get close. I've actually seen 110 of the 254 of them in Texas, not to mention the ones in other states," she said, her face lighting up.

"You keep count?"

"And a description. I keep a notebook in the RV. I plan to see them all. Some of them are down-right elegant. You should see the one in Caldwell County. The prettiest one I've seen so far. I don't like the modern ones—big square government-looking things. Ugly. Usually they've been born by fire. Makes me sad. So much history gone."

"Yeah, you're right." He didn't want to stop her. He enjoyed seeing her relaxed, and watching the emotion playing on her face.

"One of these days, maybe when I retire, I'm going to do a pictorial book of the Texas courthouses. You know, a coffee table book."

"No kidding? You think you can get it published?"

"You forgot? I know a publisher personally," she said, with a wink.

Ike laughed out loud. "A book about a woman loving courthouses? I'm not sure she'll go for it." She laughed with him.

Trudy was doing a brisk Friday evening business. It seemed that everyone that came in spoke to Ike as they passed. She wondered what it would be like to live in a place like this, where you knew everybody, and everybody knew you. Or even to be a judge here. At least Judge Green didn't have to read pre-sentencing reports—he probably knew everybody's history.

"Why don't you stay?" His question broke her reverie.

"What?"

"Don't leave tonight. Even with the full moon, those little roads between here and the Interstate will be very dark. They're only two lanes. And it's Friday. All the drunks will be out. I'd feel better if you waited until morning."

One of the But Sisters poked her head out from behind the curtain, "Remember what happened to Michael?"

Sondra startled, and a shiver ran through her. As she looked out the window, biting on her lip, she remembered asking him why he couldn't wait until morning to go get cigarettes.

"What are you rushing back to anyway? Tomorrow's Saturday."

"Well, maybe. Is there a motel around here?"

Ike tried to hide his smile. "There's one out on the highway, but I wouldn't recommend it. It's one of those little courts kind of place. Mostly truck drivers." He watched the frown gather on her face as that sank in.

"Oh. Well…"

"I've got an extra bedroom. It'd be much more comfortable."

"I didn't bring anything, except a pair of jeans. I was gonna change for the ride back."

"I'll loan you a t-shirt to sleep in. What else would you need?"

"Are you sure?" The question was directed more at herself,

than at him.

"We could play a little poker. Give me chance to win some of my money back," he said, trying to contain his excitement.

"Or give me chance to take some more of it," she said with a sly smile.

Ike put the money on the table for Trudy, then pulled the chair out for Sondra.

Outside, Ike tried to steer her toward the truck. "C'mon, ride with me. Nobody will bother your car here."

Sondra stopped. "I'd rather take it."

"This isn't Houston. And it's right across from the sheriff's office. It'll be safe."

"I know. But I'm going to leave early in the morning. I'll follow you," she said, in a tone that left no room for argument.

The winding road looked familiar. Sondra smiled when she passed the silver mailbox. She found it hard to believe it had only been a month since she first turned in there. As soon as she heard their voices, she wished she had ridden with him.

"What's she doing?"

"I don't know. What *you* think?"

"Maybe she's finally figured out that the man cares about her. Did you see the way he looks at her?"

"Yeah, girl. He looked like he would have punched holes in her tires to keep her from leaving."

"Ya'll git outta here," the mean one said. "You know he just wants to get in her pants."

"Aw, you shut up. She ain't even wearing pants." The other two had a good laugh.

"Who's side are ya'll on anyway?" the mean one asked,

pouting.

"Ain't no side. She deserves someone to care about her, to take care of her. It's been a long time, you know."

"Sista girl can take care of herself. Or hadn't you noticed? What about that lawyer?"

"Humph," the other two said in unison, arms folded across their chests.

"Well, she's got those kids?" The mean one wouldn't give up.

"Ingrates! They're going skiing. Or did you forget?"

"What about her hope-to-die friends—Angela and Eleanor?"

"Jones and Donnell," one said, making a funny face— sticking out her tongue, her eyes wide, and wagging her head from side to side.

"She's got her job. Hey, didn't you hear those people talking to her about moving up to an appellate bench?" The mean one was obstinate.

"Humph, she'd do better to take the bench down here. Did ya'll see that old geezer, playing like a judge? Bet he won't be around much longer. She could have the job *and* the man! How 'bout that!"

"All I know is, the man is *too-o-o* fine. And he's crazy about her. That's enough for me," the other said.

The mean one folded her arms across her chest, sucking air through her teeth.

Ike had been right about the darkness too. The tall pines crowded the edge of the road, sheltering it against the light of the full moon. Sondra was glad she had decided not to drive back to Houston that night. The trees ended suddenly at a wide clearing, allowing the moonlight through, illuminating the big sign that read EVANS CATTLE COMPANY. Sondra followed the truck into the long driveway that rose to the top of the hill, where the house sat. The modern ranch style house didn't fit the picture she had imagined of the farmhouse. She drove the Explorer around back and parked next to his truck.

"I guess I should have taken you to the front door, your first time here," Ike said, pushing the back door open for her to enter.

Ike turned on lamps in the living room, and the stereo. He didn't follow his recently-acquired habit of going straight to the answering machine as soon as he came in. He knew the call he had been waiting for wouldn't be there. Any other could wait until…until he got around to it.

Sondra recognized the Whispers, as soon as she heard their sweet, crooning voices.

"Sit down. I'll be right back," he said.

She sat on the couch, and surveyed the room. It was comfortable, but looked almost like an office. There was a large desk on one side of the room, with the computer and printer, and stacks of papers and files. The high back swivel chair pushed against the desk, was the same dark blue leather as the couch. The copier was next to it. Obviously, this was where he conducted his business. Funny, she had imagined a farmer's business was in the field. She'd never thought there might be papers associated with it. Ike came from the kitchen and offered her one of the small brandy snifters.

"You like cognac, don't you?" he asked, handing her the glass. Sondra remembered the rhyme, 'Beer on whiskey, mighty risky. Whiskey on beer, never fear,' but she couldn't remember one about wine. She took the glass from him.

"You want to change?" he asked, nodding at the jeans, in a roll around the tennis shoes she'd brought in from the car.

"Yes. I'd love to. I hate pantyhose."

"C'mon. Right this way. You can sleep in here too. This was my parent's room. It's the largest bedroom. I keep saying I'm gonna move in here, but I haven't gotten around to it yet. Make yourself at home," he said closing the door.

Looking around the room, Sondra thought she'd probably have liked his mother. Surely the beige embroidered lace curtains and matching coverlet on the bed had been her choice. Although Sondra preferred light-colored wood, she could appreciate the beauty in the dark and curvy wood of the bedroom suite—Country French. The highboy was a beautiful piece. Wondering what one would keep in them, she was tempted to open the little drawers at the top. She set the glass on the dresser, and changed into her jeans and the cotton sweater. She found a hanger in the closet for her suit and blouse. She put the rolled-up panty hose in her purse, and decided against donning the socks and tennis. She ran her hands through her hair to fluff it.

The cognac warmed her, as she looked at the pictures on the dresser. She could easily tell which ones were Ike, as a young boy—he had the mischievous smile even then. She studied the gold-framed portrait on the wall. His mother was seated on a maroon velvet bench, his father standing behind her, with his hand on her shoulder possessively. Mr. Evans sure had dominant genes—both his boys looked just like him. Mrs. Evans looked like Sondra's aunt—the one everyone said she looked like.

Sondra opened the door and turned the light off. As she

walked down the hallway past the other bedroom, she saw Ike sitting cross-legged in his sock-feet, on the bed—the cards in a neat stack in front of him.

"Okay. You ready to lose your money?" he asked, a challenge in his smile.

She set the glass on the lamp table and sat on the edge of the bed.

"My deal. Winner always deals."

She remembered the rules, but didn't get the cards. He cut her no slack, but he didn't get the cards either. Even so, her pile of chips was just a little taller than his.

At ten, he gathered the cards up and said "Let's watch the news. I always match my prediction against the weatherman's."

Using the remote control, he turned on the TV. He fluffed the pillows up against the headboard, sat up against one and pulled her back against the other. Sondra felt the electricity where he touched her. She wasn't supposed to feel that way. She had made up her mind.

"We get one of the Houston stations, and one from Tyler. You care which one? I'm way ahead of both the weathermen," he said, chuckling.

"I can get Houston anytime. Let's watch the other one."

The lead story was about the major drug bust by federal agents, in cooperation with local law enforcement agencies, throughout small towns in East Texas. The camera panned by so fast, she wasn't certain it was Billy Perkins she saw, in the gray Stetson, the big gun strapped to his hip. As she watched the pictures flash by of the young, Black men in handcuffs, Sondra thought in disgust, it was the same all over. Whoever was controlling it could get crack cocaine in every nook and cranny of the country, even though they couldn't seem to get jobs or training opportunities many places. Crack and prisons—the only growth industries in America. Probably the same people profiting from both.

When he caught a glimpse of Billy on the screen, Ike wondered if Donnell had anything to do with the story. He'd been shocked when Donnell told him the truth about why he'd come home, while they were filling out the reports in Billy's office after the shooting—that he was a contract agent with the DEA in an investigation of the spread of crack cocaine out of Houston.

The next shock was being served with the subpoena from the hastily-called grand jury in the matter of Michael Dwayne Harris' death. He hadn't known Big Mike's real name until then. Of course Billy and Donnell had been subpoenaed, too. As the three of them waited in the hallway on the top floor of the courthouse for their turn to testify, Ike was tied in knots with worry for his little brother. Neither of them had ever had any trouble with the law. Billy paced back and forth like a caged tiger. Donnell was the only one who didn't seem worried. When the bailiff came out and called Ike's name, Billy took his hand and shook it.

"It's over, Ike. Just tell the truth about what you *saw* and everything'll be OK," he said, as his eyes searched Ike's for understanding.

Ike understood when he was sworn and seated at the foot of the long table that took up much of the small room. The president of the bank was the head of the grand jury that was comprised of several downtown merchants, a few ranchers, and Big Joe Crowley. He thought bitterly that, except for the token Black

woman, these were probably the same people who had comprised the Draft Board, years ago. Then he thought, with
confidence, he'd survived that, he'd weather this too. He answered the questions truthfully about what he saw. Even so, he
was immensely relieved that they no-billed Donnell. He was
almost sorry that Big Mike had been killed, but Derrick's life
wasn't an even trade. It didn't make things right. If he couldn't
prevent Derrick's death, he thought in resignation, at least
Donnell had avenged it—maybe even saved some of his other
boys.

Ike and Sondra both kept their thoughts to themselves.

The weatherman came on, predicting a cold front for the
next day, chilling temperatures expected. Ike pointed to the TV.
"Won't be here 'til Sunday night. Wanna bet?" a grin replacing
the troubled look on his face.

"You ought to know, by now, not to bet with me," she
laughed.

"I am doing better against the weathermen."

"Well, I'd better turn in. I'd like to get an early start," she
said, sitting up and stretching.

"No. Don't leave," he said, grabbing her hand. "It's still
early. I've missed you, Sondra. Stay just a little while."

She looked at his hand covering hers, and then into his eyes.
Sensing her uncertainty, he leaned forward and touched his lips
to hers. He was surprised that she didn't pull away. Seeing she
had closed her eyes, Ike kissed her again, deeper this time. When
he felt her respond, he eased her back against the pillow. He felt
the tenseness in her, so he didn't rush. They had plenty of time—
the rest of their lives. He softly kissed her lips again, then
brought his hand to rest lightly on the curve of her hip. He felt

her stiffen slightly, under his touch. When she opened her eyes, he showed her only reassurance in his own deep black pools, and she relaxed more. He barely touched his lips to hers, flicked his tongue across them, to part them. At her reception, he quickly probed the depths of her mouth, then withdrew. He heard her nearly inaudible gasp, and felt her head rise from the pillow, almost imperceptibly, to prevent the warmth from escaping. So he probed again and quickly withdrew—then again, until she reached up and held his face to hers, pulled him into her, and held on. When he felt the shiver in her abdomen under his forearm, he tightened his grip and pulled her on top of him, continuing to kiss her and receive hers. He encircled her body with his arms, stroking the length of her back, her buttocks. He knew when she felt his rising hardness, because she tried to pull away. He didn't let her. She tried to say 'no', but he stifled it, with one of his hands on the back of her head to press her mouth against his, and the other on her buttocks. The tension in his loins was almost overpowering, urging him to rip her clothes from her and have her right then. He had waited so long. But he knew it wouldn't be right. Would be too soon. He wanted their first time to be perfect. She wasn't ready yet—not until every bit of resistance was gone. Smiling inside, he thought that one of the advantages of his age, was the knowledge of how to control his body, the ability to pace himself. He moved his hand under her sweater, caressing her back, up to her shoulder and back down, through the soft indented curve in her lower back. He pressed his hardness against her from underneath. She responded, breathing deeply. When he heard the soft little moans escaping from her, he worked his hand under the elastic waistband of her jeans and squeezed the delicious firmness of her bottom. The spasm that coursed through her body, told him he had found her special place. Every woman has one, sometimes in the most unlikely spots. He knew that the man who found it—and knew how to appreciate it—could have her any time. He was glad he'd found hers.

Sondra knew it too. She immediately stiffened and began to struggle against him, pushing and pulling away from him. He heard her saying "No. No. Stop. We can't do this. I can't do this." On reflex, he held her tighter—his own need almost overcoming him. Then as he felt her struggling harder, he released his grip. As soon as he did, she jerked backwards, scooting to the foot of the bed on the other side, and sat upright, staring at him. He raised up on his elbow and crossed his long outstretched legs. He watched her breasts rise and fall, her hard breathing matching his own.

"Why? Don't you want to?" he asked, simply.

She opened her mouth as if to answer, then closed it. The slight smile on his lips said he already knew the answer. She just looked down at her hands, squeezing each other in her lap, the thumb of one hand rubbing in the palm of the other, and said nothing.

"So what's the matter? You want Andrew? Is that it? Or is there somebody else?"

He was relieved when she slowly shook her head, still not looking at him.

"So, what is it? You think I won't protect you? Us? I don't want any kids, at this age, any more than you do. I've got other plans for my life now. I was hoping you'd be part of them." He raised his eyebrows slightly in a question. She looked up at him then.

"I hardly know you. I don't jump into bed with a man I've just met."

"I know. I can tell. You haven't been in any man's bed in a long time. And even if you have, he didn't satisfy you the way I'm going to." He reached out his hand to her. "Come here."

She shook her head.

"No, Ike. I'm sorry if you think I've been leading you on."

"Lead me?!" surprise showing in his voice. "I'm doing the leading here, lady."

"It's just too soon. There are lots of reasons why I can't. Shouldn't. My. . ."

"What has any of that got to do with us? We've done all that—our duty to the others. Shoulds and shouldn'ts don't have anything to do with it. At our age, it ought to be about what we *want*. This is right for us, Sondra."

Ike could tell she was considering what he had said, even though she was still shaking her head.

"C'mon," he implored, reaching for her hand.

She kept shaking her head, her eyes downcast at her hands.

"Don't make me come over there and get you."

She looked up then. Her eyes widened, then narrowed, searching his face for a sign that he was not crazy enough, or mean enough, to try to force her. She drew herself up straight, to show she had no intention of being forced.

"I'm sorry. We never should have started this," she said emphatically. "I'm going to bed. I won't disturb you when I leave early in the morning. You'll see. It'll be better this way."

"OK, Sondra. If that's the way it has to be. I can handle that," he said quietly. He saw the look of relief cross her face.

Ike sat on the edge of the bed, resolution the only expression on his face. He knew that if she walked out of that door, she would walk out of his life forever. The thought was unbearable. He had done everything he knew to do. He'd chased her, and suffered the ridicule of his baby brother for it. He'd backed off and waited for her, until his patience was worn razor thin. He'd poured his heart out to her—something he'd never done with any other woman. And the ring. Didn't that tell her—that he meant from now on? He shook his head, then stood and walked to the dresser. As he removed the items from his pants pockets, he saw her in the mirror, watching him, wide-eyed, in stunned disbelief, as he took off his shirt, then the rest of his clothes, dropping each piece in a pile on the floor.

"Have you lost your mind?!" she said, starting up from the bed.

As soon as she gained her footing, he enveloped her with his arms, pulling her body against him hard. He kissed her harder. She tried to draw away, but he wouldn't let her. She was a good-sized woman, but no match for him. When he released her lips, she commanded, "Get your hands off me. You must be crazy. Turn me loose." She was still pushing against him when he reached down and scooped her off her feet. Cradling her in his arms, he carried her into Jesse & Esther's bedroom.

Ike laid her on the big bed, covered with embroidered lace, and straddled her on his knees. When he was able to gain control of her flailing arms, he laced his fingers through hers and pinned her hands against the bed over her head. Now that he was directly over her, he saw anger—and fear—in her eyes, at being immobilized. He tried to calm her, in a soothing and imploring voice.

"Relax, Sondra. Just relax. You know I wouldn't hurt you."

She squeezed her eyes shut, and tightened her lips, as she tried to break free. He tried to kiss her again, but she jerked her head from side to side, avoiding his lips. Watching her face, Ike realized she wasn't fighting him, but something in herself. He wanted to help her win. He nibbled softly on her earlobe. When she jerked away he kissed her neck, then moved down to her breasts. Through the light sweater, he covered one with his mouth, rolling her nipple with his tongue. By the time he moved to her other breast, he didn't have to look in her face to see that the anger and fear had dissolved, had been overcome by other powerful feelings. The battle was over. He heard it, in the long exhale. He felt it, as her body ceased straining against him. Her captive fingers were no longer straight and tense, but clasped around his own, squeezing them so hard he almost winced. When his lips found hers, she received him willingly, hungrily. He freed his hands and pushed the sweater up over her breasts. When he unhooked the clasp on her bra, the black lace fell away from her erect nipples. He suckled one, then the other, as he pulled the sweater over her head. Her hands were on his cheeks, pulling him to her, then trying to push him away, then pulling again. Ike caressed her hips and thighs as he worked her pants and panties down over her legs. He eased her legs apart with his knee and stroked her thigh. She tensed when he first put his finger there, so he waited until she relaxed. When he lightly ran his finger all along the opening, she quivered all over. He enjoyed watching her pleasure, so he did it again, and again— and again. He only stopped when he felt her getting ahead of him. He knew it was finally time, when he felt her clutching at him, her nails raking across his back. He broke open the little plastic package he'd taken from the nightstand drawer. When he turned back to her, he was ready too. He laced his fingers through hers, and entered her gently, just a little way. Reflexively, her thighs clamped tightly against his. He waited, until he felt them relax, then pressed on, a little deeper each time. Her hips began rising to meet him, reaching for more.

"Easy. Easy. Not yet." he whispered against her lips.

But she wouldn't wait, so he rose to his knees and plunged the full depth, then very slowly withdrew. Her body shuddered hard. He knew he was driving her to the brink of ecstasy. He meant to. How could she have thought she was leading him!

With each slow, deep thrust, he responded to her tortured "Oh God!" with, "It's me, baby. Ike." Each time he withdrew, almost all the way, her body would rise to enfold him, desperately drawing him back. And he followed.

"Hold on baby. We're gonna do this together."

Ike felt it, before he heard it. It started low inside her, at the place no man had ever touched her before—that throbbing and pulsating place. It rose, up through the soft mound of her abdomen, taking on sound as it vibrated through her diaphragm, continuing up past her breasts and throat until it escaped into his ear.

Hearing it and feeling it, pushed him to the edge. He kissed her passionately, as he lay his full weight on her, reaching under her and holding onto her by the places he knew would take her with him. She called his name over and over, as they free-fell together, in complete abandon.

NINETEEN

As usual, at sunrise, Sondra awakened and opened her eyes. As usual, the ceiling was the first thing she saw. What was unusual, was the feel of his breath on her neck, the weight of his leg across hers, his arm across her waist, and warmth of his hand under her back. When she stirred a little, to stretch, he tightened his grip, as though he'd never let her go. She loved the feeling. Of being possessed, protected. She couldn't remember having that feeling before, not even with Michael. She felt a door closing, as another opened. There was no hesitation. She walked through.

Ike thought he was dreaming, again. It was the same dream that he woke from every morning. In that twilight time between sleep and consciousness, the recollection of the dream was more vivid today than ever before. He felt her next to him, just like every other morning. The sensation was so real this morning, the faint smell of the cologne she wore tickled his nostrils, and caused him to become erect. He didn't want to let the dream go, but he knew it was time to rise. To face another day without her. To face the fervent, but dimming, hope that she would call. To face the possibility of never having her.

When he opened his eyes and saw her, he was filled with joy. It spread across his face like the sun rising—slowly and completely. It was like the Christmas morning years ago he'd gotten the regulation basketball that he'd wanted that whole year. The look on her face was uncertainty. Then a smile started at one corner of her mouth. When it reached the other corner, he tightened his grip around her waist, pulled her hard against him, and smothered her with kisses. When she put her arms around him, he wanted to pull her right into his body, to keep her with him forever. When he felt her fingers massaging his back, he knew what she wanted. He almost lost control, when he felt her fingernails rhythmically raking across his scalp, gripping at his hair with her fisted fingers, pulling harder with each thrust. But he held back, until she thought she was completely satisfied. Then he showed her there was more than she had known.

The early birds awoke late in the morning, each holding on to the other for dear life. Ike reluctantly untangled his body from hers and rose from the bed. Sondra opened her eyes just in time to see his naked body ease out the door. He had what Eleanor referred to as 'nice buns.' The word tickled her. Buns. She decided it wasn't any funnier than 'boody.' That she had noticed his, tickled her. She could still feel and smell him, as she lay in the big bed, stifling a giggle, and listening to him moving about the house.

When he came back, wearing his robe, he handed her a cup of coffee and kissed her on her forehead.

"C'mon. Time to get up. We've got a big day ahead of us. Game's at four, and it's ten-thirty already. I want to fix the boys some burgers, for after the game. You can shower in that bathroom. I'll get you a shirt."

As Sondra wrapped the towel around her head, she heard the shower running in the other bathroom. When she pulled back the shower curtain and stepped in, Ike's initial surprise turned to a grin. She took the bar of soap from him, reached around and began to soap his back. She could no longer stifle the giggle when she rubbed her soapy hands over his…buns. She felt him rubbing the soapy cloth he was holding, all over her. As she rubbed one hand up his thigh, and dragged the bar of soap up his other thigh, across his abdomen, then down, she heard him catch his breath. He grabbed her hand and moved it out of danger.

"Girl, don't do that. Stop now. We've got work to do."

But she knew he liked it, because he pulled her to him, and his hands closed on her special places. "Not now. Later," he whispered against her lips, as he pulled her back with him, under the showerhead. The water sprayed over his head and down into her face. She jerked her face away and stepped back from him.

"You promise?"

Standing in front of the dresser in Ike's Lakers t-shirt, Sondra twisted it up and knotted it at her waist. She rummaged through her purse, pushing the gun aside, searching for her compact. When her fingers felt the little velvet box, they froze. Then they rubbed over the softness, as she remembered tossing it in her purse that Monday morning, on her way to work, planning to mail it to him when she got to her office. Then, she'd forgotten about it. She took the box out and opened it. The little pine cone was about the same size as the big diamond. Her mind was made up. After she'd exchanged the rings, she snapped the lid shut with finality, then dropped the box back in her purse.

The early flight had been a long one. The crowded plane, and the week's activities had taken their toll. Angela was too happy to be back in the warmth, to be tired. In between meetings and other business Donnell had, he took her on a whirlwind tour of the Capitol city. She had only been there once, for her high school senior trip. That time she'd toured official Washington, so this time she only saw that in passing, through the window of the rented car. She was struck by how different it all looked. The concrete bunkers around the perimeter of the White House, and other obvious security measures, made her recall pictures from some Communist country. Maybe it had all been fortressed that way before, and her child's eye, full of awe and civics lessons, had missed it.

Angela enjoyed the other D.C.—Chocolate City. He took her to hear jazz at one place, and blues at another. They danced the nights away at the clubs—some fancy, some down-home. They walked the Howard University campus and ate at the restaurant there. They ordered different dishes, and sampled from each other's plates, as had become their way. It was like a honeymoon.

The only thing that kept it from being perfect was the binding around her chest. She'd wanted to abandon it before the trip, but the doctor, and then Donnell, had insisted she continue to wear it. Donnell took special care not to touch her there, but sometimes their passion overwhelmed them both. She tried hard to keep it from showing on her face, that there was still soreness.

Each time she felt it, she was reminded of Quinton. She wanted desperately to put him out of her memory, and the soreness was all that was left. Her face, and her heart, had healed completely, under the care of her tall, gentle man. And it wasn't awkward at all.

"I hope my check is here when I get home," she said, watching downtown Houston whiz by, as they drove down the freeway.

"Don't get your hopes up. It's probably a little soon. The system's only been operational a week or so. You know, you could have had that finished weeks ago—except for your boy."

Angela winced. "He's not 'my boy.' Don't say that again."

"Well, you told me not to say his name. How should I refer to him?"

"How about, just don't refer to him at all," she said emphatically, pouting.

"OK, OK. I just won't tell you then."

"Tell me what?"

"Never mind," a little smile peeking through his moustache.

"Don't 'never mind' me. Tell me!"

"Let's see how I can do this, and still obey my instructions. A search warrant was executed at 12 Fallen Ash, New York. Computers and a bunch of records confiscated. A certain Jennifer Rawlins sang like a canary. Of course, pointing the finger at a certain unnamed party. That resulted in another search warrant at a warehouse. Large cache of drugs found."

"You're kidding! Drugs?! He didn't use drugs. He was very health-conscious," she said incredulously.

"Very money-conscious too, apparently. Anyway, he and Mrs. Rawlins are having a contest to see who can tell the most, the soonest. I know where you can get a good deal on a nice house in the suburbs—if you like cold weather."

She shivered. "I've had enough of that for this whole decade."

"Does that mean you wouldn't be interested in moving to D.C.?"

"Not on your life. Too cold."

"I'll keep you warm."

"You can keep me warm in Houston," she said laughing. Then she sobered, "Will I have to go to court?"

"I doubt it. If they have any sharps at all, they'll snitch on somebody else for a plea bargain. Even at that, they'll still do a plenty time."

"So I won't have to see him again? Ever?"

"Nope. Especially, not if I see him first."

Angela unpacked and repacked her suitcases. The condo felt strange to her, like she didn't even live there, like she was a visitor. Although her last memories of being there were more than pleasant, the ones before were overshadowing. She'd already decided to sell it. Her only regret would be leaving the Lignowskys.

"How long will we be there? In the country?"

"Oh, I don't know. When do you need to be back?"

Angela thought about it. The money from the contract would be enough to last her for a while. And selling the condo would net her a nice sum. Maybe she'd take a nice, long vacation.

"I'll pack enough for a week. Thanksgiving is next week. Maybe I ought to go home. I haven't seen my folks in a while.

We _could_ drive to New Orleans from Pine Branch. We'll see."

Angela persuaded Donnell to let her drive, so he could get some sleep.

"You know, when they get over being star-struck, those young boys will run an old man like you raggedy. You don't want to embarrass your brother," she teased.

An hour later, she turned off the interstate, to the farm-to-market road. The change in momentum, and in the feel of the ride, woke Donnell up. He stretched and wiped his hands over his face. He changed the tape to something a little more up-beat, then sat back and watched her.

"You really wouldn't move to D.C.?"

"Not a chance."

"What if I give you part of my company? We could be partners."

She thought about that for several miles.

"I've got a better idea. How 'bout I _buy_ part of your company? Then we'd _really_ be partners. We could move it to Houston. Or we could move to Dallas. We'd both be close to our families."

"I couldn't take money from my woman."

"Or let a woman drive you either," she said laughing. He laughed with her.

"That was a low blow. I told you, you're a mean little heifer. Tell you what, I'll think about it. Maybe if I marry you…"

The day took on a festive air, as Sondra helped Ike prepare for the game. Leaving didn't cross her mind. He took stacks and stacks of hamburger patties out of the big freezer, where he kept the meat he'd had slaughtered. He knew twelve growing boys could consume a mountain of food, plus there would be the six of them. He was sure Donnell would bring Angela. They drove to the store in town for buns and fixings.

Riding back, he saw her hand, resting on the seat between them. The little pine cone rested atop her finger. There was nothing to say. Only the big grin on his face, as he put his arm around her and pulled her closer to him.

At the Mansion, Sondra helped him peel potatoes and chop onions and celery for potato salad. The day was warmer than usual for November, so they worked outside on the big table. She was comfortable in Ike's big shirt, but she wished for a pair of shorts.

"There's not a cloud in the sky. Looks like you beat the weatherman again."

"Girl, I *know* what I'm talking about. I watch the animals, the trees, and the sky—in addition to their weather maps. That front'll push in here mid-day tomorrow like gangbusters. When it hits this heat, it's gonna be something." He almost added, that she should leave early in the day to avoid it, but he couldn't bear the thought of her leaving.

Ike was getting the grill ready, when the first couple of boys walked down the driveway. Disappointment stood out on their faces, when they learned Donnell wasn't there yet. They'd come early, to be the first to meet him. Ike put them to work, making sure the court was ready, sweeping the dried pine needles off the asphalt.

"Say, Mr. Ike. My folks are coming. Is that alright?"

"Sure. But you know that means you're gonna have to play

your best. And none of that hot-dogging. Just keep your head in the game, and do like I showed you."

An old pick-up truck clattered up, the back filled with kids. Four more of the team were among them.

"You boys git them chairs out the back of the truck. Ike! Good to see ya! Me and the missus thought we'd stay and watch. She brung a couple of cakes."

"Thanks, James. Mildred, you can put those cakes on the table. The boys'll be glad to have something sweet. Go on in the house and meet Sondra," Ike said.

Ike heard the noise, and turned to see a line of cars and trucks coming up the drive. Surprised, he thought his boys must have been talking the game up, in town. Since he wasn't a church-going man, he didn't know about the notice in the bulletin last Sunday. He assigned the boys to direct the parking back among the trees, to keep the driveway clear. Sondra came out and stood next to him, giving him a puzzled look. He shrugged his shoulders, then put his arm around hers. They didn't have to worry that the food they'd prepared would be enough. Soon the long table was covered with dishes that folk had brought. Ike noticed an argument had started down the drive, and went to intervene.

"But Mr. Ike said *everybody* had to park back here in these trees," the boy insisted.

"You go tell Ike that Lil' Daddy's here, and I need to park up by the house," the man insisted.

A big grin crossed Ike's face as he recognized the truck. Lil' Daddy was the best bar-b-que man in those parts. He took first place in all the competitions in the area. Ike waved him at him, then pointed him past the house toward the lake. As he passed,

Lil' Daddy leaned out the window and said, "The folk at the church sent this," pointing his thumb back toward his pit. Ike patted Lil' Daddy's arm hanging out the window, as he drove by, and walked behind the big, trailered pit, smoke pouring from its stack.

Ike was taking the stacks of patties they'd brought out to Lil' Daddy's pit, when he saw the only ones he'd invited. He walked to the lake's edge to help Jones tie the boat up. Eleanor climbed out, gave him a peck on the cheek.

"She's here, isn't she?"

Ike nodded.

"I can tell by that big grin on your face," she said, and headed off to find Sondra.

The people kept coming. The coach and several of the teachers from the school came. Even Billy Perkins. When there was no more space to park, he helped the boys push the gate almost shut, then posted a couple of them along the road to direct the parking. Cars were parked all along the road, and the people walked, most carrying fold-up chairs or blankets. Some wrestled with heavy coolers, filled with ice and drinks. The older kids gathered around a jambox down by the lake. Sondra had formed a team with some of the women, and organized a serving line for the food. After all the hugging, Eleanor volunteered to be in charge of the big canister of lemonade someone had brought.

Cheers and clapping broke out, as the brick red sportscar came down the drive. The boys surrounded the car and walked with it, to where Angela parked on the other side of the Mansion. Donnell got out and introduced himself, and Angela, to the boys. Then he took her around the crowd, speaking with the folk he had grown up with. He'd only expected the Boy Scouts. He was a little overwhelmed. In a strange way, their presence meant more to him than the crowds of strangers in the large arenas where he'd played for money. Angela ran off to find her friends.

At four o'clock sharp, Ike blew his whistle to summon the Scouts. When they were all gathered on the court, he laid out the rules of the game. It would be played like a 'pick up' game. Half court, because half a court was all they had. 'Make It-Take It' rules—the team making a basket kept possession of the ball, and possession would only change if the other team stole the ball, or got a rebound and passed the ball back past the top of the key. Two time-outs for each side. Twenty minutes halves.

Ike divided the group into two teams of six, doing his best to match the teams evenly. Each team would have one reserve player. He named the two strongest players as captains—Bobby for one team, and John-John for the other. He knew he would have chosen Derrick, had he been with them. Donnell would play one half with each team. Ike, of course, would be the referee, and Jones was appointed scorekeeper.

Sondra and Eleanor pinned the numbered squares that she and Jones had made the night before, on each boy's shirt. Blue for one team; red for the other. Angela had walked down by the lake and gathered some of the girls to be cheerleaders. She tried to teach them some of the cheers she remembered from high school, but they said hers were 'old-timey,' and did their own, to a hip-hop cadence.

The boys gathered around Ike, and Bobby told him what they'd decided. About Derrick.

Ike walked to the edge of the court and blew his whistle loudly, several times, to bring everybody to attention. The crowd quieted.

"My boys and I are glad ya'll all came. You all know we're short a player. But we feel like he's with us anyway." He was interrupted by a round of applause, peppered with "Amens" and "That's right."

"So the boys want to do this in his memory. They want this to be the First Annual Derrick Woodall Game. Let's have a moment of silence." A hush fell over the crowd, as heads bowed.

"Amen. Let's play ball!"

Even though, if asked, most of the people would say they had come to see the boys play, in their heart of hearts, they'd come to see their hometown boy do the things that they had heard about, or seen him do on TV. For Donnell, it was all about Ike's boys, of which he was only one—the first. It took a while for the crowd to understand. Each time Donnell received the ball, he passed off to one of the others on his team, for them to dribble, shoot, and sometimes score. The crowd applauded the boys' efforts. He let Ike's boys shine. As the first half was about to end, the ball was passed to Donnell, and he gave the crowd what they'd come for.

It was as though time had stopped for the other players on the court. The look of his eye and twist of his body, made everyone on the court move in one direction, while Donnell, in only a heartbeat, moved in the other. He glided effortlessly passed the stunned youth who was assigned to 'guard' him, and noisily slammed home a thunderous dunk. The crowd rose to their feet in awe, yelling and slapping palms in the air. Angela jumped up and down, clapping. When the half ended, the score was 48-34, as the team made stronger by Donnell's presence, took a commanding lead.

During the half-time break, Donnell exchanged 'high fives' with his old team—then went to huddle with his new one.

"OK, guys. We're down. Way down," he said rolling his eyes, a wry smile on his face. "But we can beat 'em. You can do it. We just need a plan. Who's the best shooter?"

"John-John," they all said in unison.

"Who's the ah—worst?" They sheepishly looked at little Robert, in the thick, horn-rimmed glasses. In the huddle, Donnell half-whispered his game-plan.

Ike blew the whistle to start the second half.

As in the first half, Donnell continued to pass the ball to the other players. It was their game. They got the ball to John-John, who made most of the shots. Each time their man went out, the ball was passed to the open man, who passed to John-John for the shot. When they'd made up the distance, and the score was 52-50, the team coalesced. They could see now, how his plan made sense. They fought to 68-66, but still trailing.

The other team had possession. Their man threw the ball toward their best shooter, waiting under the basket. In a flash, Donnell swept in sideways, stole the ball, dribbled away, then leaped high for the shot from the top of the key. The crowd went wild. Tied-68-68, less than a minute left. Donnell went out, faked to the heavily-guarded John-John, then passed to Kenny. As half the other players ran in his direction, Kenny passed to Robert, standing alone at mid-court. No one bothered to guard Robert—everybody knew he couldn't shoot. Donnell ran to the side of the court, waving his arms, yelling "Here! Over here! I got it. Throw the ball, man," drawing the other players toward him. Robert, according to the plan, faked the pass to Donnell. Robert knew he was *supposed* to throw the ball to Kenny.

Instead, he turned toward the goal, and taking his time—just like he did all those times alone in his driveway, with none of the tall guys hovering around him, poking fun at him—thrust the ball up in the air at just the right angle. The whistle blew just as the ball fell, almost silently, through the netting.

Stunned silence was interrupted only by three soft thuds of the ball bouncing on the asphalt. Pandemonium broke out, as the crowd burst into screams and yells. Donnell jerked both fists in the air. The other boys surrounded Robert, and they melded into one team, where there were no losers. All of them were patting him on the back, thumping him on his head. It was their game. Robert was their hero. That was the way it was supposed to be. When Donnell looked up, he saw Ike across the court, smiling back at him, and nodding his approval.

The boys, good-naturedly pushing and shoving each other, formed a line for the meat Lil' Daddy had set aside for them. Ike stood next to the big pit, congratulating them, commenting on each one's play. Sondra walked up, took his hand and led him away to the big table, where the plate she'd fixed for him was waiting. Ike couldn't remember a happier day in his life. As the boys joined him, Sondra got up to make room for them, trailing her fingers across the back of his neck, as she went to visit with her friends.

"She yo' woman, Mr. Ike?" Bobby asked.

Ike grinned under his moustache, and nodded his head.

"Well, what're we sposed to call her?"

Ike wrinkled his brow and pursed his lips. 'Sondra' would be too informal for the boys to call a woman her age. He knew 'Ms. Ellis' wouldn't be right. Sounded too much like their school teacher. 'Judge Ellis?' Too formal. Besides, he didn't like the sound of it. The boys were whispering around the table. As usual, Bobby was the spokesman.

"How 'bout 'Ms. Ike'?" Bobby asked. "She yo' wife?"

"Not yet," he said, with a smile.

THE BEGINNING

ORDER FORM

TITLE	PRICE	QTY.	TOTAL
THREE PERFECT MEN	$10.95	_____	_____
THE PRICE OF PASSION	$14.95	_____	_____
DANGEROUS DILEMMAS	$14.95	_____	_____
TOTAL		_____	_____

Moon Child Books
P O Box 142495
Austin, Tx. 78714-2495
(512)-452-0042; fax (512) 452-5130
Every copy autographed.

TO:

_____

Name

_____

Address

_____

City and State   Zip

From: (Fill out below and the book will be autographed as a gift from you)

_____

Name

_____

Address

_____

City and State   Zip

We'll make it easy for you, too. We'll ship directly to them—or to you.

Ship to: ME: _____   THEM: _____

Expect delivery in one week, but please allow for two

Or ask for them at your library or favorite bookstore

Other 'marvelously mature' novels by Evelyn Palfrey

THE PRICE OF PASSION
"Does it have a name?" Vivian asked Walter.
OUTRAGEOUS
What *would* be the proper question to ask your husband of nearly twenty years, when he brings home his baby by another woman, as casually as a bag of groceries you'd asked him to pick up?
BAFFLING
Who is the mother? Why won't Walter reveal her identity? What kind of woman would abandon a baby? Why hasn't she returned to claim her baby?
THE PRICE
Should Vivian stay with Walter, his political power and wealth, for the baby she's grown to love? Or, knowing that she can never have a child, should she give up the baby for Marc—the man who's shown her what love really is?

DANGEROUS DILEMMAS
AUDREY'S DILEMMA
Reeling from the ultimate betrayal by her husband, facing divorce after 25 years and questioning whether her child could actually be a killer. Should she allow a mother's love keep her from accepting the love of a real man?
MARYBETH'S DILEMMA
Survivor of a bitter divorce, alone in an empty nest, with only her career for comfort. Does she dare face the disapproval of society—and her grown children—for the love of a much younger man?
MAXWELL'S DILEMMA
The straight by the book cop. Can he forsake his duty for the sassy, full-figured woman who ignites a flame in him that he thought was dead?